A Minority of One

Derena,

To the woman behind the success of CSB's Lancaster campus — we couldn't teach 'em if you didn't bring 'em in.

It's hard to imagine a better person for the job in York. There is no question that you will be great!

T. A. B——
11/6/2002

A Minority of One

✥

T. A. Baran

Writers Club Press
San Jose New York Lincoln Shanghai

A Minority of One

All Rights Reserved © 2002 by T. A. Baran

No part of this book may be reproduced or transmitted in any form or by any means, graphic, electronic, or mechanical, including photocopying, recording, taping, or by any information storage retrieval system, without the permission in writing from the publisher.

Writers Club Press
an imprint of iUniverse, Inc.

For information address:
iUniverse, Inc.
5220 S. 16th St., Suite 200
Lincoln, NE 68512
www.iuniverse.com

Any resemblance to actual people and events is purely coincidental.
This is a work of fiction.

ISBN: 0-595-23447-X

Printed in the United States of America

I like a look of Agony,
Because I know it's true—
Men do not sham Convulsion,
Nor simulate, a Throe—

The Eyes glaze once—and that is Death—
Impossible to feign
The Beads upon the Forehead
By homely Anguish strung.

—*Emily Dickinson*

CHAPTER 1

❈

"John Lennon must be exhausted."

"Colin, John Lennon is dead!" Sandra snapped.

Colin balled his napkin and threw it onto his plate. "Yeah, but he's been rolling over and over in his grave. What's happened to people? Don't they know what rock and roll is any more?"

"Things change, Colin. The bands are different."

"These aren't *bands*," Colin raged. These are artificial quartets of little boys put together like television commercials. They don't even play instruments. They're chosen because of looks—their talent is minimal. It's all about demographics—like selling peanut butter or diet cola. They've targeted 13-year-old girls and determined what the girls fantasize about—and then they deliver. Old fat men with neckties deciding what young people will listen to."

"What's the topic?" Jack said, turning the empty seat around so that he could rest his arms on the back before joining the conversation.

The friends met at Fabulous Taco every night after work—it was a small unfranchised take-out restaurant, ironically prized for its hot dogs. Though seldom used, there were five worn wobbly tables surrounded by metal mismatched chairs. Somehow the small group of friends began using the table nearest the eternally dirty front widow as a meeting place to discuss the world and their place in it.

"Colin's dumping on popular music again."

"What now, Colin—should every new group follow in the footsteps of Arrowsmith?" Jack asked, munching on a handful of fries at once.

"I'm just saying that all this hype and commercialism isn't what rock and roll is supposed to be about!" Colin defended.

"Man, even the Beatles gave in to that shit," Jack laughed. "You think they wanted to wear those twinkie gray matching suits? Those guys were from tough working class families—but they did what their manager told them. Don't you remember the little bow they took at the end of their act?"

"But they didn't do Pepsi commercials," Colin countered.

"They sold all kinds of corny merchandise. In fact, they were the first to be really successful at it."

"Okay, okay. But they had an irreverence about them. From the first press conference here in the States, it was clear that they were smartasses. And they smoked—how many of the teen stars today do you see with a cigarette hanging from their mouths? It said something; it was a statement."

"What did it say, Colin?" Sandra wondered.

"It said: 'We're not adults. We're not part of the establishment.' It said: 'We may have used you to get here, but we think you're all a bunch of hypocrites.' It didn't say, 'Have a Pepsi.'"

"Do artists have to always be nonconformists—outside of the mainstream?" Sandra asked.

"Hell yes!" Colin almost shouted. "Rock and roll is about rebellion. The music is about decadence and desperation. It's about living for today and the hell with the future. I'll bet every member of every boy band has an investment portfolio."

"He's got something there," Jack agreed. "From the beginning, rock and roll has been about defiance and revolution."

"And making it with your friends from the garage to the stage," Colin added. "Any band that is formed from auditions cannot be called a true rock band."

"What about the Monkeys?" Sandra asked.

"You've just made my point."

"And I'll bet the self destructive behavior of the musicians is all part of the image."

"Yes, Sandra, it is. Live fast and die young—that's what Jim Morrison and Jimi Hendrix and even Kurt Cobain were all about. I can't imagine them growing old."

"You have to admit, the great poets and painters and musicians throughout history seemed to be like that," Jack said. "Smoke too much, drink too much, get hooked on drugs. And don't forget the illicit sex. Sex, drugs, and rock and roll—yeah, that's what it was all about."

"And now the groups enter golf tournaments," Colin grimaced.

"Well, I just hope that my art can be acceptable without my being manic depressive," Sandra said.

"Don't worry," Colin said sarcastically, "I think Leroy Nieman is doing just fine."

CHAPTER 2

Sandra Louder thought of herself as a painter. From the time she could remember, color and form and perspective held an attraction for her. And it was her identity. It didn't take long for the other kids in school to be impressed with the girl who could draw things like an adult. In high school, it was the caricatures that wowed them—especially the ones of teachers they didn't like. Soon, when kids would introduce her, they'd add, "She's a real good drawer."

No one knows why some people are born with artistic talent. Most of the time the individual doesn't even know he possesses anything remarkable until it's pointed out by others. After a while, he makes his innate ability part of his own image and self-esteem.

Sandra's parents were late in recognizing Sandra's gift. But when they did, there was no holding them back. Soon her mother had her enrolled in art lessons once a week at the community college. Framed charcoals and sketches began to appear on walls throughout the house.

It was only natural that Sandra would go on to study art in college. Seeing that she had good grades, a high SAT score, and an upper middle class family with the means to send her, it was no problem getting in.

Instead of going to a private institution known for its fine arts program, however, Sandra decided to go to a state school instead. Like a top high school basketball player with mediocre skills compared to big university competition, Sandra found it better to shine among the others rather than be rendered invisible by those that are so much better.

And shine she did. At State, the entire art program was built around art education—so Sandra's fellow students were future art teachers. Though these young people were much more creative and artistic than the average, art education students aren't exactly the kind that imagine themselves suffering for their calling. And though Sandra would never cut off her ear, compared to the others, she was a true bohemian.

A big fish in a little pond begins to believe its sense of superiority and, thus, begins to believe that it can hold its own in the ocean. Sandra emerged from college with the idea that she would be the real McCoy.

Therefore, any suggestion that she use her talent commercially was out of the question. No, Sandra would paint and support herself with proceeds from the purchases of the many art patrons who would recognize her ability. And because Sandra's parents provided her with a pleasant home and good meals, she was not forced to live in a cold garret to do her work.

So Sandra concentrated on accumulating canvases—hoping to approach art stores to start. Maybe eventually a show would be in order—something local.

"These are wonderful!" the fiftyish owner of the Town Gallery exclaimed as she pushed back her shoulder length gray hair, exposing a long dangling golden spear of an earring.

"Oh, I'm so glad you think so," Sandra said. "I came to you first because I thought I'd start out around home."

"Yes, yes…some of these will sell easily," the woman said, holding a still life at arm's length of wild daisies springing happily from a green vase.

"So, you'll purchase some?" Sandra asked eagerly.

"Oh, no. We don't purchase art here, honey. We're a consignment shop. We display it and take a percentage of the sale."

"Oh," Sandra tried not to sound disappointed. "Well then, should I leave them all?"

"Oh, heavens no, dear. We can only sell some of them. Our clientele would have no use for the others."

"Your clientele?"

"Yes…housewives. Women who want the pride of having originals in their homes…as long as they match the couch."

"Match the—?"

"Oh don't get me wrong. Some of them have an eye for the good stuff. It's just that there are other considerations."

"So which would they be interested in?" Sandra asked.

"Still-lifes…barns…rustic landscapes…that kind of thing."

"And abstracts?"

"Once in a while," the shopkeeper said. "It depends on the décor."

Sandra steadied herself. She was just starting, and this was a learning experience. She would place a few paintings here. They were sure to get some attention—based on the other pictures she saw in the shop—and word of her work would slowly spread. Yes…this was a beginning.

So Sandra—though not to the point of paying her own bills—fancied herself a true professional.

Sandra and Colin dated in college. Colin impressed her as the dark, brooding type—which would make a perfect addition to her conception of herself. And he was continually holding a diatribe about one thing or another. If one saw them walking between the ivy covered walls of the campus, it was usually Colin waving his hands in vehement gesticulation while Sandra listened patiently. Rarely did she get a word in edgewise.

Colin seemed eternally angry. He seemed to find injustice everywhere he looked.

"Some people are willing to accept the world the way it is," he told Sandra, "but not me...I intend to spend my life calling attention to the wrongs and inequities out there."

And Colin planned to carry out his intention by becoming an investigative reporter. He had wanted this career ever since he read Woodward and Bernstein's *All the President's Men* in the last half of his freshman year of high school. The book had motivated him to do a social studies research project on the Watergate break-ins, earning him high praise from his teacher. And the movie with Robert Redford and Dustin Hoffman gave him the romantic picture of what he would become.

Colin and Sandra had stayed a couple until after graduation. Sandra became more interested in her painting than with whom she should be seen—and she became fed up with Colin's constant ire.

"It's okay to be upset with all the bad things in the world," she told him, "but I can't be in that funk with you all the time. I like to be happy. I like to take things the way they are sometimes—forget about how unfair life is."

Colin's disposition was not helped by the fact that the only job he could land was with a local advertising newspaper. The one time he tried to convince his editor (and chief of the volunteer fire department) that they should go after important news, Mr. Jenkins laid it on the line.

"There is no room for serious news in this paper. We're here to announce garage sales and sell old refrigerators. The only stories we'll ever print will have to do with the high school's new cheerleader outfits or the baskets the 3rd grade made for the retirement home."

"What about politics?" Colin implored. "Even little towns have political scandals."

"I suppose you're right, but it's not our job to report it," Jenkins said. "About the only politics we'll ever cover will be at school board meetings—and we'll never report anything negative. Hell, they wouldn't feed us any more information if we printed anything bad."

"What kind of information?"

"You know—change in bus routes, planned building projects—that kind of stuff."

So in addition to being an angry young man, Colin was extremely frustrated.

Though Sandra and Colin were no longer romantically involved, they remained friends—or at least they hung around together with the rest of the Fabulous Taco group. Their personalities, however, were constantly clashing—they were two ends of a spectrum.

But there was something between the two of them that neither could ignore. Colin saw Sandra as someone who was pursuing her dream—she wanted to be an artist, and she was. Sometimes he was so jealous, he could hardly stand it.

Sandra, on the other hand, felt that Colin was a constant reminder that she had no depth—that her position wasn't the real thing. Though he had never been a joy to be around, Sandra had a deep respect for Colin's intensity and dissatisfaction; and she felt superficial and ridiculous around him.

So, there was a constant battle going on. Sandra would incessantly belittle Colin for his cynicism, and he would take any chance he could to mention her Barbie Doll life with her parents—smiles and happy thoughts.

🍁 🍁 🍁

Sandra and Colin arrived together at the Plank's coffeehouse—sometime in the middle of Jack's second set. Plank's was a pretty hefty drive out into the country, and Colin didn't trust his old jalopy—so he asked Sandra for a lift. Of course, during the ride, Colin picked at Sandra for having been provided such nice wheels by "mommy and daddy."

Already seated at their favorite table was Jacob "Doc" Crenshaw.

"Sorry we're late, Doc," Sandra whispered, ducking into the seat on the large man's right.

"Yeah, sorry," Colin said, taking the left. "One of us has a major problem with time."

"You're lucky I brought you," Sandra rasped across the table.

Doc's eyes never left the stage. "Remember why we're here," he said evenly.

🍁 🍁 🍁

Doc was much older than the other three—somewhere in his early forties. Strangely enough, they met him at Fabulous Taco. Doc had just sat down at one of the dirty tables, one down from their favorite, to eat his dinner alone.

The friends were in a heated discussion that night about governments. Colin maintained that Socialism was the only ethical kind of government.

"I don't know," Jack said, playing the devil's advocate to keep the discussion going. "There was something to be said for the monarchies of old."

"What!" both Sandra and Colin responded simultaneously.

"Seriously," Jack said. "If you had the right leader, the situation was very paternalistic. The king was a wise father taking care of his children. Ignorant people needed that."

"How can a ruler think so little of the people?" Colin said.

"Keep in mind, even our founding fathers considered appointing a king. And as far as allowing the people to have a voice, they didn't trust their judgement."

"That's ridiculous," Sandra said. "Democracy is the only virtuous government."

"Democracy?" Colin said snidely. "Like in what country?"

"In *this* country," Sandra said proudly.

Colin began to laugh sarcastically.

"What's your problem?" Sandra asked. "Don't you believe in Democracy?"

"Oh, I believe in Democracy, alright," Colin said, "but we don't have one in this country."

"Of course we do," Sandra argued. "We're the standard bearer of Democracy."

"Colin's right," Jack said. "Our forefathers would never have trusted the people with a Democracy."

"What are you talking about?" Sandra asked.

"A Democracy is where each person has a vote. The United States is a Representative Republic. People don't vote on issues here. They vote for people who, if elected, can vote the way they want. Hell, even the President isn't elected by popular vote—the Electoral College takes care of that."

"If we don't have a Democracy, who does?"

"I think Switzerland is pretty close," Jack said.

"Maybe the best way to go is Communism," Colin said, tired of the subject.

"Are you crazy?" Sandra asked. "Look at what's happened to the Communist countries!"

"I don't think there's ever been a *true* Communist country. The closest we've come to the real thing in recent history is the Israeli Kibbutz."

"It doesn't matter," an emotionless voice came from two tables down.

All three looked over at the man at once. He was a large heavy man with a great long disheveled mane—reminiscent of a 60's intellectual. Dressed in a black faded T-shirt with the words *Question it* printed in dirty white and blue oversized faded and spotted blue jeans, the man sat slumped in his chair, a hot dog half way to his mouth.

"Excuse me, sir?" Jack finally said.

"I just said that it doesn't matter...And don't call me sir—I'm only about ten years older than you three."

"Okay...Mister—" Colin started.

"Name's Jacob...Jacob Crenshaw. People who know me call me Doc."

"Why do you think the type of government doesn't matter, Jacob."

"It's simple lives that matter. It's people and their families. It's the daily routine—love, hate, petty arguments, laughter, music. Governments change; people carry on."

"But an oppressed people—"

"An oppressed people still live their daily lives. Government doesn't affect everything. Hell, some African countries have had wars and changed regimes, and the people outside the cities never knew the difference."

"But the laws are made by the government. Freedom of speech or religion is part of the ordinary person's life," Colin countered.

"You think every person in the Soviet Union was an Atheist? You think nobody prayed? Do you really believe that people didn't talk to each other; that truth was dead? Naw, people go underground when the weather's bad, but that doesn't mean they change."

"So you think the type of government doesn't matter," Sandra clarified.

"I think our responsibility is to those closest to us—that's what makes up our lives. The world is like a beach. That collective mass of sand seems so important when you look at it that way. But what is really important is each grain of sand and the grains coming in contact with it. If one grain of sand is removed from the beach, it just doesn't seem that significant—and it isn't to the beach as a whole.

But it affects the grains around it profoundly. There's a hole where there wasn't one before. All the sand in proximity to that hole shifts."

"Oh, my God, I didn't know I was doing so much damage with my wet bathing suit," Sandra laughed.

"So, are you saying we shouldn't involve ourselves in the grand scheme of things?" Jack asked.

"I'm saying that kindness and compassion and love and fairness must start with the individual. Those things must be kept alive. If each person keeps his own house that way, humanity will continue. The beach is made up of one grain at a time."

"Well, *that's* a different perspective," Jack said.

"It's my present perspective. Everything *now* is only for *now*. Tomorrow I may have different ideas."

"Why don't you join us over here?" Jack invited.

And the discussion group added its fourth member.

🍁   🍁   🍁

The fresh strings of Jack's acoustic guitar—his only accompaniment—rang crisply through the crowded room as Jack played the introduction to the next song. The simple chords were enhanced by a rhythmic finger-picking pattern, disguising his lack of musicianship.

The song *Jenna* was one of his staples. It was about a true love that died—Jack's version of *Love Story*. Like many of Jack's songs, it featured the plaintive whine of his high nasal voice, words desperately tugging at the heartstrings of the audience.

When it was finished, the audience went wild. It was a young professional audience who knew little about music—or any art for that matter—but were well aware of what they were supposed to appreciate. Blues were the fashionable music of their class, but drippy folk songs were their real passion.

Though he held on to his day job at the record shop, Jack made a killing on selling his self-produced CD's after the show. One could almost imagine his banal tones through the fine stereo equipment of a new model Volvo as it wound itself through the twists and turns of the city's outer drive.

After the set, Jack joined his friends at their table.

"Good set," Colin said obligatorily.

"I always cry at that song…It's so sad," Sandra said.

"Thanks. How 'bout you, Doc?"

"Sound balance was good," Doc said. "Guitar has a beautiful tone."

"You still have that Martin?" Jack asked.

"I'll always have that Martin," Doc said. "It's old, like me. Besides, I'll never be able to afford another guitar."

"How come you never played professionally?" Sandra asked.

"Got nothing to say. I just like to play for myself—usually when I'm alone and I've had a few drinks. Besides, I'm not willing to put my soul into it—it's not fair to others if you don't have much to offer."

"You're a man of many talents," Jack said. "Sell any pieces lately?"

"Sculpture doesn't seem to be in demand. I sell enough to get by. I sell enough to buy the materials to make more."

"Why don't you do more painting?" Sandra asked. "I've seen your work; it's wonderful."

"I can't seem to get my soul into that either. When I'm painting, I don't seem honest with myself. With my forms, I feel real—incorruptible."

"Welp, it looks like my break is over," Jack said after receiving the high sign from the kitchen area.

The moment Jack stood up and walked in the direction of the stage, the audience broke into thunderous applause with whistles, hoots, and hollers. Jack was a hit.

CHAPTER 3

Jacob "Doc" Crenshaw worked as a bartender at Hank's Tavern, a corner bar frequented by the working men of the community. With a Doctorate in Art History, Doc could have at least aspired to better things, but for him Hank's was the perfect place.

Unlike many of the bartenders around town, Doc didn't speak much—he never was big on small talk. He didn't smile much either, but working men set on numbing their senses don't require perkiness when ordering their shots and beers. For most people, Doc came off as rather grim.

What Doc did at Hank's Tavern was observe. Though the customers weren't aware of him, Doc was watching and listening to their conversations. The little bar provided characters with interestingly formed faces of lines and wrinkles. Noses bent and distorted. Head shapes covering every possibility. It was a wealth of configuration for his art.

But for Doc, shape and form were not all. The lives behind the worn and misshapen humanity provided the inspiration and life and essence in his work. His work was his reason for living. The reason for his creations? He did not know anymore. He was simply driven.

Jacob Crenshaw's life had not always been such. As an art student at prestigious Saint Clair University, Jacob had won many awards and scholarships. In fact, after completing his graduate work, he was offered a teaching position.

During the time as a professor, Jacob met his wife—a student in one of his classes. Most of his students were in attendance merely by requirement. Elly Zeer was intense and passionate and always seemed on the brink of a nervous breakdown. She seemed so fragile that most people gave her space. Every question she asked in class was so emotionally and sincerely loaded that the room would quiet as if a poet had delivered a line defining life. Jacob would be so entranced at her delivery, it would take him a few seconds to recover himself before responding.

It was Jacob who made the first move in their relationship by asking her to stay after class. "I find you fascinating," was his introduction; and he asked her to have coffee with him. Jacob found that he had been in love long before their first time together. Elly, having a supersensitivity for everything around her, fell in love almost immediately after. They were made for each other.

The university, however, did not care about soul mates. Policy said that instructors and students were not to have social relationships—and they were most definitely not allowed to become involved romantically. Since neither Jacob nor Elly even entertained the thought of hiding their union, Jacob was sent a letter of ultimatum. He was to either give up the girl or give up the job.

So Jacob and Elly married and began life without much direction or security.

Needing some type of regular paycheck, Jacob took a job at the local Kroch and Brentano's—they were thrilled with his education. Elly, the more fragile of the two, moved from one insignificant job to another, until she finally secured a position in an art supply store.

Their lives were not without purpose, though. In addition to the deep love they shared, they both painted. In the evenings, after a modest supper, the two would go to the living room—a space absent of furniture, turned into a makeshift art studio—and they would paint till the early hours of the morning—after which they would make love before securing an hour or two of sleep before work the next morning.

But Elly's temperament made her vulnerable to more than the unfeeling outside world. Her constant anxiety seemed to deplete what she had of a defense system in her body. Colds and a variety of common illnesses plagued her. It seemed that there was never a moment when her nose was not running or her eyes were not watering.

Eventually Elly's body succumbed to something a bit bigger. This time her cold and flu symptoms would not subside. She became so feverish that she could not rise to go to work. Jacob pleaded with her to see a doctor, but Elly had many quirks about her; and a complete distrust and avoidance of the medical profession was one of them. So, she convinced Jacob that what she had was one of her routine annoyances that had become worse because she had not rested enough. She promised to take it easy for a few days until she was on her feet again.

Jacob, used to Elly's various maladies, was easily convinced. Besides, most of us want our loved one's illness explained away so we don't have to worry. Then, when Elly's fever became so intense that she could not respond to her husband coherently, Jacob took her to the emergency room of General Home Hospital.

Elly had pneumonia. And the doctors were so alarmed at her present physical condition that she was immediately put into intensive care. All Jacob could do was visit the hospital and sit in the waiting room—this was as close as he could be to her for the rest of her life.

After Elly's death, Jacob turned to the drug with which he was most familiar—alcohol. The two of them had always had gallons of cheap wine around the house, so this was his start. When that failed to even take the edge off his pain, Jacob began to buy large bottles of cheap vodka.

Soon Jacob was in no condition to work at the bookstore. He would not bathe or change his clothes for weeks. There was no way he could concentrate. Before long, he lost his job.

This was the point when Jacob turned to painting. He found that madly slapping oil paint in representation of his anguish was mildly therapeutic. The thick lines of melancholy colors on his canvases turned out to be brilliant work.

Once in a while a dull lifeless mood of resignation would hit Jacob, and he would paint life's superficial scenes—almost as a penance because he was alive and Elly was not. He would paint flat landscapes with beaches and lighthouses or peaceful farmhouses. He would paint fruit and flowers and bowls. He would hate himself for his work—and that's what he felt he deserved.

Jacob's work was not about profit, but he found himself in a position where he could not survive without some meager income. Eventually, he asked some art dealers if they would consider his work. And his paintings sold—sold enough so that his current lifestyle could continue.

Ironically, however, the paintings depicting his emotional genius were rejected. It was his other work that sold—the canvases of self-flagellation were what the dealers wanted. But that was fine—this is what he deserved. He would stay alive on the thin, fraudulent crap he produced as self-punishment for his continued existence. This made the pain even sweeter.

His paintings sold and sold, and Jacob began to see quite a bit of return on his hurt. This, he thought, was not what he had intended. In his mind, the purpose of selling the superficial work was to punish himself by keeping him alive—but barely alive. He could not tolerate any major benefit from it.

Finally, Jacob ceased painting—not just the dull lifeless landscapes and still-lifes, but painting altogether. He no longer picked up a brush.

A true artist is driven by his calling. If he does not have a canvas, he will find himself unconsciously creating on a dinner napkin or scratching an image on a tabletop. Thus, Jacob needed another creative outlet. This is when he turned to sculpture.

Sculpture offered two things to Jacob: he would create works that defined himself, and he could not possibly sell enough to become comfortable. And he was right. Few of his works were purchased, necessitating his job at Hank's for survival—thus offering true atonement for his sin.

CHAPTER 4

❈

Fabulous Taco was open all night. It was the custom for the four to meet there after attending one of Jack's performances. Jack needed to unwind, and all four needed a release.

"The words to *Daylight* are beautiful," Sandra said.

"Yeah, great," Colin said with a mouthful, about to stuff another bite of hot dog in.

"It's not just the meaning," Sandra said, "it's the words themselves that get me."

"You mean the sound?" Jack said.

"Yeah. Sometimes I like words because they feel good to hear or say."

"You mean like 'bird, bird, bird—bird is the word'?" Doc asked.

"Well, I never cared for that song...but yeah...something like that."

"All there is to that is an exercise. It's nothing more than when an infant delights in repeating syllables over and over," Doc said dryly. "Only when the baby sees some response to a particular combination of sounds is there any value."

"Don't you think words can have a charm or attractiveness on their own. You know...like the way Dr. Seuss would rhyme."

"I don't believe in the intrinsic value of words—especially at the risk of communication. Too often do we confuse poetry with jump rope songs. Rhyme and meter can inhibit meaning."

"How do you figure?" Colin asked.

"Well, if you're looking for a word that will rhyme instead of one that will convey a meaning, rather than one that gives the clearest understanding of the thought, you will probably lose something."

"So, are my songs communicating clearly?" Jack asked, afraid of Doc's straightforward answer.

"Absolutely. Nothing lofty. Nothing profound. But there are definitely ideas and emotions transferred in your songs. Kind of like Jan and Dean's *Deadman's Curve*. You felt something."

"Now you're making fun of me."

"Not at all. To the adolescent, *Deadman's Curve* would strike intense feeling, clear empathy. This was the purpose of songs like that, and that's what they did. Just like a love song turning a couple to mush. That's real communication. But words for the sake of sound or the way they fall off the tongue? I don't think so."

"But isn't that why Shakespeare has been considered so wonderful—because of his graceful language?" Sandra asked.

"Only those who are truly ignorant of what Shakespeare did talk of the innate beauty of his words. Shakespeare's genius was in his understanding of psychology. And when he used one of his famous metaphors or similes, he conveyed something that the ages could relate to—that was his genius. The man had insight. We quote him because his words are true, not because they are pretty to say."

"There are scholars, men with many degrees, who disagree," Jack argued.

"Listen, Jack, this is an invention of society. Society creates little artificial pockets of useless expertise. Combine a little pretense with a little inventiveness, and you've got wine connoisseurs, opera analysts, clothes designers—you name it. More artificial pockets."

"What *isn't* artificial?"

"That's a good question: What isn't artificial? I guess pain and survival—basic life needs."

"Doesn't leave much substance to the human existence," Colin said.

"No, no it doesn't," Jacob Crenshaw said quietly—sadly.

🍁 🍁 🍁

The next day, Sandra paid a visit to Town Gallery to check on interest in her work.

"Oh, they love what you do, dear," the owner said, twirling the round metal bracelets on her left arm.

"Then you've sold something?"

"Possibly. I'll tell you what I want. I need three small paintings of flowers—you know, for an arrangement. Now, they should be done in subdued colors—blues, grays, purples. One, the one we'll be using as the center, should have just a tad more vividness than the other two."

"You want me to paint three flowers to match someone's room?" Sandra was incredulous.

"After the customer saw your work here, she agreed that you were perfect for the job."

"But couldn't she find some existing painting she was interested in?"

"Oh, she loved what you've done," the proprietor said, "but there was nothing just right to fill the space that she has."

Sandra turned and started for the door.

"I told her they'd be ready by Tuesday," the lady called after her.

🍁 🍁 🍁

"What the hell is this!" screamed Calvin Jenkins from across his editor's desk.

"It's the school board meeting report," Colin said.

"What's this about a parent's group?"

"There was a large group of people—I'd say about 40—who were at the meeting to protest the closing of one of the elementary schools. They saw no reason for the busing of their children across town."

"But you mention 'anger' and 'frustration.' My God, Colin, you describe Dick Norbin, the school board president, as 'cold and indifferent to their plight.'"

"He told them he would not hear them because they were not officially on the agenda. When they insisted, he threatened to have them removed by the police."

"He has that authority."

"These were not anarchists—they were parents!"

"I told you a long time ago—we do not look for scandal. We do not make waves."

"Then you won't print it?" Colin asked.

"You have to ask me that?"

"Then I quit!" Colin stated.

"Then that makes things easier for me because I was going to fire you."

❦   ❦   ❦

Colin was already slumped in a metal chair staring blankly though the dusty window when Sandra entered Fabulous Taco. For some unexplained reason, each was drawn to the dirty little food shop—possibly to lick wounds or find solace. Possibly it was a location where the truth was sought on a daily basis—not found, but contemplated. Possibly the two viewed the little fast food restaurant as a haven from the falsity of the world that had just injured them.

There was nothing to say, so they sat in silence. Not even a terse greeting was shared when Sandra joined him. What had happened to each was unspeakable—converting it to words would make it too real to endure.

After as much as ten minutes of silence, Colin was the first to speak.

"You'll be paying for the hot dogs."

CHAPTER 5

❀

The inside of a neighborhood bar is a world of its own. It has to be. This is where the men and women with real lives find escape. And the escape they find is not in booze alone.

It starts with darkness. Never has a man walked through the door of a tavern and seen an iota of sunlight entering from the outside. No matter what the time of day, the magical darkness exists in this fortress of night. Only neon beer signs and bar lights bring the slightest bit of illumination, and these reflect only shadows of the visitors, providing an anonymity to those who desire it and a new identity to those who would be lowly in the sunlight.

Of course, the eternal darkness of this pleasant cave also hides imperfections. Just as it hides crumbling plaster, worn floors, and dirt, it also hides the scars of work and misery and time on its denizens. A combination of darkness and alcohol makes used women beautiful again, beaten men young and strong. It erases wrinkles and bad teeth and melancholy.

As Doc served his customers, he was reminded of Hawthorne's story "Dr. Heidegger's Experiment" in which three elderly people who have blundered in their early life get another chance at youth by drinking a magical elixir. Naturally, their return brings the same mistakes.

"Fill 'er up again," a sixty something man in a ragged green work hat said, lifting his glass toward Doc as if in toast.

Without a word, Doc prepared another rum and coke and placed it on a coaster advertising Schlitz beer in front of the man, picking up the money that was left on the bar in almost the same motion. Then he put the bill and change in the same place on the bar. It would not be picked up. It was there to pay for future drinks.

"Ain't you the guy who's an artist or somethin'?" the man slurred.

"Yeah…*or somethin'*," Doc said.

"What kinda stuff do you paint? I hope it ain't any o' that modern art shit, 'cause I can't see how nobody can understand that. I like pictures that looks like what they were…you know what I'm sayin'?"

"I know," Doc said impassively.

"So?" the man demanded.

"So what?" Doc asked.

"So what kinda pictures do you paint?"

"I don't paint. I do sculpture."

"You mean like them naked statues around buildings and such?"

"No naked statues…at least not recently," Doc was still without emotion. "I just like to make form of all types."

"Uh huh," the man said, not understanding. "You make any money doin' that?"

"I'm working here, aren't I?"

The man looked up and studied Doc's face. "You don't look like no artist," he said squinting in doubt.

"What's an artist supposed to look like?" Doc said, forcing a slight smile.

"Not like you," the man said with conviction.

On the other side of the room, a couple moved and twirled in the fox trot type style of their earlier days. Forgotten were the man's work clothes, stretched over an aged beer belly, and the woman's distorted body and sagging breasts, covered with a faded pink and blue print dress. They were Ginger and Fred for the moment. Their transition to another time was complete. And though short lived, they were emersed in the seconds they had.

Along the wall nearest to the bar, a crowd was gathered around an ancient pinball machine; they shouted and laughed as if at a Vegas craps table watching a high roller. The champion at the controls held a smiling look of concentration as he kept the ball in motion. Here he was the center of attention. Here he was better at something than anyone else. Tomorrow he would pick up the morning shift at the sewage filtration plant at the end of town.

Doc recognized that souls were never burned out. A time and a place was needed for everyone to bloom for awhile. Therefore, he did not look at these people as pathetic or pitiable. Instead, he cursed the world for making it so difficult for them to shine.

At the same time, however, he celebrated their spirit. He envied their durability. *He* was the one whose essence was smothered beyond recovery. So he used them as inspiration for his creations. Their inebriated vitality, their ability to steal away for a few hours, their life force was what he copied in his work.

Unfortunately for Doc, he had to return home after work. By law, the bar had to close by 2 a.m., and he was forced to return to his rooms just down the alley behind the packaged liquor store.

Opening the steel door, which was padlocked, Doc entered the two-room art studio where he lived. Except for a filthy old blue Lazy-boy and a cheap twisted metal table tray with some type of fiberboard top, there was no furniture in the place. The rooms were used for creating and drinking—never both at the same time. When he finally had to give in to sleep, Doc used the chair.

One would think that obtaining liquor when one lived near to a storeroom full of the stuff would be easy. On the contrary, the owner of the establishment was extremely careful with his wares, bolting the door from Doc's rooms to the backroom of the store with three locks—counting his supply every morning.

Doc got his drink from the bar. At the end of each evening, Doc would cop the end of one or another brand of whisky, replacing it with a new bottle as if it had just been depleted. Accountability is difficult when doing inventory at a bar. Booze is splashed into glasses in sometimes unmeasured amounts, drinks are made over, complimentary shots are handed out to police and other influential people. Besides, Doc's bosses would not have cared anyway since he was probably the hardest worker they had ever had.

So Doc used the remainder of his purloined bottle to force himself to sleep each night. His demons always seemed to be their most wicked in the wee hours of the day; and without the drink, he would probably have fallen asleep during his art time.

Recently Doc was using clay to make his shapes. After an initial rough form was begun, Doc would work on the blank with a fervor. During his times of artistry, he needed no drink, for he was totally immersed in his composition. Doc involved every nerve ending as he worked frenetically on his images—any less intensity and he would have considered it a failure.

Doc would work at this pace, never pausing for sustenance, until he would drop into the tattered blue chair from exhaustion. Here he would sleep until he awoke in the late afternoon when he would go out for fast food dinner, lately at Fabulous Taco.

This was not a life. It was only an existence. But aren't they all to some degree? Don't we all fill our days and evenings only to sleep and start again? Wouldn't we all be terrified if left only with our mind's devils? How much does each of us seek to suppress with habitual activity and inane entertainment?

🍁 🍁 🍁

Doc joined Sandra and Colin on the afternoon of their deep funk. And since Doc was not a greeter or a back-slapper, or even the least bit effusive, he simply sat down next to the reticent pair and began to eat his hot dogs in silence.

"Hi, Doc," Sandra acknowledged him, for she was the most tied to social obligation.

"Sandra. Colin," Doc said, showing no interest in their obvious depression.

"Doc," Colin began with no prerequisite salutation, "how does someone keep a job and his integrity at the same time?"

"That's simple," Doc said without a hint of inflection. "Sacrifice the integrity."

"How can you, of all people, say that!" Colin exploded.

"Because I have," Doc said with equanimity.

"But you've given up everything for your art," Sandra protested. "You live a life of pure honesty."

"Nobody has *pure* honesty," Doc's voice became gentle. "Even when we've made a concentrated effort to be straightforward with the rest of the world, we're never totally honest with ourselves."

"Doc, that's not true," she argued. "You've sacrificed a lot of comforts so that you can do the work you do. You're a true artist."

"I don't know if I am or not. I don't know if there is such thing. I'm not sure I even understand what art is. When did we attach such importance to representations of humanity? Let's face it, that's all paintings and other art is. Are we trying to show ourselves how important our presence on earth is? Are we trying to convince ourselves that we find part of our being here beautiful by showing it from our own perspective?"

"You can't explain it because it's pure," Sandra said.

"So what you're saying," Colin addressed Doc, returning the conversation back to his own interests, "is that to have integrity, one must take himself out of the phoniness of society."

"I'm not saying that at all. Removing oneself from others is a bit arrogant, don't you think? How does arrogance and integrity go hand in hand?"

"So how does a person live without compromising himself?" Colin asked.

"One doesn't."

CHAPTER 6

❀

Working at Spece's Records was the closest Jack could get to making a living with music. At least here he could talk the talk all day—keep his head in the game. It also provided him the opportunity to dream.

Often, while stacking CD's in the bins, Jack would evaluate the album covers for eye appeal and style. Some attracted attention with near naked women (he would never stoop to that), others featured off-the-wall artistic composition. But the type Jack favored was the musician himself, perhaps holding his instrument, with some kind of deep, meaning-packed expression. Yes, that's what he would choose.

Jack's imagined video of his latest hit would also be a straightforward presentation of his music. He could picture an intense performance in front of a microphone. Maybe scenes here and there representing the song's story or message, but nothing more.

Jack pictured himself as an entertainer with class. He didn't see himself as brooding like Dylan or Van Morrison—he would be personable. He would share his God-given talent with the people who appreciated it, and he would do it with a giving attitude. But he would always realize its importance—never trivializing it with hype.

Often the aspiring superstar was awakened from his reverie with a mundane question about location or price. Jack was always pleasant, but inside he felt the stab of a person of greatness interrupted by menial talk.

Jack gained quite a following while playing his small circuit of clubs. Often he would be recognized at the store. He tried to tell himself that it meant nothing, but the small touch of stardom would always give him a thrill.

He wasn't quiet prepared, however, when a middle-aged man in a dark business suit approached him at the front counter.

"You are Jack Benson, aren't you?" the man said in a strong confident voice.

"Sure am," Jack smiled. "What can I do for you?"

"I've seen your act, and I'm extremely impressed," the man said.

"I appreciate it," Jack said, wondering at the age spectrum of his fans.

"Ever do any recording, Jack?"

The man's well-modulated voice and business approach began to communicate that this was no ordinary fan conversation, and Jack became the musician.

"Actually, I had a friend who dabbled in it. He had kind of a little studio in his basement where he recorded me. For awhile I sold copies of that recording at shows—actually, I still do."

"Well, I think it's time to introduce myself. My name is Chuck Henderson. I'm a field representative for Comet Records. I've caught your show a few times, and I've convinced the company to give you a chance to record."

"Comet Records?" Jack said, trying to hide his excitement.

"We're small, Jack. Small, and very independent. What we do is cultivate musicians. Then we often sell them to a large label. We've had quite a few successes."

"Sounds pretty interesting," Jack said, shaking on the inside.

"We'd like to talk to you about developing you as a personality," Chuck said, handing Jack his business card. "Please give the office a call on Monday, and we'll arrange to get you started…if you're interested."

"Oh, I'm interested," Jack said, losing any pretense of cool.

🍁   🍁   🍁

Jack couldn't wait to get to Fabulous Taco that afternoon to tell his friends.

"What do they mean by 'developing you as a personality'?" Colin asked. "What's wrong with your personality now?"

"I think it's all about presentation. It's the recording part that I'm interested in."

"And I'll buy your first record," Sandra said.

Doc, who had been quietly observing the conversation, said, "What are you willing to do for success, Jack?"

"What do you mean, Doc?"

"I don't really mean anything. I'm just curious. Have you thought it out?"

"I don't think anyone thinks it out," Jack said. "It usually just kind of sweeps you up all at once. Besides, all he's offering is a beginning—no one knows where things will actually go."

"Well, I, for one, think you will go far!" Sandra exclaimed.

"At least one of us might be successful," Colin muttered.

There was something different about Jack's performance at the coffeehouse that night. He seemed to smile more, relate more to the audience—he seemed to shine somehow. Already there was something bigger than life beginning to take hold.

And when he left the stage, Jack didn't hurry over to their little table as usual. Instead, he lingered awhile in front of the stage, chatting with customers. And there was an air of assurance, poise—a bearing that was calm and secure, but somewhat condescending.

Even through the rest of the evening, while the friends chatted about the world, Jack could be seen with a slight smile to his lips, his eyes indicating a great sagacity. He seemed to suddenly see the triviality in it all.

Just after saying their good-byes (they never stayed for the last set), Doc uncharacteristically lingered with Jack for a moment as the others made for the door.

"What is it, Doc?" Jack found himself saying aloud.

"Stay outside the situation, Jack. Look at it as if you were a stranger."

"What do you mean, Doc?" Jack asked, a look of confusion and humility on his face.

"Just that. Nothing more."

❦   ❦   ❦

Though Jack's music consisted of drippy love songs and cute, happy ditties, this was not exactly his taste when attending other performances. Jack preferred raunchy, electrified Chicago Blues.

Most of the appeal of this particular genre was the rawness, the realism. No song was ever played the same twice; musicians improvised and created as they played. And the voices were raspy and crude. It was all about honesty; it was all about heartfelt communication. Sometimes the lyrics were so rough, so direct, Jack felt exposed and vulnerable.

Jack found his music in a little club in the run-down section of the city near the old can factory—a place called Buddy's. Here he could go after he finished his own show because they were opened illegally after hours.

Jack would sit with a coke and become drunk with the sounds that surrounded him. He would find himself shouting out praise like the rest of the audience, not the least bit abashed. It was like those massive religious revivals where the audience abandoned their inhibitions and became one with the Holy Spirit. This was Jack's church.

Finishing his last set at the coffee house would leave Jack wired; but finishing the last set at Buddy's left him happily, gratefully spent.

He could then go home and catch a few hours sleep before work at the shop the next morning.

Jack's favorite act at Buddy's was a group called Johnny Frost and the Snowmen. Johnny was a blind singer/guitarist who was so immersed in his music that every note came directly from his gut. Jack would sometimes find tears in his eyes at the end of a set.

But the Snowmen did not have Johnny's authenticity. They were simply there to provide the right accompaniment. They were bored with their role—it was just a steady gig—and to relieve their boredom, they made fun of their leader. Of course, the audience did not know what they were saying to each other and why they were giggling and snickering during an otherwise soulful song, but they could somehow guess. Jack hated the back-up band for this.

Still, even they could not detract from the impact of the blues—the way it hit you between the eyes with its honesty. It was like breathing after being under water for too long—or eating after having skipped meals for a couple of days—or good, unreserved, intense sex.

Now, one would think that Jack's admiration for the truth of the blues would make him examine the core of his own music—and it did. When writing, Jack would begin by telling himself to dig deep and uncover the soul. Unfortunately, there seemed to be no treasures to be unearthed in Jack. He feared that the thin layers he presented were all that he had.

So Jack's songs continued to be about romantic love and sunshiny times. When he would wail to his audience about the girl he lost, he would touch the superficiality of their souls too—and they would allow their thin emotional veneers to respond. Of course, an "up" song would always follow a sad one, so one needn't worry about becoming too dispirited.

And whenever Jack would feel bad about having no depth to his work, he would use the reaction of the audience to convince himself that he was truly touching others. And because they loved him, he loved himself.

※   ※   ※

Jack called Chuck Henderson on Monday. As expected, Chuck's voice was just as enthusiastic as the last time they had talked. Jack was reminded of the stereotypical used car salesman, but he dismissed it.

"So, Jack, are you ready to hit the studio?"

"Yes, sir," Jack said.

"Then we start tomorrow at 8 a.m. Be prepared for a long day," Chuck said with a cheerful warning.

"How many songs will I be recording?" Jack asked.

"Oh…bring a handful of those 'young love' things you do. I think they're real sellers," Chuck said. "And we've got a couple of our own we'd like to try on you."

"But I just do my own material," Jack protested mildly.

"Sure, sure…and that's great…but we've got to put together a base for you. We'll talk about it when you get there. You'll have a great time."

Jack smiled somewhat weakly when he hung up the phone—and then he shook off any negative thoughts that were nagging at him and returned to work.

CHAPTER 7

❀

"I guess it's just me and you, Doc," Colin said, setting his hot dogs on the little table. "Sandra and Jack have got work to do."

"You get another job yet?"

"Naw. It's just too hard," Colin said morosely.

"Too hard to find a job?" Doc was surprised.

"No, that's not it, Doc. It's just that…well…even though I wasn't working for a real paper, at least before—"

"You could *pretend* you were a journalist," Doc finished.

"Yeah…that's about it," Colin admitted.

"And it didn't matter so much that you really weren't."

"Oh, it mattered. I complained a lot. But, I could still…pretend. If I get a job at a hardware store or work at the iron mill, I'm out of it. I'm just like anybody else."

"And you don't ever want to be like everybody else."

"I want to be seen as special in some way," Colin explained guiltily.

"Even if you aren't really, truly anybody special."

Colin didn't answer right away. He looked down, as if ashamed. "Yes."

"I understand."

"You do?" Colin was a little amazed.

"Yeah," Doc said, "because that's how the *real* players feel too."

"The real players?"

"Writers, artists, musicians, professors, experts of all kinds—they all know they're frauds," Doc said.

"They can't all be frauds," Colin argued.

"They can, and they are—because they're human. I'm not saying they choose to be. All I'm saying is that none of us with any kind of special image can live up to it. It leaves no room for the doubts and imperfections that make our species. Even the best of them fudge a little—bullshit a chapter, pad a paragraph, fake a solo."

"Even the geniuses of their fields?"

"Sometimes I think a genius is made rather than born. I mean, if enough people call you one, you are. It doesn't really matter if what you produce is junk. It's almost as if people need perfection in others—to prove that we are, indeed, superior on this earth. How could we think of ourselves as spiritual—children of God—if we weren't able to sometimes come close to that heavenly quintessence?"

"So you're saying that even the great ones have doubts about their veracity?"

"All people do," Doc said. "The difference comes when a person begins to convince himself that what others perceive in him is correct. You know, like sublimation—a person releases unconscious thoughts in different ways. An author never really means something to be symbolic, but his readers interpret it as such. Later, he actually convinces himself that that's what he meant in the first place."

"Okay then," Colin concluded, "then some really believe in themselves."

"Not down deep. In fact, some, like Stephen Crane or Mark Twain, questioned their motivation—but that can drive you crazy. Most persuade themselves that they truly possess some extra-human talent. But there's always a guilt deep down inside."

"But how about you, Doc. Isn't your art real to you? Do you question the inspiration for your art?" Colin asked.

"Every day. Every hour. Every minute."

Doc had a way of making Colin feel guilty and extremely disappointed in himself. It was like meeting your conscience daily over hot dogs and a coke. Looking into one's depths is never pretty. Discovering the true purpose behind one's actions is painful. But the worst part was that it didn't seem to serve a purpose. Never did Doc's observations cause a change that would create something good or positive. All Doc ever seemed to do was to call attention to one's self-deception and hypocrisy. Doc never offered an alternative road.

Colin continued to stew in his own juices for another week before looking for a new source of income. He ended up taking a job that at least made some use of his special skills—he became a proofreader for an advertising magazine.

Oddly enough, this new position served a second purpose. Colin was now part of the manipulative media—out to brainwash an unsuspecting public with ideas that they thought were of their choosing. This was a way Colin had of punishing himself for not having the integrity that he so much aspired to.

To Colin's credit, though, he never gave up his dream. He was still bound and determined to be a proper journalist. He felt as if he were bursting with ideas that would reeducate the public to the truth of things. When he found an outlet for this information, the world would be taken up in a storm.

🍁   🍁   🍁

For some reason Colin was still drawn to Sandra. Here was a woman who represented the antithesis of everything he believed in—and what's more, she rejected him. Still, her approval seemed extremely important.

Though he told himself that Sandra was the last person he wanted to see now that his self-esteem was at an all time low, he found himself at her front door, knocking with the expensive brass doorknocker.

Sandra's father answered the door in the same way he had when they were dating. He would eye the suitor with suspicion before opening the storm door. Without a sound, Mr. Louder would return to his chair by the lamp and raise his paper over his face. Only then would he say something like: "Sandra will be right down" or "She's in the kitchen." This time he said, "She's in her studio painting."

Sandra's studio was in the remodeled basement of the home. Her father had it done in style so that Sandra would be happy working there. It was very important that Mr. Louder made his daughter happy.

Sandra stopped her work when she heard footsteps coming down the stairs. When Colin's face appeared above his body, a slight unconscious thrill ran through her.

"Hi, Sandra," Colin said in his eternally depressed voice. "Mind if I come down?"

"Of course not," Sandra said evenly.

Colin walked noiselessly toward her and came to a stop behind her working canvas.

"That's really nice," he said perfunctorily.

"I know you hate it," Sandra said. "You know," she said defensively, "it's *okay* for people to enjoy the beauty of flowers."

"I didn't say a word," Colin said.

"Yeah…but I know what you're thinking. You don't approve of my work. You think I'm a sell out."

"Sandra, I'm in no position to judge anyone else."

"You don't ever have to say a word. You're like my conscience. I check everything I do with how you will evaluate it. And I'm constantly asking myself if I am being true to my work. You're like my conscience incarnate, Colin."

"That's ridiculous," Colin protested.

"Is it? Well, it doesn't matter—it's how I feel."

Colin walked around in front of the easel and sat on an old kitchen chair next to Sandra's table containing tubes of oil paint.

"I just wanted to talk to you," Colin said quietly.

"Me? Why, Colin?"

"I don't know myself. I mean, I'm at an all time low. You're the last person I want to know about how bad off I am—yet, you're the first person I wanted to see."

"Why is that?" she said, picking up her brush again.

"I don't know, exactly. Somehow I feel you have something to teach me. I can't imagine why, but somehow I think you've got answers."

"Gee," Sandra said, "*that's* a shocker. How much have you had to drink tonight?"

"I know I don't seem like myself—whatever that is. I just wanted you to know that I'm not giving up."

"You don't ever have to tell me that," Sandra said, looking at him over the top of the canvas. "You're the one person in the world that never has to convince me of that."

"But I still need some answers," Colin said.

"Well, you've come to the wrong place for those. All I've got are questions."

❦   ❦   ❦

Having nothing to do, Colin spent a lot of time just hanging around. First he would walk for hours on the lakefront, balancing on the large rocks as the waves lapped just beneath his sneakers. The industry in the area had made this particular part of the lake useless for recreation. In fact, the boulders he balanced on were actually large cement slabs. There were fish out there, but few anglers cared for the product of these polluted waters. Besides, part of fishing is the natural setting; and this area wasn't something to inspire paintings.

Amazingly, when we're depressed, we seem to be attracted to depressing situations and environments. Walking in the rain or sitting in the dark is common for the gloomy. Maybe it's only that misery loves company. Maybe it's part of the downward spiral that melancholia begins. In any case, despair and despondency seem to feed on themselves, growing a monster that becomes too overwhelming to ever have hope of defeating—thus proving that there was never any possibility of escape.

So Colin knew what he was doing when he walked along with his thoughts, growing them into large demons. It was like picking a scab till it bleeds. You know it's harmful, and it hurts while you're doing it; but you continue to pick until there is no chance of it healing for a long time.

But there is method to the madness. As long as one is falling into the deep pit of despair, one may as well let go. Struggling in free fall is futile. The only hope is to hit bottom so there is no longer anything to lose. It's a tremendous weight lifted from the individual to give up completely—almost the perfect calm. Desperation no longer plagues you—you've dropped as far as you can go—there is no need for a fight—there is no hope for a savior. All is dull and dead and numb. One finally can get outside of oneself. A knowing smirk takes the place of the painful grimace.

However, try as he might, Colin had too much spark in him to lose himself in hopelessness. Just as he was beginning to give up, anger stepped in and saved him. And his anger was aimed externally, giving him respite. Then his anger cleared his head, and he took a direction—any direction—to save himself.

Colin knew that he must be around life. Desolation would destroy him.

About a half-mile down the shore, where a park met the water instead of concrete, was a tiny county zoo. At one time in the city's past, the little zoo boasted lions and giraffes and elephants. Now it dealt mostly with birds and other small animals. There was even a petting zoo for children.

But there was still one great beast left in the little menagerie: the bear. Actually there were three of them. They were located near the entrance, as if to disguise the insignificance of the rest of the park.

Colin, like most people, had no idea what kind of bears they were. They were simply brown bears like one thinks about when he envisions the creature, and Colin saw no reason to search for a placard with any further information.

In front of the bear cage was a small square machine. At the front of the machine was a rounded place where one could place a quarter. Then, turning a knob to the right—much like a gumball machine—a biscuit was dispensed. Apparently this was zoo-approved bear cuisine.

Colin was stingy with his money of late, but he figured he could part with 25 cents to make the big creatures happy. So he reached into the little coin pocket in his Levi's and pulled out one of two quarters. This he put into the machine, turning the knob. A small clunk sounded, and Colin opened the little metal door to retrieve his prize.

The biscuit was the size of a small dinner roll, so Colin broke it into four pieces. He tossed the first section high through the bars, wondering if the bears would even see it. To his surprise, not only did one of the large animals see it, but he used his comrade as a ladder to move higher, and dived for the small morsel.

Tossing the remaining pieces into the cage, Colin was treated to a real show. These heavy, lumbering creatures became quite agile with the hope of a treat; and their antics brought an unconscious smile to Colin's face.

As soon as the last piece was consumed, Colin eagerly fed the next quarter into the machine. Again, he was not disappointed. The biscuits must be delicious, he thought, as he witnessed more unexpectedly graceful moves.

This was the first joy Colin had experienced in a long time, and he did not want it to end. However, he had no more coins to waste. Then, staring absently toward the interior of the zoo, Colin spied a wishing well. In Colin's mind, the wishing well would be a source of coins for the biscuit machine; money would be provided by the zoo for the zoo animals. It was perfect.

Upon reaching the little structure in the center of the zoo, Colin peered in to see round silver shapes of all sizes. Without hesitation, he went in, head first, until he reached water. Unable to see clearly, Colin simply felt around for the money, judging denomination by size.

When he was sure he secured a quarter, he heard a loud voice overhead. Thinking it some wise guy or busybody, Colin continued his quest. The next sound he heard, however, was clear as a bell.

"Get out! Get out now!" the deep voice commanded.

"I'm getting quarters for the bears," Colin called up behind him.

"Now!" the voice said as someone grabbed him by the back of the belt and lifted him up.

When Colin's eyes refocused, he found he was staring at the angry face of a city policeman.

"What the hell do you think you're doing?" the man said.

"Oh...well...these bears over there," he pointed, "like the biscuits...so I needed quarters—"

"The zoo feeds the animals plenty," the policeman said. "You're going to have to come with me."

They walked together until they rounded the corner of the souvenir building, headed toward "back stage." The cop nodded for Colin to walk ahead of him when the path became narrow because of overgrown vegetation. Then Colin came to a stop in front of an extremely small Quonset hut.

"Go on in," the officer instructed.

Inside there was only enough room for a desk and a chair. Apparently this was the zoo "interrogation room."

"Okay, buddy," the policeman said as if he were talking to a made man in the mob, "put the money you stole from the well on the desk."

The scene would have been laughable had there been an audience, but neither the cop nor his perpetrator found this amusing.

"But I've—"

"I said, put all the money you've stolen from this zoo in the center of the desk," the man said emphatically.

Colin put the quarter he held in his hand on the desk. It might have been a thousand dollars, judging by the grim expression on the officer's face.

"Now empty your pockets," the cop said.

"Honest, sir," Colin pleaded, "that's all I took."

"I know that, but I want to see if you've got any drugs on you."

"Drugs? I don't do drugs, sir."

"Listen," the large man sad, "any guy your age who steals from wishing wells to feed bears is a suspect for carrying illegal substances."

Colin emptied his pockets, hoping the policeman's mood would change when he saw how ridiculous the whole scene was. But the man of law and order continued his role.

"Let's walk," he told Colin.

This time they went back up the path and made a sharp left just before it widened. Behind a large tree and some overgrown ferns sat the cop's black and white.

"Get in," he directed.

"You're taking me to the station?" Colin said in disbelief.

The man looked Colin directly in the eyes, as if he were talking to the scum of the earth, before answering, "I'm taking you out of my town."

They drove to the city line where the officer pulled across both lanes. Then he walked around to the to other side of the car, the side away from the city, and opened the door.

"Now get out, and don't come back."

Colin, sensing that an argument would be useless and might set the man off, proceeded to walk down the center lines of the road toward the country. Then as soon as he had rounded a curve in the road where the policeman—who stood watching a full five minutes now—could no longer see him, he dived into the woods, cut around in back of the zoo, and headed toward the mall to hang out with Jack.

CHAPTER 8

❈

"You're a hit," Selma Woods said as she paid Sandra for her most recently commissioned flower paintings. "It seems that my customers can't get enough of you."

"You mean a lot of people like my work?"

"All you have to do is get your stuff in the right living rooms, and you've got it made. They've been coming in here asking to see more. How much can you get over here?"

"Well, I've given you all the still-lifes and landscapes."

"Bring me anything. I think your pocketbook is going to be quite full, dear. The customers are asking for your work by name—that's the key for any artist."

The word "artist" was all that Sandra's ego required to blot out any doubts about the honesty of her work. She had been discovered, like Monet or Picasso or Pollack. Perhaps all her doubts were unfounded. After all, every artist looks a little too hard into himself—it's a creative person's nature. And even the best of them had done commissioned art, like portraits, to make ends meet until they could be free to produce what they were really meant to do. Yes, she was a true painter.

And just as Selma had told her, Sandra's paintings sold like hot cakes. She could barely keep up with the demand. In fact, her work became so sought after that she was interviewed for the *Times* Arts and Entertainment section of the Sunday paper.

Selma, always the businesswoman, exploited the interview and announced a show of Sandra Louder's work the following weekend.

❧   ❧   ❧

Sandra wasn't sure what to expect when she walked into Fabulous Taco the Monday after her interview appeared. She was especially worried about Colin's reaction. Here she was, feeling on top of the world, getting exactly what she had always hoped for—the last thing she needed was for someone to make her feel bad about her success.

So Sandra was quiet that afternoon. When she did talk, she spoke of trivial things—trying to direct the subject matter to the interests of one of the others at the table. Just when she thought she might get away with it, Colin spoke up.

"We all read your interview," he said, beginning a sarcastic smile.

"I was pretty sure you would," Sandra said.

"I, for one, think it came off great," Jack said enthusiastically. "Looks like you're getting there, Sandra."

"One way or the other," Colin said, with more than a hint of bitterness.

"Well, I suppose there are different ways to get started. At least I'm going in an upward direction," Sandra said innocently, but knowing her statement contained a sting for Colin.

"The important thing," Jack said, "is that you are doing what you were meant to do. You were put on earth to paint—it's your destiny."

"Destiny? What the hell is that?" Colin sneered.

"I believe that we all have a purpose here on earth. We all must contribute something to the world."

"I'm not sure man really has any purpose here," Doc said quietly. Of course, when Doc spoke, all heads turned. He was one of those individuals who seemed to say nothing if not profound.

"Then why are we here, Doc?" Jack asked.

"Well, now you're getting into something a little too deep for our little group. All I can say is that everything else on earth seems to have some sort of balance. Destruction of an insect or a pesky animal seems to throw all of ecology for a loop. But Man? Well, I'm not sure that his absence from the mix would make much difference."

"That's because man is unlike the rest of God's creatures," Sandra said. "He is intelligent and spiritual. He brings a soul to the universe."

"Are you saying that animals have no souls?" Colin asked.

"Yes, I guess I am. The world is populated with plants and creatures to serve man. They are linked in a balance because they exist together in man's dominion."

"Oh, brother," Colin shook his head. "What did they do to your mind in Sunday school, anyway."

"Man is a freak, a mutation, an aberration," Doc said, his voice becoming slightly more expressive. "He serves no function. He must rationalize his existence somehow, so he calls himself a higher being when indeed he is inferior."

"But what about art and music and drama and literature. They prove the depth of man," Sandra argued.

"And what is the principle subject matter of art and music and literature? Man. Even when the subject appears to be linked to nature, it is only about Man's reaction or relationship to it. Man's sole occupation is the celebration of himself. From the cavemen to the Egyptians to the present, man has been preoccupied with creating representations of himself—on stone, on walls, on paper. While other animals unconsciously function on earth, man consciously celebrates his being. It's the only way he can justify his existence."

"But people buy paintings of flowers and trees and—" Sandra argued.

"Artificial representations of the real thing—minus the irritating bugs and poison ivy and bad weather—to decorate his ugly shelters. Everything about what we call our 'culture' is synthetic."

"You make things sound so bleak," Sandra said.

"Yeah…and they call *me* cynical," Colin added.

Doc looked around, quickly studying each face. "Sorry," he said. "Sometimes I get carried away."

"That's okay," Jack said. "You make us think. It's just that sometimes a person doesn't want to analyze things—it's depressing."

"I think you've hit on something," Doc said.

"I have?"

"Yeah. If you think too hard about the charade and futility of it all, you spend your short time on earth in a funk. It's best to ignore it all and go with the flow."

"You, of all people, can't mean that!" Colin reacted.

"Of course I do."

"But you analyze everything to death. You question *everything*," Colin said. "I thinks that's something to be proud of."

"We've been through this before. What does it bring me? Sometimes knowing the answers, seeing through the veneer of everything is not a good thing."

"How can knowing the truth *not* be a good thing?" Colin asked.

"It's kind of like a ride at Disneyland. The artists and animators put you into a whole fantasy world—which is quite enjoyable. But if you start looking for the air conditioning ducts or start noticing thin wires and machinery, it ruins things for you."

"So?"

"So, it's like that with life. If you keep searching for the truth behind everything, it ruins the ride. And the ride is a short one, so why wreck it?"

Sandra couldn't help staring at Doc through his treatise. "Then why do you do it?" she asked softly.

"Because one cannot easily turn his back on the facts once he knows them. The key is to never uncover the truth—because there's no turning back."

※ ※ ※

It was always lonelier returning to his little apartment after discussions at Fabulous Taco. They saw him as so wise. They envied his sagaciousness. And he envied them. What they didn't understand was that all his philosophy, all his understanding of the world brought him only misery.

If the three young people only knew that the time he spent with them was the highlight of his life. Until he met them, his life was an inescapable darkness—a hell on earth. And he cursed himself for living it—for not having the courage to die.

Because he could not accept the deception and hypocrisy of the world, Doc could look forward to nothing else. Not like them. They had the whole world ahead of them…if only they didn't listen to him. Was it his jealousy that made him share the underside of life with good people? No, he *told* them that knowledge brought heartache…but did he truly think they would believe him?

Doc was doomed to his life because he did not accept a false existence. He was cursed because he could see through the smoke and mirrors. Thus, Doc's being consisted of the satisfaction of basic needs—like an animal or a street person. Everything else was an obvious sham.

Of course, basic needs have to be met. Doc had to eat, but he did not eat for pleasure—he ate from necessity to fill his stomach and to give him what energy he needed. The same with sleep—he did it so that his body would not shut down. As far as shelter, the hole he inhabited kept the rain off him and his work.

But there's another need that man has involving the female of his species. This was a requirement that brought more self-loathing than anything else in Doc's pitiful endurance. He had loved a woman with every molecule of his miserable self—and she was taken away. There could be no substitute. Yet, once in a while Doc's natural urge would take over his body and mind; and he could not think clearly until it was satisfied.

Now, man has always had the puritanical idea that sex, unlike eating and drinking, can be controlled with mind over matter. History has also characterized the carnal act as something wicked—except in matters of procreation. Doc knew different, of course. After all, he was extremely intelligent. But intelligence has little to do with the guilt and shame that society has filled our minds with. And even though Doc knew better, understanding did not diminish his self-reproach.

Therefore, Doc's sexual episodes could not be construed in anyway as human relationship or companionship. It was absolutely imperative in Doc's mind that satisfying his appetite for fornication must be understood as an animal act.

Every other Wednesday, just after leaving Fabulous Taco, Doc would walk East on Mulberry Street for about ten blocks until the homes began to look shabbier, and the inhabitants began to look pathetic or desperate. Here the businesses changed from gift shops and insurance agencies to adult bookstores and peep shows. People visiting the area were shadows, preferring to blend in with the gloom. And shame and desire were equally heavy in the air.

Doc walked to the corner of Mulberry and turned the corner at Peach. Here he was met with the filthy yellowed windows of Pete's Porno Palladium. Just after passing Pete's store front, Doc opened a door leading up a flight of dark stairs. He climbed them slowly as if an execution awaited him at the top.

When Doc reached the top, he made a sharp right. Immediately he confronted a glass door, its painted window protecting the secrets of the room beyond. Opening and entering, the room was not much lighter than the hall. It was lit only with scented candles and lava lamps, placed occasionally on covered wooden boxes serving as end tables for the three couches that lined the walls.

Scantily clad women sat on the couches, having close, whispered conversations with visiting men. Every so often a woman would rise, taking her man by the hand, leading him through a door at the back. Doc just stood at the entrance, taking the whole of his degradation in, when he was approached by an older woman who was obviously in charge.

"You're here for Corrine, aren't you?" she said knowingly.

"I don't know her name," Doc snapped.

"Hell, you take the same girl every time you stop by—you ought to know her name by now."

"I want the same woman—if she's available."

Corrine was a tiny woman with an innocence about her face. That innocence and a child-like voice put Corrine in a category apart from the others for Doc. And though Doc wanted to believe that she was just a whore that he used, there was a tenderness he felt when he was with her. His awareness of his affection for Corrine caused Doc much consternation so that he was rougher with the little prostitute during the sex act. Then afterwards, to his chagrin, he would worry that he had hurt her. And, of course, then he was angry with himself that he cared.

On this night Corrine looked particularly soft and vulnerable. Her perfume, unlike the strong scents that the others used, was gentle and fresh with just a touch of jasmine. Doc did not know if he could even approach her.

"What's wrong, Jacob?" she said in her juvenile tones.

"I don't want to talk," Doc said.

"Then you don't have to," Corrine said as she began to remove the few things she was wearing.

"I...I'm beginning to think of you as a person," Doc stammered.

"Is that so wrong?" Corrine said gently. "I *am* a person."

"No...no...I can't," Doc said, placing his hands over eyes that had begun to tear. Then he dropped his hands and turned toward the light switch by the door. Soon an overhead light in the center of the ceiling illuminated every inch of the filthy room, with its cracked plaster and stained furnishings.

In the middle of the room stood Corrine, a look of shock on her face. At least Doc assumed it was Corrine. The woman before him appeared worn and used. She wore caked makeup and dark eye shadow—giving her a movie vampire look. Her sagging breasts and flesh were marbled with stretch marks and discoloration. Corrine quickly pulled the top blanket off the bed to cover herself as if exposed naked before a man for the first time.

"Why did you do that?" Corrine asked, bewildered, exposing gray rotted teeth with large gaps toward the back of the upper set.

"Because now I can live with myself for another week," Doc smiled sadly, placing money on the bed table. Then he left and walked until he somehow found himself at the door to his own rooms.

CHAPTER 9

❀

Colin knew that if he continued to exist the way he had since leaving the paper that he would destroy himself. He knew he must do something to survive. He needed to put his angry energy to work somewhere so that he did not turn it back on himself again. It was not the first time that Colin had gone through the stages of disappointment and pulled through.

Taking any old job would not be the cure. If he were to work somewhere that he thought demeaning to him, he would only begin to sink again. No, it wasn't necessarily a job that would save him; but he had to fill his days with something by which he would be consumed.

Colin made the decision that he would write. At first he envisioned penning thick philosophical novels; but a blank page and virtually no experience put an end to that aspiration. Then he thought he might like to express his frustration with the political climate, but that would necessitate much research before actually attacking the keyboard—and Colin needed to strike immediately.

What he did was use a channel where his voice could be heard almost at once. He began sending contributions to the "Letters to the Editor" section of the daily news. This way Colin could pontificate on just about any subject and was sure to have a readership. In addition, he would get reaction by the next issue.

A newspaper usually picks the most provocative but well-written letters for this section because it is a main stop for most daily readers. Therefore, if someone familiar with the language and trained in persuasive writing sends contributions, the editor is glad to print them. Colin had no problem getting published.

In fact, the paper printed a number of his essays in consecutive papers; and the response was staggering. There were so many calls and letters in reaction to Colin's ideas that the paper began to generate some talk in town. This was quite exciting to an otherwise dull periodical, and they even found the sales began to increase.

Now, Colin's letters were seldom conservative, and they did not reflect the feeling of the community by any means; but they were controversial, and soon he became the man the town loved to hate. Colin's submissions were eventually given top status and continually selected for a small dark headline.

"My God, Colin, you're famous," Jack said at the meeting place, with a mouth full of hot dog.

"No shit," Colin said with an enthusiasm that had been lost for a good while. "People recognize the name wherever I go. I've been cursed in grocery stores, parking lots, and even at the dentist's office. It's great!"

"I'm not sure whether it's good or bad for us to be seen associating with you," Sandra laughed.

"I know—but I've always brought out the worst in people."

"Maybe you're getting people to think for a change," Jack said.

"Or maybe they're just digging in deeper to some of their twisted convictions," Doc suggested. "You know, people love a common enemy. It brings them together—solidifies their beliefs. I'm sure you've brought strangers together all over town."

"I do what I can," Colin grinned broadly.

🍁　　　🍁　　　🍁

Water coolers and lunch tables all over the city buzzed with ire over whatever Colin said the day before. Soon the paper realized that they couldn't let a good thing get away.

"They offered me a column," Colin said over the phone, with no other introduction.

"Colin?" Sandra asked sleepily. "It's 2 o'clock in the morning."

"I know, I know. I was gonna wait till tomorrow to tell you. I've been keeping it in since yesterday afternoon—but I just had to tell someone."

"I'm so glad you waited until this hour."

"Sorry…I just couldn't sleep."

"I know what you mean."

"They're even going to print my picture," Colin said excitedly.

"I thought you weren't into vain, pretentious things like that," Sandra chastised.

"It's all part of the image thing. They want a face to hate while they're thinking about what I've said. Anyway, they're paying me a regular salary, so who gives a shit."

"I'm happy for you," Sandra said sincerely. "But I'm going to have to go back to sleep now."

"Okay. I'll call you first thing tomorrow."

CHAPTER 10

❀

Jack looked from his pillow to the digital alarm clock on his bedside table. Only 4:15. This night seemed to last forever. His excitement over the first day in the recording studio made it almost impossible to sleep. It was like Christmas Eve, he thought. He couldn't remember one night before Christmas when he had had a minute of sleep. Up until now, it was the only time he had ever wanted the morning to come sooner.

According to Chuck Henderson, they would be using professional musicians on whatever tracks they would lay down in this session—just to see what it sounded like. Jack's music, though not particularly cerebral, had always consisted of just his voice and the honest tones of an acoustic guitar. He wasn't sure what the adulteration of other instruments and recording effects would have on his songs, but he reasoned that the pros must know what they were doing.

Jack arrived at New Horizons Studio an hour early. The secretary laughed at his innocence and provided him with coffee while he sat nervously flipping through trade magazines, wondering at the next stage of his career.

Finally someone walked through the heavy glass door of the reception area.

"Hi, Sam," the secretary called out from her cubicle.

"Hey, Candy," the man responded as if half awake. "Got coffee? I don't know why the hell these things gotta start so early. Most of us played jobs last night."

"Sam," Candy introduced, "this is Jack Benson. He's the guy you'll be recording with today."

Sam turned toward Jack as Jack jumped from his seat, hand extended.

"How're you doin', son. You gotta pardon my attitude this mornin'. I didn't get home till three."

"Oh, I understand, sir," Jack said, close to hyperventilation.

"Sir? Shit, son, I ain't yer daddy's age. You just call me Sam."

"Sure…Sam."

"I'll be playing guitar behind you today—just to kind of dress your stuff up a bit. After my eyes open a little, we'll go on in so I can get familiar with the songs you'll be doin'."

"Well, I don't have anything written down. I don't write music," Jack said almost apologetically.

"Hell, you ain't the first one. You just do what you do and leave the real music to us."

It was another half-hour before the other musicians showed up. Murphy Devlin, a short man with a mad shock of uncombed red hair, walked in first and immediately took a seat on the throne of the drum set before saying a word to anyone. Snore Atkinson walked in a few minutes later, a sullen demeanor behind a thick cloud of cigar smoke—he would be playing keyboards. Last was Ian Smith, the most personable. He would be playing rhythm guitar on a huge twelve string Guild. Ian would also share the bass duties with Sam.

By the time Chuck Henderson and the engineers arrived, Jack had played four or five tunes to the backup musicians. Jack had become used to impressing people with his little songs, and was extremely disappointed when, upon completing the first for these backup men, not a comment was made. In fact, each song was met with blank faces.

"We got it," Sam finally said. Then before the musicians took their places in the studio, they huddled together and talked quietly. Jack scanned their faces for any sign of smile or ridicule, but they continued to keep their expressionless demeanors.

"Okay, Jack, you ready?" Chuck's car salesman voice came from the booth.

"Sure am," Jack said, realizing how like an adolescent he sounded.

"Sam," Chuck said, "show Jack where to sit and what to do."

Sam indicated a stool in front of a microphone behind a round filter.

"Put the head phones on there, boy, and just sing when they tell you."

"But there's no mike here for the guitar," Jack observed.

"You concentrate on yer singin' just now," Sam said. "Ian here will take over yer guitar chores."

Before Jack could object, Chuck was talking from the booth again. "Let's run through the first number for a check," he said.

Jack could hardly believe his ears as Ian played the acoustic introduction to *Jenna*, exactly as Jack would have done it—but much, much better. As the rest of the band kicked in, Jack just sat open-mouthed at the record-quality background they had put together with their short conversation.

"I've got no voice from Jack," the engineer said from the booth.

"Sorry," Jack said.

"Okay," the engineer said. "Let's try her again."

This time Jack came in on cue, hearing his voice through the headphones float beautifully atop a professional background of perfectly balanced instruments.

"How'd that come off, Sarge?" Sam spoke to the glass.

"Got the sound," the engineer said. "We'll need another take on the song to smooth the edges."

After four more takes of what Jack thought perfection, they were finally able to move on.

"I'd like you to try one of the others now, Jack," Chuck said.

"The others?"

"Yeah. We talked about that on the phone."

"Oh, yeah," Jack said, a little dejectedly.

"Come on, Jack, you've got to leave some of these decisions to us now. Let's try one; I think you'll like how it turns out."

Jack listened to the demo three times before he thought he had it. He was able to follow along with the words until he indicated that he had the proper phrasing.

"This is close to rock and roll, don't you think?" Jack said to the air.

"Jack, a performer has to show his versatility. You can't have an album of one folksy love song after another. This will show another side of you."

"Okay. Do you have the music for the band?"

"The band already knows it," Chuck said.

The song *Ripping Through* was an angry tune about social injustice and the disenfranchised. It began with semi-power chords and a biting solo by Sam before Jack was to start.

Of course, Jack's mushy James Taylor/John Denversish voice missed the mark completely.

"Jack, can you get a little roughness to your voice?" Chuck asked after the first take.

"I can't sing that way," Jack argued.

"Sure you can," Chuck said encouragingly. "Let Sam take it through once and show you. Sam?"

Sam gave a weak smile to Jack as he stepped up to the microphone. If Jack hadn't been uncomfortable and sensitive as to his role in this session up to this point, he surely was now. He took a seat almost hidden by an acoustic divider and prepared to listen.

Sam belted out the song effortlessly in some of the most driving, soulful notes that Jack had ever heard. He couldn't believe his ears. Here was a man who possessed more talent in his little finger than Jack had developed in his entire time as a performer, and he was relegated to the position of backup musician.

"My God, you're great!" was all Jack could say.

"I'm just a session player," Sam said. "You're the man that has to sing this. You think you got her?"

"I think I know what he wants," Jack said, not happy about singing the same song after Sam's rendition.

But Jack did sing. He pushed his thin melodious vocal chords as much as he could. Of course, there was no way he would have the raw power of Sam's sound. Hell, he didn't even have the volume. When he finished the take, Jack's head dropped in disappointment.

"Fantastic!" Chuck blurted from the booth.

"What?" Jack was incredulous.

"It's exactly what I wanted."

"It didn't even come close," Jack said.

"It wasn't supposed to. We're selling *you* here, Jack—not just your songs. There's much more to the music business than music."

What a horrible thing to say when all the people in the studio could hear. Jack didn't think he could look at anyone again. All he wanted was to leave, and leave quickly. But he did sneak a glance behind him at the band, half expecting them to be in a group snickering. Instead, he saw four noncommittal faces standing ready for the next song.

After the session, Jack met with Chuck in the lounge at the back of the studio—even the engineers had gone home.

"I think we've got something big here," Chuck said, handing Jack a Dr. Pepper from the machine.

"Yeah," Jack said, heavily.

"What's wrong Jack?"

"What did you mean when you said that the music wasn't all we were selling here?"

"Oh, don't get me wrong, Jack. The music is important. But in this business it's the face, the personality that sells."

"But that song—the one Sam sang—he was great. Why doesn't *he* have a recording contract?"

"It's like I just said, Jack—he doesn't have the look and the manner to go with it. Hell, he'd scare people if they saw him on an album cover. Besides, that was his kind of song. He can't do anything else."

"But it wasn't *my* kind of song."

"Yeah, but the girls will go nuts when they hear that gentle voice try for a nasty edge. It's going to work, I tell you."

"So you're grooming me to be some kind of teenage heart throb?"

"Listen, Jack. It's a way to get your foot in the door. You're lucky you've got it. It doesn't mean you can't take your music seriously. On the contrary, the plaintive love songs are gonna break hearts everywhere."

"But…how do I face session musicians when I know they have so much more talent?" Jack asked.

"Jack, you must understand that you and only you are the star. They understand that. They know their place—you've got to know yours. Stars have a quality that transcends sound—they know that too. A good session man has long gotten over that comparison thing. *You* are what their job is all about, and they know that only *you* can accomplish things out there on the concert tour. You're gonna be big, Jack; and every backup musician will have been proud to play on your songs."

CHAPTER 11

❀

Sandra strained to get a good look at her buttocks in the full-length mirror by her bedroom door. The washed out blue jeans still fit pretty well, she thought. And they didn't look bad with the oversized black sweater she had chosen. Of course, black leather Doc Martins would complete the outfit. She only wondered if some kind of headgear would be going too far. After all, she was an artist—not someone dressing for a costume party *as* an artist.

It was a beautiful day, and the show at the Town Gallery would be able to extend to the garden in the back. She could envision herself walking among the paintings, hearing people whisper, "That's her…That's Sandra Louder," as she passed. With the sun shining down through the vines entwined around the Town's trellised enclosure, she would sit on a wooden chair and observe the crowds—it would be like Paris.

Of course, nothing turns out like we imagine; but this time things were very close. Arriving an hour after the show began, Sandra's heart beat quickly as she saw that there, indeed, was a crowd behind the little art store. As she pulled up, women in expensive leisure clothes were getting out of cars and walking down the cobblestone walk which led to the back. And it was all for her. It was all about what she created.

Sandra had to take a few deep breaths to calm herself so that she could affect the "cool" that she wanted to show her admirers. Then she walked with a slow deliberate confidence to appear before the many patrons of the city's upper middle class.

There was Selma Woods standing at a weathered wicker table, handing out glasses of wine. What would a day's adventure be for these amateur art connoisseurs without the obligatory alcohol? Naturally, it would be only a few glasses, just to keep the laughter and the conversation flowing.

Selma spotted Sandra out of the corner of her eye, and raising her own wine glass in Sandra's direction, she announced in a voice that all had to attend, "Here she is now. Here's your artist—Sandra Louder."

Sandra's knees went weak as the entire population of the back garden turned and applauded—at least those ladies who could find a place to set their glass for a moment. It was a dream come true. Sandra's art was being appreciated. No…not appreciated. They loved it…and they loved her, for it was an extension of her.

When the ovation ended, many of the customers continued to browse through the canvases. A group of three ladies trotted up to Sandra excitedly.

"Oh we just love your paintings," one of the women said. She was a rather plump lady, but she wore her weight properly under clothes that draped just right.

"Yes, yes," her friend said from beneath a straw sun visor. "Debbie and I already have one," she bubbled, sharing a grin with her fat friend. "And we're looking for one for Mindy now."

"Oh? Well, is there something in particular that you like?"

The shorter woman smiled up into Sandra's face. "Browns," she said. "I need something with just the right shades of brown."

Not all the show's visitors were interested in matching furniture and wall hangings, thank goodness. Some were even well stocked with arty "buzz words" that—if not overanalyzed—allowed Sandra to feel credible about her work.

Though we want to believe it, most of us are initially skeptical about praise that we're not sure is deserved. But because it's how we imagine ourselves, we don't give all that much fight to other's claims about our great ability. Soon, we're more than willing to believe it. *Perhaps there was just a bit of virtuoso in that work after all. Yes…yes…that's what you meant to convey from the first.* Sometimes one's head can swell quite a bit from the praise until one reaches the point where criticism is now foreign and, therefore, ignored as anomalous and thus incorrect.

Fortunately, God plants mines of humility just when we're most secure in our ascendancy. For Sandra, this came in the form of a large, somewhat portly gentleman sitting in the very back of the garden on a large landscaping rock.

"What are you doing here?" Sandra said to the stubble-faced man in the faded khaki T-shirt and rumpled baggy jeans.

Doc hadn't noticed her walk up, and he turned his head slowly to his left when he recognized the voice.

"I wanted to see your work."

"You don't seem to be looking at any paintings way over here by yourself," Sandra said.

"I was at the show when it started. I've been through your things at least three times now."

"And you're disappointed," Sandra said dully.

"Disappointed? No."

"It's what you expected from me then."

"You sound as if you're not happy with what you've produced," Doc said, the shadows of a small Japanese maple falling across his considerable forehead.

"You think it's trite, don't you?"

"Trite? That's an odd word to come up with."

"I mean," Sandra's shame was making her defensive, "that you don't think it's real art. You know, *from the soul.*"

"You're wrong, Sandra. I think there's a definite place for your work."

"But it's not legitimate."

"Another very interesting word. Listen, Sandra, painting must be appreciated by the *people*. After all, opera and symphony were not directed at the elite. Even Shakespeare was written for the common man. It's the *groundlings* that are important, Sandra."

"What's that supposed to mean?"

"I mean," Doc said, "that it's what the population thinks at the time that is important."

"So if everybody's buying up velvet paintings, then that's legitimate art."

"There's that word again. My point is that your work is legitimate if it is viewed as such. I don't think velvet painting is ever going to reach that status," he smiled.

"Okay," Sandra gave up her aggression, "I give up. What I really want to know is whether you like it."

"Yes."

"You do?" she was surprised.

"Sometimes an artist, a musician, a writer gets so caught up in the calling that he creates masterpieces that only he himself understands. Sure, everyone recognizes the mastery, the ability; but not everyone likes it."

"You're losing me, Doc. Aren't you just trying to weasel out of an explanation."

"Haven't you ever heard a simple country song that hits you just the right way. I mean, it's simple and didn't take much musical knowledge or ability to produce, but it hits you just the right way."

"Yeah…I have."

"The guy that recorded it becomes famous. I mean, you could find better singers and musicians in the lounges of most of the Holiday Inns in the city—but they never make it."

"That's true."

"And sometimes a guy that has interested people with his little song begins to grow as a musician, as an artist himself. He begins to expand his horizons. And the people hate it."

"So, you're saying that what I do is like that little song."

"I'm saying that what you do has a purpose higher than decoration. And if it's what you do with all your heart, then you should be proud of it."

Sandra pondered the point and was just about to ask for clarification when Selma Woods walked up and grabbed her by the arm.

"Where've you been, dear? There are so many people that want to meet you. You must be so proud."

🍁 🍁 🍁

Often one or two of the members of the Fabulous Taco group would be late or have some other plans. Discussions were always best when everyone showed up, but that was not always possible. Lately, every member arrived just around six and stayed until midnight, if not later.

Strange that as the members of the little circle would be more regular in their attendance just as each career was taking a jump and there was so much to do. But oddly, Sandra, Colin, and Jack valued their little band more because of that fact. All three seemed to be swept up in things that were uncontrolled and artificial, and they needed grounding. In other words, Fabulous Taco became the site of reality check.

"The hot dogs are on me," Colin announced to the table. "And eat what you want; I'm finally gonna get a paycheck."

"Great…I'm starved," Sandra said.

"I got drunk last night," Jack defined non sequitur. "Alone."

"What the hell for?" Colin asked.

"I don't exactly know. I've been all keyed up lately. I'm not much of a drinker, you know, so I bought some pop wine, figuring it would mellow me out a little."

"Man, you should know better than to drink by yourself," Colin shook his head.

"Yeah...that's what alcoholics do," Sandra said.

"No...no...it was good for me."

"You mean you got high and felt better," Sandra scolded.

"No. I mean...I got outside myself. I was able to see things more clearly."

"Was that *acid* wine?" Colin laughed sarcastically.

Doc rubbed his eyes, both elbows resting on the table. "I understand what he's talking about. I do it all the time."

"Well, then, maybe you can explain it to us."

"Jack, remember when I told you to look at things as if you were a stranger?" Doc asked.

"Sure...I remember...Now I know what you were talking about."

"Sometimes when I'm just drunk enough," Doc explained, "I look at my hands and just wonder at how old they look—like I'm looking at someone else's hands. Sometimes I'll go into the bathroom and just stare into the mirror."

"I never took you for narcissistic," Colin said.

"Far from it. But sometimes when I've had quite a bit to drink, it alters my perception so that I'm almost seeing what others see."

"Is that really a good thing?" Sandra asked. "I know when I see myself on video tape or hear a recording of my voice, I'm usually very upset."

"It's always a good thing to view yourself as just another person—one of the crowd. It gives you a better perspective on things and forces you to see your relative insignificance in this world. It's never a bad thing to understand that the world does not revolve around you."

"It's a little bit frightening," Sandra said.

"Yeah," Colin said, "it scares me just to think that I'm one of this race of mutants. Ever sit on a bus and watch people get on and off? Could I possibly be that disgusting?"

"I think that misanthropy of yours is going to make you very successful in your new career," Sandra said.

"And it's just so easy to find fault with the way things are," Colin agreed.

"Too easy," Doc said wistfully.

CHAPTER 12

❀

Jack had attended a good number of concerts at Municipal Park Stadium, but never one like this. Unlike most shows where the stage is turned toward the athletic field so that the seating includes even the nosebleed seats of the stadium, this concert was held on the end of the field. The stage was made so that it could be converted to face in either direction, so for small shows only one end of the field was used.

Most of the entertainment in this area were acts that appealed to a mostly older, more mature crowd. Jazz and blues groups, big bands, and oldies groups were among the acts one could see in this venue. Of course, this didn't sell as many tickets, and there was not as much money to be made as with the rock bands; but the smaller shows produced enough revenue to make them worthwhile.

Entering the concert area was quite different than with most shows. Because an older crowd would be attending, beer and wine stations, complete with long-stemmed plastic glasses, were set up just inside the entrance. Also, right before the stage came into view, a makeshift bistro was set up with tables and waitresses for pre-show socializing.

As Jack and Chuck walked up from the parking lot, Jack was struck by the age of the crowd headed toward the entrances. Groups of couples ranging from their 40's to their 60's strode slowly up to the gates and then stood patiently in line, smiling and joking comfortably with others of their generation.

It's tough to get older, and most people fight it—so it's interesting to watch the many ways middle age people face their dilemma. It seemed as if each had his own idea of the proper concert-going attire. This was based mostly on an individual's perception of what was currently "cool"—and always mistaken. It was like thousands of people having their midlife crises in the same spot all at once.

Jack saw everything from white-haired men in Hawaiian shirts and pleated-front shorts with little gold necklaces to old hippies in their jeans and cutoffs, their long hair blowing in the breeze or tied back in a ponytail. The women wore T-shirts purchased from *Wireless* magazine, printed with clever sayings or observations. Their neatly pressed bluejeans were made loose for comfort, and the denim was still very dark—which only accentuated their stark white sneakers.

Once seated, the audience was as excited as impatient adolescents waiting to see the newest teen idol. Ladies whispered to each other with the word "remember" coming up over and over in their conversation. They seemed to be actually wiggling in their seats in anticipation of what they would soon experience.

"I'm still a little confused about why you wanted me to go to this concert," Jack said.

"Come on, Jack, you must've heard of Little Wonder and the Beachbums."

"Sure, I have. They're part of rock and roll history—but why are *we* here?"

"To make a point, son. How do you think an act like this could stay around for decades and still draw crowds?" Chuck asked pedantically.

"They were good."

"Lots of people are *good*!" Chuck corrected.

"Okay…they were great."

"Wrong, wrong, wrong, wrong!"

"Well, it couldn't be because they were bad," Jack said, a little puzzled.

"Listen, Jack…Little Wonder has just been admitted into the Rock and Roll Hall of Fame. His peers have recently been honoring him with banquets and television specials."

"I'm sure he deserves it."

"They herald him as a musical genius, Jack. They're taking the little catchy tunes that he slapped together in a bus seat or a dressing room, and they're calling it great art. They've even recorded a couple of Wonder's ballads with orchestras—as a kind of tribute. Can you imagine that! Here's some guy in the Chicago Symphony Orchestra who has spent his whole life studying music—theory and harmony and all that shit—and he has to play a bunch of trite notes strung together, originally composed to accompany pubescent love lyrics. And he's got to keep a straight face while doing it."

"So, if Little Wonder is not the maestro they give him credit for being, why is it so important that we see him tonight?" Jack asked.

"Because they *believe* he's a genius. Because *he* believes he's a genius."

"Huh?"

"Just enjoy the concert," Chuck said, handing Jack a five-dollar cup of beer he just purchased from a traveling vendor. "We'll talk later."

It wasn't quite late enough to be dark, but the lights were still able to color the stage in a fantasy blue as a bodiless voice announced in the deep professional tones commonly heard before a wrestling match: "Ladies and gentlemen, let's give it up for the greatest rock and roll band in the world—LIIIIIIITLE WONDER AAAAND THE BEACH BUMS!

As the recognizable bass part at the beginning of Wonder's biggest hit *Sleepin' on the Beach* began, the crowd went wild and immediately lept to its feet. Without a doubt, this audience was ready to throw themselves into the mood of the evening. Hands went into the air and clapped to the rhythms, as hoots and whistles emerged from the mouths of businessmen, shoe salesmen, and grandparents.

In front of Jack were three 50ish women dancing the same steps, shaking rear ends that had more than their share of cellulite—moving their torsos in remembered sexually suggestive motion. My God, Jack thought, in their youth these were the type of women who would ride their boyfriends' shoulders at concerts and bare their bosoms. Jack prayed that wouldn't happen tonight.

When the first song finished, the audience returned to their seats as Little Wonder greeted them with almost as much hype in his voice as his announcer. Little Wonder had to be in his early 60's, but with hair coloring and just the right lights, one could almost imagine him in his better days. The Beachbums, however, looked like the beer-gutted slobs that you see in the better seats at NBA games.

The second tune was not recognizable to the audience. Little Wonder was trying to make a kind of comeback and had just released an album of all new tunes. The new tunes, however, were not the simple innocent adolescent anthems he had produced many years before. Little Wonder, believing in the musical prowess attributed to him, composed very serious and what he thought as musically complex songs for the new CD.

The audience was in a mood to party, so they didn't judge Little Wonder's attempts at serious art too harshly. Though they remained in their seats, they still clapped and hollered and swayed to the foreign sounds.

It was apparent that Little Wonder was going to plug his new endeavor by stringing a few of these songs together at this point in the concert. Jack wondered if this might be a mistake in showmanship—that maybe he would lose the momentum of his performance. Then all of a sudden young girls began to pop up in various places among the crowd. These young women seemed to be big fans because they began to dance with wild abandon to Wonder's new sounds. And they didn't sit down after a number. They continued to move with no sign of wearing down, as Wonder did unrecognizable song after unrecognizable song.

Jack was surprised how women so young could be such enthusiastic fans of Wonder's music. And it seemed odd to him that these young fans appeared to rise to the beat at the exact same time. And they were so well spaced among the concertgoers.

Soon others in the crowd became infected by the ardor of the youngsters and began to dance along. One by one, the crowd rose to its feet in movement until they functioned as a single being, giving of themselves, immersing themselves in a spirit they did not totally understand. Soon having no sense of self.

How could this happen? Jack wondered. The dancing girls were apparently "plants" to get things moving—but how could mature, intelligent people be taken in by such a ploy. Jack thought of the television religious revivals where thousands of people would relinquish their individuality to a manipulator on stage who would have them waving and swaying together to the Holy Spirit.

Later in the concert Wonder returned to the oldies and then finished with a medley of his best. Obviously his management knew what side the bread was buttered on and had insisted that he do what he was known and loved for.

There was a sense of exhaustion when the last note of the last song ended. The audience had been whipped up into such a frenzy that they now experienced the pleasant feeling of release that one feels after intense sex. And to some of them, this was the closest they had gotten to intense sex in quite some time.

"Okay," Jack said, the two of them remaining seated in the plastic chairs as the crowd filed out. "Now you can tell me why you brought me here."

"I was hoping at this point I wouldn't have to explain," Chuck said, shaking his head but smiling.

"Well, you do."

"It's simple. It's not about the music. It's about image. It's about perception. It's about aura. It's about promotion."

"Are you trying to show me that my music is not the thing that will sell my records?" Jack asked.

"The music has to be somewhat catchy. Even the best of them has to make sure they have relatively good material. But it's much more than that."

"Explain," Jack said skeptically.

"Do you really think Madonna has all that much singing ability. Yeah, sure, she was in *Evita* and surprised the hell out of us all; but for the most part she's a hacker."

"A hacker?"

"She's got this little thin voice that sounds like all the other little thin voices. Her tunes are provocative, and young people like that. But most of all, it's her attitude—her image. The lady knows how to cultivate celebrity.

"Ever notice how some sports figures get all the commercials and some don't get any? Sure, part of it is based on how they perform as athletes—but sometimes it's the second and third best that you see all over the television. You know why? It's because they're interesting. I mean, let's face it, Dennis Rodman made a couple of movies. Do you think he deserved that?"

"Yeah, you're right about the sports world," Jack conceded.

"I'm right about the entertainment world too. Do you really think that Arnold Schwarzenegger is an actor—or even Tom Cruise, for that matter? It's image that sells."

"And you want me to develop an image."

"Jack," Chuck said patronizingly, "I'm not asking you to forget about your songs. I'm not even asking you to discard your personality. I'm just asking you to think about the marketing game as part of your development. Would you do that for me?"

"Sure, I guess."

"That a boy," Chuck said with a big white grin.

CHAPTER 13

The little metal diner was built sometime in the 50's by a company who was putting them all over the country. Though it may have been an eyesore at the time, the place had become an historic building. There was something comforting about a structure that was stainless steel inside and out—clean and comforting. And the little metal restaurant seemed to trap the smells of the wonderful food like no brick or wooden building ever could. Whatever the attraction, Chef's Dinner was always packed.

Colin made it a habit to take his lunch about 45 minutes earlier than everyone else so that he was assured a seat. And like the writers of old, Colin had his favorite booth in the back. Here he would enjoy the tasty greasy dishes that could be found nowhere else, while he read the *New York Times* or *The Washington Post*.

Of course, after awhile the waitresses know your name and even what you're likely to order. Seconds after Colin sat down, a large ice tea was placed before him as chesty Daisy Wenk stood over the table, order pad in hand, making sure Colin would still be having the "regular."

"I'll have the Deluxe Platter, Daisy," Colin said, smiling around his paper.

"You know, Mr. Morely, you really should try something else once in awhile. The Turkey Club Special is one of our most popular lunches."

"I'm afraid of what my stomach would do if it didn't get its daily share of grease," Colin said, placing the paper in his lap.

"You're a real character," the tall, solid blond said, pushing the wisps of her tied-back hair out of her face.

"That's what they pay me for."

"I wouldn't do what you do for no amount of money," Daisy said, the corner of her lips blowing up at the continually falling strand of hair.

"Oh, it's not so bad," Colin said. "It's kind of fun coming up with something that will set people off every day. You'd think they'd ignore me by now—but they just keep coming back for more."

"What you got written across your T-shirt?" Daisy observed, putting her book in the pocket of her small apron.

"*Iconoclast*," Colin said, waiting for a reaction.

"What's *that* mean?"

"Oh, it's just another way of getting people pissed off at me," Colin said, suddenly realizing that most people wouldn't even know what to make of it.

"You're a real *character*," Daisy repeated, departing for the kitchen.

Colin immediately lifted the paper and started perusing the editorials, when he felt someone's presence. Thinking that Daisy had returned, Colin lowered his paper smiling."

"You little fuckin' shit," a portly woman holding the hand of a small child spat at him.

"Ah, a fan," Colin said calmly.

"All you do is tear everything down. What kind of a person spends every day of his life making fun of everything that good people care about!"

"And what exactly makes you a *good* person?" Colin asked, his eyes in mock curiousness.

"I'm a Christian lady with old-fashioned values."

"And that's it?"

"That's all there has to be," she said.

"Don't you ever question anything about your existence? Don't you ever wonder if some of your ideas could be wrong?"

"Thinkin' about every little thing only causes misery. I accept what life gives me and the ways of my people. That's what a good citizen does—that's how you get along. But you…you always got to make waves," she said, yanking the child back as he pulled away.

"But don't you want to know the truth about things?" Colin asked.

"The truth is what you believe. Shakin' all that up makes it harder for a soul to live from day to day. And then you got to come along and start tamperin' with our notions."

"You know," Colin said sincerely, "what you just said is quite profound."

"There you go again," the lady said angrily, her face now turning a bright red, "criticizing what people say." And she turned, yanking the poor arm of the child again, and stalked off down the diner floor toward the door.

❦   ❦   ❦

"We hardly ever do anything as a group except meet here to eat," Sandra said that evening, paying for her order at the counter of Fabulous Taco.

"What's wrong with that?" Colin asked.

"Nothing's wrong with that. It's just that friends should do something together besides constantly analyzing their lives over pork byproducts. I was just thinking that we could spend a day doing something that had no deep meaning—something that is just for fun."

"What have you got in mind?" Jack asked, reaching for his next fry.

"I was thinking about us going to an amusement park," Sandra announced in expectation of enthusiasm.

"An amusement park? What the hell for?" Colin asked.

"For no reason. That's the beauty of it—we go and have fun with no reason except to enjoy ourselves."

"You should have been head cheerleader in high school," Colin scowled.

"I think she's got a point," Jack said. "We've all been under a lot of pressure lately—I know I have. It might do us some good to do something totally non-cerebral—something that doesn't have to make any sense."

"Okay, okay," Colin conceded, "maybe a day away wouldn't hurt."

"How about you, Doc?" Sandra asked.

"I'm afraid you'll have to count me out."

"Why? Don't you like to have fun?"

"I'm just not very good at it," Doc said.

"But maybe a couple of roller coaster rides and some cotton candy will clear your mind—give you a new perspective."

"I've never understood why anyone would choose to terrorize himself with an amusement park ride. Life seems to be full of so many frightening situations, why would one want to partake in artificially induced fear?"

"Because," Sandra explained, "it has nothing to do with reality. It's a way of losing yourself for awhile."

"Why do people find that so necessary?" Doc asked.

"Why do people drink?"

"Touché," Doc said.

🍁 🍁 🍁

Even for the most cynical, walking into an amusement park holds an excitement and a nerve tingling sense of expectation. The promise of adventure hangs in the air as smiling faces enter the numerous turnstiles, heads turning up at the first sights of a fantasy trip.

And modern theme parks do their best job at the entrance, creating a feeling for its customers of having left the real world. Faux buildings from storybook times with their stucco and beam walls and thatched roofs; or empty castles, their colors flapping in the blue sky line; the main path leading to the midway area.

Of course everyone knows that behind the doors of the counterfeit fairy land are the first of many, many souvenir shops. But knowledge of the setup doesn't deter the crowds from visiting the little air-conditioned stores and spending only the beginnings of the hard-earned cash they brought.

Next in sight, of course, are the food vendors with the usual fair: hot dogs and cotton candy and ice cream and even pizza. Naturally no one can resist the sights and smells of the overpriced food, so there is a second stop before even getting close to the attractions one paid to experience.

It's funny how people are with food. Eating seems to be an integral part of recreation for Americans. One can't go to a sporting event and really, truly enjoy himself without a four-dollar hot dog and a five-dollar plastic glass of beer. A circus just isn't the same without cotton candy. And who in his right mind would sit through a movie in a theater without at least one box of popcorn. Even sidewalk and garage sales have some successful entrepreneur offering a hot dog, fries, and a coke for some outlandish amount. Feed you're face: enjoy the day.

Fabulous Taco had made the four friends hot dog aficionados, so their first stop was the Weiner Wagon. As the group sat around the little umbrella-covered metal table, they offered their expert opinions on the food.

"I have to admit," Colin said, still chewing his food as he talked, "these are great hot dogs."

"It's just because we're out in the fresh air," Jack said. "Food always tastes better outside."

"I think the smells and the atmosphere are just doing a job on you," Doc said, almost smiling.

"They're too rich or spicy or something," Sandra said, taking a long drink of her soda.

"Food can't be plain anymore," Doc said. "They have to bombard the senses. Everything has to have more sauce, more bacon, more cheese. Then when all that gets boring, they have to come up with something else. In the mean time, our taste buds have become numb."

"Well, you know what they say," Colin said. "Build a better hot dog."

"That's *mousetrap*," Sandra said, missing the joke, "and I don't think these are better."

"It's not just with food," Doc said. "Everything has to be bigger and better and more colorful. Take these roller coaster rides," he said nodding over his hot dog to the top loop of the Terror Titan. "People used to get a thrill out of going up and down on a few little hills—but then they wanted more and more and more. Some of these rides today are just about pushing the ceiling of safety."

"Yeah, like that bungee jump they have on the other side of the park," Jack said. "They take you up to this amazing height, and then they just drop you—with nothing but an elastic cord to stop your fall and send you bouncing around in the air. Who needs that?"

"I think the problem lies in the fact that we're deadening our sensory organs so that they are not able to tune into to the small, fine, delicate messages. If a smell doesn't knock you over nowadays, you don't even notice it's there. We're missing sounds and feelings all over the place because they've been drowned out for so long."

"That's true," Jack said. "The other day I was just sitting at home with everything off—no television, no music, nothing. I just felt like I needed quiet. But there was no quiet. The traffic and sirens and blasting car stereos never let up for a minute. Pretty soon I got pretty irritated by the fact that it would just never be silent—*ever*."

After one more hot dog, they made their way past the kiddie rides and games and down one of the roads leading off the central area. The place was beautifully landscaped. Clear creeks twisted in and out around the rides and concession stands. Tree shaded rest areas were evenly spaced throughout. There was even a peaceful duck filled pond with lily pads and cattails under the swinging bridge on the way to the Death Defier, the newest and scariest ride in the park.

"Oh, my God...Look at that!" Jack exclaimed while staring up at the anti gravity track at the top of the ride.

"Yeah, they say you get lifted off your seat when you hit the top," Sandra said excitedly.

Colin squinted up into the sun. "And then you come down backwards."

"You can leave me out of this one," Doc said.

"Oh, no, Doc," Sandra said, "we're all doing this together."

"What is it with women and roller coasters?" Colin quipped.

"A better question is, Why men are so afraid of them?" Sandra said.

"I think it's a control thing," said Jack. "I don't mind riding on daredevil vehicles as long as I'm driving. I don't like putting myself where I am at the mercy of others."

"It's just a ride," Sandra laughed. "And it's safe. It gives you a chance to just let go without worrying about being hurt."

"I think you hit on the best explanation there," Doc said.

"I don't like to drop," Colin said. "I don't mind being jerked around, but I don't like to drop. I see no fun in that."

"The fun is when it's over and you're exhilarated because you got through it. You feel really alive because you faced something so terrorizingly overwhelming and survived. It's a rush."

"Don't you think it's kind of sad that it takes this kind of experience to feel alive?" Doc asked. "Shouldn't someone feel alive because the sun is shining and the birds are singing? Why does someone have to have a brush with death?"

"I guess the world is so fast and furious that it takes something pretty frightening to put you in another place for awhile," said Jack.

"Another place? You mean on some other plane? Some other level of consciousness?"

"Something like that, Doc," Jack smiled.

"Maybe you have to feel like life could be taken away from you to really appreciate it, even if it's only an artificial threat," Colin said.

"That's pretty profound, Colin," Doc said, nodding his head.

"I once knew a guy," Jack said, "that told me he felt nothing most of the time. I mean, his emotions were flat. This guy used to skydive just to feel something. Can you believe anyone could be like that?"

"I'll tell you what I believe," Sandra said. "I believe that the line has just gotten longer while we've been standing here yapping. Come on, let's go."

Part of the anxious anticipation that people feel for one of these thrill rides is accomplished through the long wait in line where one watches the screaming faces of the current riders and wonders how he will respond. Doc chose not to watch. He would go on the ride because somehow it would please his friends, but he would not allow himself to be psyched out by the whole thing. After all, he knew he would survive it. Everybody did. Even little kids would get in line over and over again with no fear whatsoever. And as Sandra pointed out, it was safe. It was all a case of mind over matter.

When they were put into their cars, Colin and Sandra were paired in the front, so Jack was seated next to Doc. Suddenly, as he crammed himself into the little seat, hands on the padded bar in front, an uncontrollable panic came over the sculptor; and he wasn't sure he could go through with the whole thing. And then, to make matters worse, the attendant pushed the bar down into his lap until he felt it lock. There was no turning back now unless he would cry out for help.

Of course, every roller coaster starts out with a long, high climb, just to get that heart pumping. Doc told himself that the drop on the other side couldn't possibly be that bad—that men and women of far less courage than he had survived this ordeal, so he could too.

But Doc underestimated the drop. Once he began to fall, a feeling of helpless terror came through him so that all he could do was look down and press forward on the bar as if he would somehow be able to slow the descent. Only once did he look up when, to his amazement, he saw both Sandra and Colin raise their hands above their heads along with most of the riders in front of him. Jack did not join in, but Doc, glancing quickly to his right, could see the young man laughing uncontrollably with joy.

Then it happened. A spasm of distress and nausea overtook Doc, and he had no time to consider its implications before turning his head to the left and vomiting uncontrollably. Interestingly enough, the vomit was caught in the rushing air and seemed to swirl and jettison into space, destination unknown.

Now embarrassment replaced fright, and Doc was only semiconscious about the remainder of the trip. To his surprise, however, no one said a thing as he lifted himself off the seat and made for the platform.

"Didn't you just love it, Doc?" Sandra said, almost shaking with enthusiasm. I told you that you would!"

Apparently Doc's episode of regurgitation went unnoticed, and the hot dog filled contents of his stomach had disappeared into another time, another dimension. Doc had survived both the ride and his humiliation, and he felt a curious sense of being more alive, more in touch with his environment. He smiled unguardedly.

CHAPTER 14

❀

Sandra sat on a wooden stool in the center of her studio looking at the various sized canvases around her. Lately Sandra produced countless pieces. Though she loved her work, she had never turned out so much. She told herself that it must be because she was now painting for others—that was a good thought. She also wondered if she was painting to *please* others—that was bad.

Sandra had always done a good number of the kind of paintings that were in such demand—flowers, barns, still-lifes—but she had never done them exclusively. Now she feared that she was painting for commercial value, because she was no longer doing anything else. It was nice to be appreciated, part of her reasoned. It's nicer to be accepted, she countered.

Often Sandra's father would visit her downstairs. The man was always supportive, but Sandra feared that he was not quite objective. Since she was a little girl, anything that she produced—from dioramas at school to Christmas tree ornaments—was celebrated as great art. Her father only saw her as the best in everything.

Her mother, on the other had, was not so easy. She, of course, was also supportive; but she cautioned Sandra that one must have substance to succeed. And to get this substance, her mother would remind her, one had to work her hardest. People were not rewarded in this life because they possessed some undeveloped natural talent. Sandra's mother was her motivation for going to art school. And, more importantly, her mother taught her to step back and examine the real intent of her actions.

"Mind if I come down?" a voice attached to some feet and legs asked as someone started down the basement stairs.

"Hi, Dad," Sandra said just before his face became visible.

"Taking a break, Sandy?" Only her father could get away with this shortened name.

"Just for a few minutes," Sandra sighed.

Her father walked toward her and then stopped and turned around slowly.

"My God, Sandy, they're so beautiful. How can one little girl produce so much beauty?"

"I'm not a little girl," Sandra laughed, "and you're a *little* prejudiced."

"No I'm not," her father said sincerely. "And you'll always be my little girl."

"I was wondering, Dad," Sandra said, "is everything in the world done for profit or praise?"

"What do you mean, baby?"

"I mean…is it possible to ever do something for yourself and nobody else?"

"You always did your art work for yourself—from the time you were little," her father said, his eyes staring up for a moment as if imagining Sandra as a girl.

"Sometimes I think I did it for *you*. I mean, would it have been half as rewarding if there was nobody around to appreciate it?"

"Maybe that's how we know the quality of our work, but I'm not sure that's why we do it," he said.

"But in the art world…in the art world it's not only important that something comes from inside, but that it is cared about by others. Sometimes those two things fight against each other."

"Well, lots of us produce things from the heart that people wouldn't be impressed with. You ever hear me sing?" he laughed.

"Then it's only good art when someone *else* appreciates it?"

Her father looked down in thought. "Sandy, I think art is just a real powerful bit of communication. It's just like language—if I talk to you and you don't understand, there's no thought being passed along. If you write a poem and nobody gets it, you're defeating the purpose, aren't you?"

"So art has to reach out and say something to people," Sandra clarified.

"I think it's safe to say that."

"I just wonder if my paintings are speaking to anyone," Sandra whispered wistfully.

"They're saying lots to me," her dad assured her.

🍁   🍁   🍁

It was the best day Jack had ever had at the record store. Jack worked with gusto at stocking the bins, singing at the top of his lungs as if alone. Every customer that walked in was greeted with the cheeriest salutation he or she had heard from any of the "cool" young folk who worked at the shop. Jack helped the customers with all the enthusiasm of an owner. He was walking on a cloud.

The night before, Chuck had called with the good news. The record people had listened to Jack's record, watched the promotional video he made, and were very excited. They wanted to release his album immediately and start a public relations tour. Jack's dreams were coming true.

Great things were definitely happening for Jack—and not just in terms of his music. Jack was also in love—truly, deeply, pathetically in love. He was always very popular with the women and always seemed to be in some type of relationship; but until now, nothing had meant much. Michelle was the real thing.

Jack didn't meet Michelle while performing, like he met most of his other girlfriends. In fact, Michelle had no idea that Jack was involved with music. To this quiet raven-haired beauty, Jack was just a clerk at a record store. But something about him caught her eye; and as she frequented the shop and got to talking to the young man, she was taken by his genuineness.

Naturally Jack couldn't resist a pretty face, so he asked Michelle to join him for lunch at the TGI Friday's in the mall. His original intentions were hormonal; but after they got to talking and laughing over a couple of hamburgers, Jack was stricken. He was so smitten with her that he thought about her all the next day—she just wouldn't leave his mind. And the attraction was her easy laughter and odd perspectives on things. Never had he enjoyed the company of another human being as much.

It's rare when two people are enamored with each other to the same degree. Usually one or the other of a couple—even when clearly in love—still has his or her feet on the ground. Not so with these two. Both fell hard after that first meeting, and soon they were inseparable.

Michelle was a legal assistant in the law firm of Denhey, Bilger, and McGuire, located in the Concord Bank building downtown on the square. Though quite a haul from the mall, Jack began leaving a little early and waiting for Michelle outside her building at noon time. Then they would eat bag lunches under the trees in the park area in the center of the square.

One usually pictures people new to love doing nothing but mooning over one another when together. With Jack and Michelle, it was constant dialogue. Both had so much to say to each other that there was rarely a second of silence. And laughter was always part of their meetings. They would laugh and laugh until tears came to their eyes. Jack, who had never been particularly witty, seemed to think of a million clever things to say when with Michelle; and Michelle, who would have been enough just to look at, had a wry sense of humor that broke the young musician up.

Interestingly enough, Michelle didn't seem all that impressed with Jack's career. Oh, she was happy for him, and she wanted him to succeed; but his future stardom held little importance for the pretty brunette. Her interest was only in the person that Jack was.

Now, most people would find this to be a wonderful thing—to be accepted for who you are. But remember, Jack was just beginning a career in show business—an area that requires a certain amount of ego and self-involvement. What Jack had difficulty with was Michelle's relative indifference to the beginnings of his dream. It was not that he was angry at her attitude, or even hurt; but the two things Jack loved most in the world had very little in common—yet both experiences were now intensely powerful for him. It was as if he were living two lives.

Jack made a number of attempts to join the two meaningful paths his life was taking. He asked Michelle to accompany him at recording sessions or wait for him during photographic shoots. Michelle, however, let him know that when she was with him, she wanted all his attention and that waiting around for him as he "worked" was boring for her.

"But you *do* like my music?' he asked her as he drove home from the studio.

"Oh, yes, your songs are very nice."

"Very nice?"

"I think you have a lot of talent, Jack," Michelle said.

"But it doesn't knock your socks off."

"*You* knock my socks off, Jack. Isn't that enough?" she asked.

"But my music," Jack argued, "isn't it part of who I am?"

"That's just it, Jack. It's only a *part* of who you are. I love all the other parts."

And that was how most of their discussions of Jack's show business career went. But that didn't stop Jack from wanting Michelle with him, even when pursuing his other love. He was constantly frustrating Chuck, always wanting a place or a ride or a ticket for Michelle.

"You know, Jack," Chuck said, "there are lots and lots of girls on the road."

"I've already met lots of girls. There's only one I really care about."

Chuck shook his head. "This could be a problem?"

"Problem? What problem?"

"We'll talk later."

CHAPTER 15

Sandra wasn't quite sure why she had agreed, but she and Colin had a dinner date at the Journal Room, an exclusive restaurant two doors down from Colin's paper. It seemed that they were the least likely couple—at opposite extremes of the spectrum, personality-wise. But there was something that always tied them together. However, when they were with each other, they were like water and oil—Colin being the oil.

Sandra's parents, though they did not dislike Colin, had always thought him a bit strange, but even they were a bit taken aback by Colin's new carefully constructed image.

Colin was dressed in blue jeans and old Converse black and white high top sneakers, topped by a ratty-looking black sport coat. The coat parted just enough so that one could read the message printed in large white letters on his black T-shirt. *Nihilism,* it read.

In addition to the look of his costume, Colin came off as rumpled. Not only did his clothes appear old and unlaundered, but they had a disheveled look. This was topped off by his unshaven face and a long wild mass of uncombed hair.

"Are you ready?" Sandra said, quickly grabbing her jacket and herding Colin toward the door.

Colin, who genuinely liked Sandra's parents, was in no hurry to leave; but Sandra, seeing the confusion on her mother and father's faces, knew that she had to get Colin out before any extensive discussion took place.

Sandra's father was extremely conservative, and her mother dutifully followed his lead. Some of the things Colin had written lately had disturbed them. Now, with his strange appearance, she knew there would be questions; and she knew Colin would not hesitate to get into some big debate.

"What the hell have you got on?" Sandra asked when they were safely in the car.

"Sandra, it's not like you to curse," Colin mocked.

"I thought we were going to a nice restaurant...and you're dressed for Fabulous Taco."

"This is who I am, Sandra. The people expect me to express myself," he defended.

"This isn't who you are, Colin; this is who you think you're *supposed* to be."

"How do you know that?" Colin asked.

"I've known you for a long time—maybe better than most people. You were never pretentious."

"How could this outfit ever be considered pretentious?" Colin laughed artificially.

"Because you did it on purpose...for effect. You're dressing the part of the controversial columnist. You've become a caricature of yourself."

"Maybe," Colin said in patient condescension, "I'm finally allowing myself to be who I truly am. Maybe you should try that."

"Who you really are?" Sandra said. "Oh, Colin, I've read your pieces. Most of it is just to provoke people, and you know it. Whatever they hold sacred, you attack. It' got nothing to do with how you really think. It's all a show."

"Well, then maybe I should be taking you to Fabulous Taco instead of the Journal Room," Colin teased.

"Maybe that's exactly where we should be going."

🍁   🍁   🍁

Doc and Jack were already at the table when Sandra and Colin arrived.

"Michelle busy tonight?" Sandra asked, pulling a chair out.

"I just needed some time to think," Jack said.

"I'm not sure this is really brain food they serve here."

"Doc and I were talking about who we really are," Jack said.

"You mean, you've been incognito all this time?" Colin wisecracked.

"Doc here thinks there's no such thing as knowing yourself," Jack explained.

"I just said that we're a number of people," Doc said.

"Kind of schizophrenic, you mean," Colin quipped.

"Yeah…pretty close," Doc said seriously. "We react to our environment, we react to our mood, we react to society's expectations. We play roles. Who we 'really are' is just all these people put together."

"That's kind of upsetting," Sandra said.

"It doesn't have to be. It seems like we're all trying to have this one personality—something that identifies us. Why is that so important? If we all just relax and react to what's happening around us—understanding that we have no stock role to play—life will be much simpler."

"Then aren't we just reflecting and reacting rather than *being*?" Colin said.

"Why fight it?"

"All our lives we're taught that we're individuals—one of a kind. We're told to think for ourselves and be independent. Now you're saying that this isn't natural?"

"That was all bullshit from the beginning," Doc said. "Ever think about who told you to be yourself? Teachers? Parents? And when you actually took a step to the right or the left of society's line, weren't those the same people that pulled you back and told you that you had to get along with others and work within the system?"

"But, Doc, you're one of the most unique people I've ever met" Sandra said.

"Being original can only bring you pain. Working at it is asinine."

"But you—"

"I am a fool."

CHAPTER 16

❁

The best thing about when the bar was busy was that Doc didn't have time to think. But, oh, those down times were murder. Now, like so many nights at the little tavern, while he wiped the counter down with an overused rag, he had time to contemplate what *God hath wrought*—and it wasn't pretty. The pathetic lives before him were a reminder of the futility of it all. There had to be a purpose, he thought. Life, the earth, all of it had to have a purpose; but it was just too elusive for mere human beings to ever grasp.

Just as Doc approached total isolation with his thought, he was awaken from his reverie by the angry voices of two men.

"You was lookin' at her!" a short, stocky man in a thin ratty looking T-shirt with "Grab a Heiney" written on the front.

"Why would I look at *her*?" the second man said, a large biker type with a sleeveless blue jean jacket, hairy tattooed biceps bulging from its ripped armholes.

"What the fuck is that supposed to mean!" the smaller man demanded.

"It means," the large man said, rising from his stool to stand at least a foot taller than his accuser, "that I don't need to see no skinny, ugly skanks."

"You apologize to the lady right now!" the first man said as the lady covered her eyes crying at the insult.

"You go screw your mamma," the biker said, turning away and starting for the door.

As he walked away, the short man stared a hole in his back, his eyes glaring pure hatred. Then, like a wild animal, he tore toward his enemy and attacked his back by leaping on him and grabbing him around the throat.

The larger, stronger man was apparently in shock, and his first reaction was to pull the smaller man's arms from around his throat; but like a feral beast, the other would not let go nor loosen his grip. It was almost humorous the way the biker struggled, the little guy attached to him like a child's piggyback ride gone amiss.

Then, as the patrons of the bar watched in wonder, the big man's face began to turn blue, then darker, almost a purple. Then he went down hard on the floor. Once down, he tried to recover, but to no avail because now the stocky man used his opponent's incapacitated state to his own advantage—kicking the other man's large head with his heavy work shoes. He kicked and he kicked, over and over again, making a bloody pulp out of the Goliath's head.

Finally Doc was able to shake the trance he was under, watching the surreal scene; and his heavy, out of shape body leaped over the bar to help. Doc was able to grab the attacker from behind, pulling the kicking, twisting little ball of anger away from his object of hate.

The small man would not give up; but, unlike the biker, Doc was at an advantage, and he threw the small man's body against the front wall. The compact frame bounced off the paneling like a rag doll and hit the floor. There was no more motion.

Without even needing to look to see if his move was effective, Doc went immediately to the phone around the bar and dialed 911.

"We need an ambulance," Doc said loudly over the wails of the peaked looking bag of bones whose honor had been defended, her stringy streaked hair shaking with the throws of her sobbing. "Make sure the cops come too."

When he got home that night, Doc immediately went to work, molding and shaping and carving his clay into the face of the "damsel in distress" at the bar. He realized as he worked that the incident with the fight had truly been her moment to shine. She would have expected nothing less of her boyfriend, and she would feel a happy triumph if the biker were to die.

Nausea overtook the artist for a moment, but he was able to fight it off.

CHAPTER 17

❀

Jack's first album was released about a month after it was recorded. Chuck explained to him that making the product was the easy part. What it took now was promotion, and the first line of attack would be the radio stations.

In the '50s, over aggressive marketing men would provide plenty of payola for any disc jockey who would play their product. There has been much hypocritical head shaking about those times ever since. How could the world of music have ever been corrupt? And when dealing with art forms, how could anyone hope to sell it if it wasn't good?

The fact is, people like to hear things that they're comfortable with. In other words, the public loves songs that they've already heard. Anybody that doesn't believe this can stop at any Moose Lodge in the country and witness the worst bands ever allowed on the stage playing familiar songs and getting away with it. All the audience wants is something close to the original, and they're happy.

Now this is ridiculous when it comes to album sales, because any newly recorded music couldn't possibly sell millions based on this premise. The trick is to get your songs heard over and over again by an unsuspecting public. One can go about this by providing contributions to a movie sound track, backing up a commercial of some type, or simply playing the music as often as possible.

Of course, anyone who thinks that disc jockeys are still not influenced by the promotion men is not in touch with the times. Money and other favors are not limited to those lobbying our elected officials. And big record labels have influence—they get the publicity that they need to make the audience curious and the radio stations obligated. With the right handlers, screaming pigs could produce something that would go platinum.

And perhaps screaming pigs would have a better chance than most singers and musicians because of the attention farm animals on a concert tour would attract. So the next important thing is to have a hook of some type for the act. This could be the way band members dress or wear their hair—after all, the four mop tops got plenty of mileage from appearance. And sex is always, always a good sell—does Janet Jackson really have that good of a voice? Or it might be life style. Rock and rollers have always been known for their decadence and rebellion. The problem here is to be more insolent and bolder than the next guy—and that's getting harder and harder to do.

Jack didn't know why so many disc jockeys wanted to interview him on their shows, and he didn't want to ask. All he knew was that he would be covering the country doing nothing but radio and fan magazine chats. The idea was to let the youngsters know there was a new kid in town.

The whole idea was exciting to Jack. He had just received his last check from the record store, and now he would be introduced to the nation. The only problem was that he would have to be away from Michelle for at least a month. Though he was caught up in the whirlwind of his coming celebrity, he was also caught in the chains of a new love; so this was tough. He decided, however, that he would insist that Chuck make accommodations for his girlfriend.

"I might as well tell you right now and get this over with," Chuck said. "A girlfriend is not something we want as part of your image. We're trying to appeal to young women who want to fantasize about you while they're listening to your songs. They don't want to know you've been taken."

"But I have been taken, Chuck; and that's not a part of my life that I want to compromise," Jack said firmly.

"Then I'm afraid I'm going to have to insist. See her all you want, but a traveling girlfriend is out."

"Who are you to tell me that!" Jack almost shouted.

"Who am I? I'll tell you who I am. I'm the guy that's gonna make you a star. I'm the guy that's gonna make your dreams come true. I'm the guy that's gonna make you rich. Is that enough?"

"I thought *I* was the guy who was going to do all these things—that *my* talent and your help were going to make it for both of us."

"Your talent?" Chuck sneered. "You think it's talent that makes a singer big today? Haven't you figured it out yet? Do you think Little Wonder made it on pure talent? Or the Rolling Stones? Come on, Jack, there are lots of people with talent. We're trying to make you a star!"

"Okay, okay," Jack said. "So you know how to work the business. But she still comes with me."

But, of course, Jack didn't discuss his plans with the most important person.

"I can't just pack up and leave work for that amount of time," Michelle said. "Besides, I've got a life too."

"I thought I was a big part of your life."

"You are, when you're free to be."

"What the hell does that mean?" Jack asked.

"It means that our relationship has nothing to do with your career. I thought I made that clear before. Listen, Jack, I'm not stopping you from following your dream. I'll miss you for the time you're gone, but I'll survive. When you get back, and we're with only each other, the relationship will continue."

"It doesn't sound like you care much about me," Jack said childishly.

"Jack, you're all I care about. You're going to meet people who care about everything else but who you are—your fame, your music, your looks. I'll always care about *who* you are."

"It's hard to be angry with that kind of an argument."

"Then don't be," Michelle said. "Just have a good time on your trip."

❦   ❦   ❦

And, though at first he troubled over not having Michelle with him, he did have a good time. Jack was treated like a king on the trip. He was a guest at many expensive dinner parties, he met big famous personalities connected with the label or its parent company holdings, and he was ogled by some of the most beautiful women in the country. In addition, he was asked questions over the airwaves as if his previously mundane life interested everyone.

Jack didn't care much for the photo shoots, though. They were embarrassing. Before he was even allowed to see the public, Chuck made sure Jack was dressed in the trendiest clothes—a small fortune was spent on a wardrobe that Jack felt silly and uncomfortable wearing. Then he was expected to stand in front of cameras in various settings wearing "cool" looks in "with it" poses. He wondered what the photographers and PR people really thought of him.

His days and nights were exciting and hectic, but once back in the hotel room, things were lonely. Here he was left with a television and a Gibson flat top that he traveled with. For some reason watching television by himself always made Jack feel lonelier, so he used his time to compose more songs.

Soon it got to the point where Jack's creative run made him want to get back to that room and instrument as soon as possible. Actually, his songs were a tie to the real purpose in all this, and it was comforting to go back to the music after a day of make-believe. And he succeeded in coming up with enough good material to record another album when he got home.

But Jack would not be returning soon. While on this small promotional tour, his record took off big; and the frenzied days became chaotic. Crowds of girls began to wait outside the radio stations so that plans had to be made to sneak him in and out safely. Once the media caught on, he was never left alone anywhere. Soon the fun waned and the pressure became a strain on Jack. The only thing he kept telling himself was that it would be over soon.

"Thank God this will all be over next week," he said over coffee with Chuck at the table in his room. "I'm really starting to stress out."

"Then take a pill, man. We're not going home quite yet."

"What do you mean?" Jack said, with more than a hint of alarm.

"I mean that you've taken off. Things are happening faster than we thought. We've got offers for television spots and talk shows all over the country. You're a star, my boy!"

"But I gotta get some rest," Jack argued. "And I want to see Michelle."

"Welcome to show business, Jack," Chuck said. "Once you've made it, there's no turning back. This is what you wanted, isn't it?"

"Well, yeah," Jack admitted, "but I'm really worn out."

"When I said to take a pill, I meant it literally. I'll get you some stuff to help you sleep better. And as far as energy, I know exactly what you need."

"Nope. I'm not going that way. Okay, I'll play the game, but I'm gonna do it as myself, not some load of chemicals."

"Sure, sure," Chuck said, palms out in agreement. "I wouldn't want you messing with that stuff if you don't have to…but it's available if you need it."

"When all this is over…when I make it…I just plan on being myself," Jack offered.

"I don't follow you," Chuck said.

"I mean, I'm doing all this to get there…but once I'm there, I want to concentrate on the music."

"Nobody really ever gets there, Jack," Chuck said a bit cryptically.

"What are you talking about?"

"You'll only know after you've traveled the road for awhile."

❦   ❦   ❦

Doc sat on the floor as the early morning light filtered through the slats in the cheap blinds covering his only window. He was playing on his old Martin six string for the first time in many months. The song Doc was playing was his own. All the songs Doc played were his own compositions. And though he must have written close to a hundred of them, nobody but his wife had ever heard one. He composed for himself.

CHAPTER 18

❀

Colin rarely worked downtown at the newspaper building, but he did have his own office. He used it at first, but he quickly realized that his pariah status was not limited to the readers. The first day upon opening the door, there was a stench of garbage so pungent that he backed up unconsciously. But his nose was correct. Someone had placed garbage cans from the cafeteria along the walls and then turned the air conditioning unit off. The 90 degrees heat and the sun pounding through the exposed windows did the rest.

Another time a neat pile of dog feces lay in a ring on his desk blotter with a note that said: "Add this to the shit you write." And sometimes the messages were not as clever—just notes on this door telling him to leave town or wishing him an early demise.

On his last visit a sign hung outside the door that said: "Take the hint!" When he opened the door, he was greeted by what looked like all the realty signs in the city. On his desk was a pair of outdated bus tickets.

So because he worked at home now, it was unusual for Colin to be climbing the marble staircase of the Chesterfield building. He was not headed for his own office, however. That was on the 11th floor.

No, he was here for a meeting with his boss, Mr. Keetering—a man that he had spoken to once just after he was hired.

To Keetering, it was important for the public to reach him without an elevator ride to a penthouse of some type, so he kept an office on the ground floor. Keetering had some fantasy that people had access to his ear. The truth was that reaching the Oval Office was easier than getting through Keetering's battleaxe administrative assistant who sat on guard behind her desk in the anteroom.

"Yezz?" she said, rising as Colin entered through the pair of beautifully carved oak doors. Even the outer office was like entering a palace. Colin didn't know much about period furniture, but the two couches and the chair arranged around a beautifully carved cherry table reminded him of old France. The green and gold leafy wallpaper reached up to the ceiling, outlined with an ornate crown of gold trim. In its center was a chandelier that Colin thought could have hung in Buckingham palace.

Though Colin was as intimidated as easily as everyone else, he went out of his way to conceal it. And what he concealed with was pure impudence.

"I got an appointment with the head honcho," he said, examining the room with distaste in his face, his hands jammed into the pockets of his wrinkled baggy slacks.

"Do you have an appointment?" the fiftyish woman with the tight hair asked, her contempt undisguised.

"Yep. Got an appointment," Colin said, picking up an expensive porcelain carving of a swan from her desk.

"Please," she said as she reached over for the object. "What is your name?"

"Lady, don't you read your own paper?"

"Certainly," she said haughtily.

"Then you must have seen my picture on the editorial page," he said grinning with all his teeth to torment her.

"You're...you're..."

"That's right, ma'am."

"You're that horrible man who upsets everyone."

"See, you *do* know me."

"Just a minute," she said, standing straight up, looking Colin in the eyes. Then she turned on her heals and went behind a large potted plant down a small hall.

When she clicked back into the room, she positioned herself behind her desk before announcing the news. "You are to go right in. Just down that hall to the end."

"Maybe we'll have some time to get to know each other after," Colin said with a silly smile.

Behind the large white door at the end of the hall sat Mr. Keetering, a huge antique desk before him. In front of the desk, to Keetering's right, sat another white-haired distinguished looking gentleman.

"Come in, Colin. Come in," Keetering motioned with his hand out. "We were just discussing you."

"Discussing *me*?" Colin asked, his wiseass act on hold.

"This," Keetering motioned to the man looking back at Colin, "is George Whorton Seeger. Have you heard of him?"

"Heard of him! I've studied his career all my life. You, sir," Colin said in deference, almost bowing, "are the classic journalist."

"Oh, my career as a writer," Seeger said in modesty, "was over many years ago."

"George is here to see *you*, Colin," Keetering announced.

"Me?"

"He wants to offer you a job," Keetering said.

"But I work for you, sir," Colin said in false loyalty.

"And *I* work for him," Keetering said. "The *Boston Scroll* has owned this little rag for years. Gone are the days of the many individual news gatherers. Everyone belongs to one of the big boys now."

"I'm here," Seeger started, "because of the reaction to your work."

"Oh, well, let me explain what I—"

"We think you're ready for the big time. We'd like you to work for the *Scroll*. What do you say, son? This could be the beginning of big things for you."

"I...I...well," Colin sputtered.

"It's the first I've known him to be speechless," Keetering laughed.

"Then you will?" Seeger asked.

"Of course, sir...yes...yes...I will."

"We're going to need you at the beginning of next month. We'll make a big thing about you joining the paper. Hell, they'll want to strangle you before you write a word when we get through."

"You want a column...like the one I write now?" Colin asked blankly.

"Of course. That's where your talent is, Colin. You do want the job, don't you?"

"Oh...yes," he said absently, "yes, of course."

"Okay then, our business is through."

"Pardon us now, Colin," Keetering said, taking a bottle of expensive scotch and two glasses out of his bottom desk drawer, "but now two friends from the old days are going to get soused while we talk about better times."

"Sure, sure," Colin said, understanding his exit cue. "Yes...well...thank you again, sir," he said, backing out the door as if leaving royalty.

As he walked down the hall somewhat stunned, he heard raucous laughter from behind the large white door.

🍁   🍁   🍁

"Why'd you ask me to meet you here?" Sandra asked. "Aren't we stopping by Fabulous Taco?"

"Naw. Jack isn't in town...and I'm just not in the mood for Doc tonight."

"What's wrong with Doc all of a sudden. I thought you liked his challenges to our thinking."

"It's just that I wanted to tell you about my new job without feeling guilty about it," Colin admitted.

"You got a new job! How wonderful! I never liked what you had to be with that column. I think it was changing you with all the anger. It wasn't you, Colin. It wasn't you at all."

"Well…my new job is with the *Boston Scroll*," he said awkwardly.

"Oh, Colin, you're finally going to do what you've always wanted," Sandra said, folding her hands and closing her eyes as if in a thank you prayer.

"Sandra," Colin interrupted the rapture, "I'll be doing the same thing—on a bigger level."

Sandra opened her eyes and looked at him in poorly hidden disappointment.

"I know," Colin said, "that you hate the column. But this is a big opportunity for me. Maybe after awhile I can change over to straight news."

"I see why you didn't want Doc around," she said.

"He wouldn't even have to speak," Colin said. "I would know what he was thinking."

"Will you be leaving town?"

"Not necessarily. A lot of what I do can be done from home at first. Of course, there are social obligations associated with a Boston columnist, so eventually I'll be moving."

"Well," Sandra said unenthusiastically, "if it's what you really want, I'm happy for you."

"Sometimes we don't always get what we want," Colin said, obviously paraphrasing Mick Jagger's lyric, "but we can get what we need."

🍁　　　🍁　　　🍁

Fabulous Taco seemed especially dirty that evening. Doc could feel the grit under his shoes as he unconsciously moved his feet while contemplating his next hot dog. The windows were so bad that the accumulated dust had taken on a brownish hue—perhaps colored by the cooking smoke from the kitchen. And Doc's left sleeve slightly stuck to the table every time he would raise it to lift his hot dog for another bite. The grime coating on everything in the place seemed to be made worse by the emptiness of the little restaurant.

This is where it all started, Doc thought as he sipped his coke, and this is where he would be left in his eternal loneliness. But that was okay. Doc expected it. He always expected the worst, and he was never disappointed. Besides, there was an advantage to loss: you could now wallow in your own pity without blame.

But somehow the hot dogs were just not as good.

CHAPTER 19

❀

Unlike most young adults, Sandra always spent time with her parents in the evening, usually watching television. Now, for a young hip intellectual, watching TV was not cool at all, so she never mentioned her habit to her friends. But the fact was, she loved the tube. She especially liked situation comedies that made her laugh, or those mini-series things that captivated her for two or three nights at a time.

The value Sandra got from television was mostly diversion. She liked to sit in the comfortable green chair in the living room, her legs curled under her, and let the electronic entertainment take her to other places and situations. This way she could lose herself and forget her cares for hours at a time. Of course, Sandra wasn't a brooding artist; but, like all of us, she had her frustrations, so the TV worked for her.

Lately, however, there was a problem with her favorite media. It seemed that the networks had discovered a new genre of programming they termed "reality TV." Reality television featured real people in contrived situations and their reactions to the circumstances and to each other. One group was trapped on an island, another locked in a house together. Still another was put in an artificial crime situation. In all the shows, people would begin to get on each other's nerves until there would be coalitions and shouting matches. It was like looking through a window at a dysfunctional family, but not close to as exciting as most voyeurism.

Then there were other shows with horrible stunts where people would engage in intense competition for money. Sometimes they were the worst.

"What some people will do for a buck, huh Sandy?" her father commented as one of the screen's contestants ingested the gonads of a goat.

"What gets me," her mother said, "is that they are so serious about it. It's like winning is everything to young people today—regardless of what it takes. Shouldn't people have *some* self-respect? I mean, isn't there anything people won't do today for fame or money?"

"The sad part," Sandra said, "is that they don't consider some of the humiliating things they do as lowering themselves. On the contrary, they think it's a statement of fearlessness and domination. They don't think of it as groveling for a prize; they think of it as being victorious in a competition—like it was the Olympics or something."

"Even real athletes seem to be taking themselves a little too seriously, don't you think? After all, aren't they just playing games?" her mother said shaking her head.

"It's all about getting yours before somebody else does," her father added as the commercial for a sport drink blasted through the speakers. Somehow we've done this to young people. Living simply with some semblance of integrity is for losers today. It's always who you can conquer and how much you're going to get."

"It's the looks on their faces when they defeat their opponent that gets me," Sandra said. "It's almost an evil satisfaction. It scares me what's happening with people."

"Let's change the channel," her mother said pleasantly, "and see what else is on."

Jack finally accepted the fact that staying on the road was important for his career, but he was not happy. He had dreaded making the call to Michelle—but her response was worse than he had imagined.

"Okay, Jack, then I'll see you when you get back," she said.

"That's it? That's all you have to say?"

"What do you want me to say?" Michelle asked.

There was silence on the phone for a moment. "I guess I wanted you to be upset about it."

"Weren't you afraid to make this call because I'd be upset?"

"Well…yeah."

"Then you should be relieved," she said.

"Am I not understanding something here about our relationship?" Jack asked.

"What do you mean?"

"I mean, I'm upset about not seeing you; so shouldn't you be upset about not seeing me?"

"Jack," Michelle said calmly, "I'm very unhappy about it. But since I can't really change things, I felt I should just make things easier for you."

"Maybe too easy," Jack said cryptically.

"What do you mean?"

"I'll call you again," he said, ending the conversation.

Just minutes after hanging up the phone, a knock came on the hotel room door.

"Jack, let me in," Chuck said. "I've got someone I want you to meet."

Jack opened the door, and a pretty young thing in a tight blue T-shirt that didn't quite meet the top of low riding jeans stepped in.

"Jack, I'd like you to meet Jennifer Green, the mayor's daughter."

"It's Jenny, and I'm more than the mayor's daughter," she said in an attractively confident voice.

"I'm happy to meet you," Jack reached for her hand. "The mayor's daughter? The mayor of—?"

"Jack forgets what city he's in," Chuck apologized.

"It's just that we've been in so many places in a short time."

"I can understand that," Jennifer said. "He's the mayor of South Cambel."

"I'll bet it's a nice place," Jack said politely.

"It is a nice place—a *very* nice place; and if you had time, I'd show you around and prove it."

"If I had *time*?" Jack asked.

"Chuck tells me that you have a tight schedule and was kind enough to get me up here to meet you for a few minutes. I'm very impressed with your music. I'm not often taken with songs I've just heard, but your CD is incredible," she said, articulating in a manner much older than her years.

"So, you liked the music? Had you heard any of the interviews or read any of the publicity before you became interested?"

"Sorry, no. I didn't even know what you'd look like. I just wanted to meet the man responsible for the fantastic sounds."

"So, it's really a nice place?" Jack asked.

"Excuse me?"

"Your father's town. Is it really nice?"

"It's wonderful," Jenny said. "And it's my town too."

"Then would you have time to show me around this afternoon?"

"Jack," Chuck interrupted, "we have a very busy schedule."

"Don't worry, Chuck, I'll be where I'm supposed to be when I'm supposed to be there."

Jenny was extremely self-assured for her years. Just the way she moved so naturally in those faded well-fitted jeans—nothing for show, she was who she was. She led Jack down to the parking garage where they climbed into an early model Porsche. In what seemed like one movement, she started the engine and backed the little car into the lane of the garage. Then she took off like a shot down the aisles, causing Jack to unconsciously grab the dashboard and push. When she squealed out of the garage and hit the street, her foot became lead; and Jack could almost imagine G-forces pushing his body back into the bucket seat.

Down the narrow residential streets of brownstone townhouses they went at breakneck speed until they hit the entrance ramp to the highway. Jack didn't think that Jenny's foot had anywhere more to go on the accelerator; but when they reached the highway, they must have hit warp speed.

Up until that point, there had been no conversation. Jenny was intent on her driving, and Jack was hanging on for dear life. Now, though she never let up on her speed, she visibly relaxed in her seat and began to talk.

"Hungry?" she asked.

"After this ride, I don't know what kind of condition my stomach is in."

Jenny smiled, "I thought I'd take you to a little place I know on the East side of town. Like tacos?"

"I've never had one," Jack laughed, thinking of his hometown hangout.

"Well, then you're going to start with the very best."

The neighborhood they were entering was run down in contrast to where Jack was staying. In fact, as Jenny cruised up and down the little streets, Jack was a little surprised the mayor's daughter was familiar with this part of town.

"If daddy knew I spent any time here, he'd send a bodyguard with me. For a man of the people, he just doesn't really *understand* the people."

"Oh yeah?"

"The people on the East side are good people—hard working, genuine people. Their values are a thousand times better than you'd find in the classier parts of town. Family, love, loyalty—that's what they care about. These are things that many people abandon for money and success. I find that I'm much safer walking these streets than in my own neighborhood."

"Really?" Jack wished he wouldn't have said.

"The folks down here know the difference between right and wrong. Oh, sure, there's a lot of wrong going on, but people here are not afraid to step in and correct it. In many parts of town they just turn their heads."

"And how did a young person like you discover all this?"

"By skipping classes. I convinced daddy that I wanted to go to school nearby. Of course, a father never objects to his daughter living at home. So I enrolled in Laurence State, just across the river."

"And you didn't go to classes?"

Jenny laughed. "I've always found my studies to be easy. It was no big deal for me to do my reading and study without some of the boring lectures, which were a rehash of the chapters in the book anyway."

"And then you just explored the city?" Jack asked.

"Basically, yes. I wanted to experience all I could—and that was not possible in my everyday environment."

"So you just visited parts of the city and kind of…went with the moment?"

"Exactly," Jenny said.

Before Jack was able to make another comment, Jenny made a hairpin turn into a little parking area next to a shabby brick building with a faded message about food painted on the side.

"Here we are," she announced.

"And we'll be welcomed in here?" Jack said unsurely.

"You're only welcomed where you make yourself welcomed. Just because people aren't totally trusting at first doesn't make them bad people. After awhile, everybody realizes that there isn't much difference between us. Don't worry, they know me here. I've broken the ice long ago."

Loud brass music hit them as they entered from the tiny foyer area into the restaurant. Jack was taken aback by the immediate contrast between the outside of the building and its interior. Inside, the room was attractive with colorful wall hangings and neat little tables with starched white cloths. Everywhere there was movement—the waitresses, the animated table conversations, and even two couples dancing in an empty area to songs of a culture that they found comfortable in an otherwise strange and sometimes hostile world.

"Ah, Jenny," a heavily accented voice shouted from the kitchen. "I see you are bringing me more business."

"Whenever I can, Hector," she smiled brightly.

"Then sit, sit. We'll bring you your favorite."

"They even know your usual?" Jack said, incredulous.

"I have a weakness for certain things—the spicier, the better."

"Somehow I could have guessed that."

"How about you? Do you like hot, seasoned food?" Jenny asked.

"Lately I've been eating a lot of hot dogs," Jack said.

CHAPTER 20

Being by oneself is the worst situation for an introspective individual, and Doc was always alone. Of course, this was of his own doing. Even the least desirable human form on the planet can find friends if he wants. Doc was smart enough to know this. He knew what he was doing to himself through his isolation, and he thought he deserved it.

Though feeling sorry for himself was probably part of his objective, even that became too painful to bear at times; so Doc had to come up with distractions in order to have even short periods of respite from his self-torture. There was always booze, naturally, and sometimes that worked really well. But there was something about alcohol. Once in a while it had a different effect on a man. While most of the time it provided a better viewpoint, other times something would go wrong—a man would go deeper into is his sorrow. Sometimes Doc just couldn't take the chance.

Music was a help, but it only involved one sense. True, one could react emotionally to a piece of music; but with Doc's collection of recordings, the emotion was bound to be depression. Besides, Doc could never just sit and listen to music; he had to be engaging in some other activity, or he would be too defenseless when his demons crept in.

The only thing that Doc could really escape with was literature. Reading took all of one's thoughts, and one could escape to other places and other times. Sometimes the initial plunge into a book was not an easy one. Doc's mind would fight it, and he would end up reading the same page three or four times. Then, without his really knowing the exact moment, the transition would take place, and he would be immersed in the story.

Doc read a lot of philosophy and quite a bit of history. He was also very interested in politics and government. But this was not the material he chose to read when he needed to avoid himself. At these times he would insist on a writer of good imagery whose story pulled you through by the ears.

Steinbeck had been one of his earlier favorites. The times and situations were so different from Doc's that the fact that Steinbeck may have written a social message wasn't important. Doc could imagine camping on the road along Route 66. He could see pearl divers coming up with their prize. He could even picture Salinas, California, and the ranches that might have been. Steinbeck's characters were men who worked and lived hard, but who could appreciate small comforts.

Unfortunately, John Steinbeck wrote only so many books; and Doc had to move on. His search for a replacement author took him all the way from Sinclair Lewis to Kurt Vonnegut Jr. There was even a time when he tried the Russian novelists—although they're not much help for depression, and the different names for each character can drive a reader crazy.

But when Doc really needed a fix, when he really required a trip away from his reality, he turned to Stephan King. This was not for the same reasons that most people value the novelist. Doc was convinced that Stephan King was the most honest writer of his time. While some were fans because of the author's disgusting descriptive passages and terrifying people and animals, Doc liked the books because they were comforting.

Doc liked to read about friends and how they related—it didn't matter that they came across a dead body. He liked the closeness between the survivors in *The Stand*. He wished he had had childhood companions like those in *It*. It was King's simple innocence and open values that Doc liked in the writing.

So Doc would spend hour upon hour reading. Sometimes he would fall asleep with a book in his lap, only to wake and take up where he left off. He loved his trips into other lives. If he could have had his way, Doc would have stayed within the lives of others until his own was mercifully over.

The problem was that Doc was not hardened by what he perceived as a cruel world. Try as he might, he just could not develop the calluses necessary to place between himself and the hurt that he experienced. Leaving his hovel of a home for even a short while was like going into a winter storm bare naked or like walking through fire. And Doc's pretense of cynicism did not help to protect him. So his alternative was to stay away.

❦   ❦   ❦

It was just after three in the morning when Doc heard a noise at the back door—his only door. Probably some drunk bouncing off both sides of the alley on his way home, Doc thought. Then when the semi consciousness of sleep wore off, Doc realized it was a knock.

Nobody wakes from a deep sleep and is truly happy about a knock on the door, regardless of where he might live. In Doc's neighborhood, a visitor at this hour could only mean trouble or danger. Besides, Doc could not remember the last time anyone asked entry to his abode.

"Doc, it's just me. Let me in!" the voice shouted from the other side of the steel door.

"Who is it?" Doc tried in as gruff a voice as he could muster.

"Doc, it's Colin. I need to talk to you."

Doc's voice changed to concern as he quickly unbolted the door. "Colin, are you alright?"

Colin had a red gash just above his left eye and a large bruise forming around his right.

"Damn, Colin. What happened to you? We're you in a fight?"

"I wish," Colin said.

"Then what happened to your head?"

"I was in a car accident. I hit the steering wheel when I came in contact with the house," Colin said flatly.

"You hit a house?" Doc was getting excited.

"Well, I was hit by another vehicle, and then I lost control, and then I hit the house," Colin said with little emotion.

"So some bastard hit you? Was he drunk?"

"Not exactly…you see…I was the one who was drunk. I…I started to make a left hand turn from the far side of a four lane highway, and I was clipped by a guy in a van going my direction. Then I just kind of skidded or something across the other two lanes and went up on someone's front lawn and hit his house. I was lucky I didn't get hit again by the traffic going the other way."

"Did the police come?" Doc asked, now under more control.

"Yeah…and they had me sit in the back of a squad car for a long time while they talked to witnesses."

"So you were charged with drunk driving?"

"No…for some reason I wasn't," Colin explained. "They had to know I'd been drinking—hell, I must have really stunk up that squad car—but they didn't say anything. They just asked me a lot of questions about the accident. I guess they could tell that I was in control by my answers. Shit, I sobered up big time when I came in contact with that building."

"That surprises me," Doc said. "The cops around here are really tough on drunk driving."

"It didn't happen here."

"Where the hell were you?"

"Boston," Colin said a little sheepishly. "Or at least some suburb—I'm not sure."

"You drove your banged up car all the way back here from Boston."

"Not right away," Colin said shamefacedly. "First I went to a few more bars."

"A few more bars!" Doc was excited again. "What the hell is wrong with you, Colin? That doesn't sound like you at all."

"Then I took Route 3 home," Colin continued, "only I was pretty drunk by then. Then I got real sleepy. Luckily the highway was fairly deserted at that time 'cause I kept dozing off. I'd wake up to find myself almost going off the other side of the road."

"You're lucky you're not dead."

"Yeah. Strange thing. There was an eighteen wheeler behind me for my whole drive down—just me and that trucker on the highway. He could have gotten around me a number of times or called the state troopers or something—but he just hung back there. Then when I got to my exit—I'm surprised I even found it—he blinked his lights twice and sounded his horn. But it wasn't like an irritated blast—it was kind of like a signal. I think the guy was watching out for me."

"There are still a few of those kind out there, but they're getting rare," Doc said.

"Anyway, as soon as I got to that little diner between here and the highway, I just stopped and had something to eat and at least a pot of coffee. I didn't get back into the car 'til I was dead sober."

"Well, I'm glad you stopped," Doc said, going to the stove. "We'll have a little more coffee while I put something on that cut. You've had one hell of a night."

"But I didn't come here to tell you my story, Doc. I came because I need to talk to you about something—get your advice maybe."

"Possibly a lawyer would be a better consultant in this case," Doc said.

"Oh, I'm not here to talk about the accident," Colin said. "I got so drunk because I got something on my mind, Doc."

"It must be a whopper."

"Doc, you know this column I write? Well, it's been starting to get to me. I've had to have this sardonic attitude as part of my public image. At first it seemed to fit like a glove. I mean, I've always been kind of a cynical guy—but nobody should ever be that mordant. My insides have had so much bitterness lately that I'm all tight and sick inside."

"I never thought you were cynical. I just thought you had an overly healthy skepticism about the world. I enjoyed it," Doc said. "But I have seen a big change in you lately. You aren't the man you pretend to be in this new role."

"In my mind, it was just a way to get a foot in the door," Colin said. "I figured that eventually I'd become a legitimate reporter when people saw that I could write. Then I got offered this job with the *Boston Scroll*. I thought my big break had finally come, and then I found out they wanted me to do the same thing on a larger level. I could have a big career if I took it."

"But you don't want fame and fortune that way—is that it?"

"It's alright for awhile…but if I do it for the *Scroll*, I'll be stuck in that genre forever. Then I would truly have to be the son of a bitch that I'm portraying now," Colin said dejectedly.

"So what's the problem?"

"The problem is that it may never happen my way," Colin explained. "If I don't take this opportunity, I may never have any chance with newspapers."

"You understand, don't you, that a job is not who a person is," Doc said. "You don't go about trying to change yourself to fit the job; you find the job to fit who you are."

"But I'm a writer," Colin protested.

"You're not a writer. Shit, you're a *thinker*," Doc corrected. "Your stuff is good because it examines things from different points of view. The problem is that if you're always expected to shake people up with some controversial stand just to upset them, you're not doing what you do best. It seems to me that they want you in Boston to cause trouble to sell newspapers. If you were to write what you really feel, it might not always be contentious enough. Then to keep your job, you'll write what you're told. That's not who you want to be, is it?"

"I'm not sure who I am anymore," Colin said, looking at his feet.

"Well, I'll tell you who you aren't. You aren't a drunk. You aren't negative. You aren't a bad person. And you don't deserve having so many people angry at you all the time. This is your decision," Doc said, "but you asked, and I told you what I thought."

"Thank you, Doc. I don't think I like what I've become."

"Never ever become what you think you're supposed to be. Life may be a role playing game, but play the roles you're comfortable with. Unfortunately, that may bring even more pain—but hell, at least it's honest."

"It's just that I've got to make *something* out of my life or I'll turn out like—"

"Me?"

"I wasn't thinking that, Doc. Not at all," Colin protested.

"But it's true, isn't it?"

"Well," Colin admitted, "I guess you're the only guy I know who examines his motivation for everything. I guess you're what honesty is all about."

"No, I'm not honest with myself. No human being can be. But I do look at my reasons for doing things; and if the reason offends me, I just don't do it. You can see, however, where that has gotten me."

"If you would have been a little more flexible with your values, you could have been just about anything you wanted," Colin said.

"Sometimes I wish I could—but I'm not made like that, Colin, and neither are you. Most people can put scruples right out of their minds. They don't even have to go through the rationalization game. They just accept. It must be a wonderful way to live."

"You've got to be kidding, Doc," Colin shook his head.

"No...not really. I mean, what's life all for anyway? What are we achieving by trying to remain true to ourselves? And what *are* we that we're remaining so true to."

"Well...it sounds like you're saying to go with the flow then. Have you changed your mind?"

"You and I can't go with the flow," Doc said, "and it hurts to even try. That's what I'm saying to you. You couldn't live with yourself in that job—just like you can't even live with the *idea* of it."

"So I should reject anything that would challenge my integrity."

Doc laughed, "That would be just about everything. No...just be selective in your compromises."

"But you never seem to compromise," Colin said.

"Oh, I compromise...and I *hate* myself for it afterward."

CHAPTER 21

Sandra couldn't remember being this nervous since she had to give a three-minute speech in her sophomore year of high school. How she had ever gotten herself into the speaking engagement, she did not know. Well, yes she did. It was her mother who had mentioned her to a friend who had recommended her to the City Ladies' Club.

The City Ladies' Club was an anachronism in this day and age, but they were still going strong. The original women who joined to bring more meaning to their lives besides being wives and mothers had encouraged their daughters, generation after generation. It was now larger than ever before.

The difference, of course, was that the women meeting in the prestigious group now held down jobs—mostly as professionals. The club had always been relatively exclusive. Only women married to successful businessmen in the community were asked to join. Since you had to be sponsored by a member, recruits were very select individuals. But now a woman needn't rely on her husband's reputation for the club to consider her. Today's woman often became part of the elite on her own credentials.

Because the City Ladies' Club concerned itself with culture, the meetings were mostly built around a musician or artist of note. The artist would be expected to give a sample of his or her work along with an enlightening talk about his or her calling. This would, of course, be followed by a long question and answer period while the women had a late desert of only the most expensive pastries.

Sandra would be speaking about the sources of her ideas that she brought to the canvas. Her inspiration was what they wanted her to express—and they wanted it to be great and noble. No one would ever admit that he did what he did for money—even if it were true. And never, never would the artist confess to falling into what he did by accident. The women of the City Ladies' Club had convinced themselves that there was something divine connected with art and culture—that it assured one of the high ranking of man in the universe. In short, the artists were "witnessing" before them to validate the members' superiority.

Sandra's voice actually shook as she started her talk about her early introduction to the arts and how she had always known what she would pursue. Then she began to calm a bit as smiling ladies would nod their approval of her words. By the time Sandra got to how she came up with her subject matter, she was convinced that the truly attentive audience was in the palm of her hand.

"I like the simple things," Sandra explained. "I like the way an old barn looks with natural flowers growing alongside. Maybe a cool pond on a summer's day. Maybe just an old milk can with some pussy willows stuck in the top.

"I don't want to copy my world, though. I mean, what I paint is what I feel about the objects around me, but I'm not interested in realism. I guess what I'm saying is that I paint the world as I see it through my own filters."

Murmurs of assent and the sight of whispered approval let Sandra know she was on the right track.

"So in a way," Sandra was encouraged, "you all get to see a little of what's inside of me."

This was met with laughter, and Sandra decided to quit while she was ahead.

"So, are there any questions?"

A squat little lady with just the hint of a moustache stood up. "What advice," she asked, "would you give those of us who aspire to be good painters?"

"Well," Sandra thought, "I guess I'd have to say that you first must learn the fundamentals…and then you have to be true to yourself."

And this met with an enthusiastic ovation. Each of these pretentious women liked to think of herself as possessing integrity, as well as a sensitivity to the finer things. Each also liked to feel liberated and fulfilled and in touch with herself. A sisterhood was felt in the room—a sisterhood emanating from the success of one of their own. You could almost hear Helen Reddy singing "I am woman; hear me roar" behind the applause.

Afterward, there was cake and coffee and lots of chatter. And just like her first art show, Sandra was the center of attention. Women were almost standing in line to tell her that they owned one of her works. And then there were those who fancied themselves an artistically sophisticated cut above the others, who talked perspective and color with the tone and attitude of insiders.

Sandra enjoyed the attention. Most people blessed with a talent for art or music or anything else are quite surprised when first told of their ability. Because it is so natural to them, they are puzzled that everyone does not have the same capability. Then as time goes on, and the artist realizes his uniqueness, he feels happy in his identity as someone apart from the rest. Like a great athlete or a superior intellect, the artist begins to accept himself as being unusual and special—though he knows he is in no way responsible for his uniqueness. There still remains the confusion, however, that people are so impressed with his capability.

Then, as money and fame become associated with one's talent, one starts to believe in one's own genius. This is good in the fact that it allows the artist to relax about his calling, and bad because it tends to take that edge of insecurity off that is so necessary to the product.

Soon even the artist believes that anything he produces is worth praise—that he can't help but show his brilliance.

The next unfortunate step is the belief that the piece of art or music has been constructed by hands akin to the gods—even when the work is far inferior to that with which he gained his renown. But being celebrated for anything feels good to people. And the guilt that one might experience, knowing that not that much effort was expended, is soon ignored. Soon one believes that he deserves the praise he is receiving.

"You, Sandra," the president said as she closed the discussion, "are the best that we've had speak to us so far. And we're so excited that you're one of our city's own."

While the ladies filed out and Sandra picked up her things, she experienced a kind of euphoria she had never felt before. Funny that her art had brought her something she hadn't even considered—love. It wasn't just admiration she felt while standing behind that podium—they *loved* her. Sandra didn't analyze the feeling much—she knew it would end if she did. She just went with it for as long as it would last.

Strangely, once she was alone in her car and cruising through the wealthy neighborhood where the City Ladies' Club was located, she was hit by a lonesomeness, a sense of desolation that she couldn't quite understand. Wasn't she just the "bell of the ball," the most important thing in town? What had happened? Why this feeling of despondency? It was as if she were coming off the high of some drug, needing another fix or she would fall into dangerous melancholy.

For some reason, Sandra decided to stop at Fabulous Taco for a late meal. She wasn't drawn there by the promise of hot dogs or even company. It had been a long time since the friends had met in their usual hangout. But somehow she felt that a trip to the dirty little eating establishment would help to allay her present doldrums.

But then, to add to her new found misery, her Ford Escort sputtered and died in the middle of the busy intersection of 176th and

Minneapolis Boulevard. Of course the drivers of the cars she was inconveniencing were not as taken with her as the members of the Ladies' Club had been. So there she sat as the lights changed and the horns blasted.

Then, as she hopelessly tried the engine over and over—it was all she could think to do—a knock came on the driver's widow. When she looked up, she saw the face of an extremely clean cut, but handsome, man smiling at her. He was wearing a smart striped tie over a starched white shirt and unnecessary suspenders—the current sign of the well-dressed professional.

Since he was obviously an individual Sandra could trust, she rolled down her window.

"Having a little problem?" he grinned, teeth as white and straight as any move star.

"Just a little one," Sandra managed a weak smile.

"Let me try," he said, opening the door.

Sandra never hesitated as she relinquished her driver's seat.

"Ah, I've located your problem," the man said with another Hollywood grin.

"Are you some kind of mechanic or engineer or something?" Sandra asked.

"I don't think you need a mechanic for this one…You're out of gas."

"Oh, my God," Sandra said, covering her face in embarrassment.

"Don't let it get to you," the man assured her. "It happens to everyone."

"I'm so sorry," Sandra said. "What do I do now?"

"Just get back in. I'll push while you steer for the curb there on the other side," he indicated by pointing over the still honking cars.

After some awkward maneuvering, Sandra finally got the little car safely parked.

"Thank you so, so much," she said when the man walked up to her window.

"I'm Sean," the young man said. "Sean Brady."

"Sandra Louder," she said, putting her hand out the window to shake.

"Where're you headed?" he asked brightly.

For some reason Sandra felt she had to protect her real destination. "I was just going to look for a place to pick up something to eat."

"Isn't that amazing—so was I!" Sean said. "How 'bout if we have dinner together."

"Well," Sandra hesitated.

"Please," Sean said. "I really hate to eat alone."

"I know how you feel," Sandra said. "Sure…but we'll have to take your car."

Sean's laugh was as perfect as his teeth, as he took Sandra by the hand and walked her back to his silver BMW. "How about Jeffery's?" he suggested.

"Jeffery's?" Sandra said, impressed at how easily he mentioned such an exclusive eatery.

"I really like their veggie platter."

"Sure, sure," Sandra said, calculating her funds quickly in her head.

"And it's on me," Sean said, as if reading her mind.

"Oh, no, I couldn't," Sandra objected. "You've been so kind."

"Then you owe me," Sean said. "The least you can do is let me buy you dinner."

"Well, if that would pay you back," Sandra laughed.

Conversation between strangers always begins with an inquiry about the other's profession. Sean was visibly impressed when he learned that Sandra was an artist who had just come from a speaking engagement.

"What about you?" Sandra said politely.

"Me? I'm a salesman," Sean said modestly.

"Oh, what is it you sell? Maybe I could buy something from you some day."

"Industrial machinery. Can I put you down for something?"

"No," Sandra almost giggled, "I don't think I'll be starting a factory in the near future."

"It's interesting at times," Sean sighed, "but sometimes I wish I was involved with something a bit more exciting—like you are."

"How did you get involved with industrial sales?" Sandra asked.

"Family business. My grandfather owns the company. Soon my father will inherit everything."

"And then you," Sandra finished.

"I'm next," he said.

Later Sean took Sandra to a filling station near to where they had left her car. He purchased some gas in an emergency container they provided for just such problems.

"See," Sean said when they got into his car, "I told you it happened to everyone."

Then after he put the gas into her car and followed her back to the gas station where she filled up, Sean insisted on accompanying her home. Since it was dark, he said, he would just feel better.

When they got to the house and Sean walked her up to the door, he didn't leave immediately.

"Aren't you going to invite me in?" he asked, teeth displayed.

Sandra got a surprised look on her face. "First," she said, "we've just met. And secondly, I live with my parents."

"Yes, you mentioned that at dinner," Sean said. "That's why I want to come in—so I can meet them."

Sandra always had the look and personality of the fresh-faced All-American girl. In high school she was frequently dated by her jock and clean-cut-preppy counterparts. Needless to say, her parents were delighted by her choice of escorts. But by the time she got to college, Sandra was bored with the Izod shirts and Dockers that wanted to take her out. Her life lacked adventure.

True to her personality, however, Sandra could never do anything too dangerous. That's when she met Colin. He was different, mad at the world—interesting.

But now meeting this obviously prosperous man was pretty attractive to her. After all, she was now meeting many of her goals as an artist. Her image was no longer of importance. In fact, she doubted that the City Ladies' Club would have wanted anyone too bohemian. Maybe she was finally accepting who she really was now. She had always felt guilty that she had the wrong personality for an artist. Well, maybe her way of thinking was just fine after all.

Of course, Sandra's parents were thrilled with Sean. Her father couldn't seem to get the smile off his face; and her mother kept offering refreshments. Naturally parents want the best for their daughters, and Sandra's parents felt that she had finally brought home a keeper.

"Are you going to be seeing each other again?" Sandra's father asked as the whole family walked Sean to the door.

"Dad!" Sandra exclaimed in embarrassment.

"I plan to spend as much time with your daughter as I can. It's all up to her."

"I'm sure there's no problem there," her father assured him.

"Dad!" she shouted this time.

"What about tomorrow?" Sean proposed. "It's Saturday. And the weather is supposed to be great. Why don't we go out to South Harbor for the day?"

"That sounds—" her father started before getting a look that could kill.

"I'm not used to being asked out in front of the whole family," Sandra said. "But I think that would be nice."

"Good," Sean said, his smile never leaving his face. "Very nice meeting you folks."

"Yes, yes," her father said, ignoring Sandra's dirty look. "I hope to see you again and again."

CHAPTER 22

❀

"It's late," Jack said as they pulled up in front of the brownstone where Jenny lived. "Chuck is probably already having a heart attack."

"Good," Jenny said, "then he won't bother you anymore."

"Everything's all business with Chuck. Sometimes I get so stressed I feel I'm going to explode."

"Exactly. That's why you need some down time. Come on up. I've got some good wine and some of the best smoke you'll ever toke."

The rest of the evening was a beautiful blur. Floating on the most pleasant high Jack had ever experienced, the couple listened to music and laughed and made extraordinary love. It was all a dream—nothing seemed even close to real; but Jack was flowing with it.

The next morning Jack awoke alone in Jenny's bed. A bit disoriented, he took a few minutes to focus. Then, hearing movement on the other side of the door, he quickly dressed and went to find Jenny.

"Hello," she said happily while crunching on a piece of toast. "I thought I'd let you sleep. You needed the rest."

"The best night I've had in a long time."

"Good," she said, gulping her coffee. "Just take your time. Find something to eat in the frig, take a shower—there's no hurry. You can hang out all morning if you want."

"Where are you going?"

"Got places to go. Busy, busy, busy. Sometimes I wish I didn't have so much energy."

"I've got to leave for Springfield this afternoon," Jack said sadly.

"Ah, that's too bad. Well, I've got to be off," she said pecking him on the cheek. "It's been great."

"Wait," Jack said. "When are we going to see each other again?"

"Depends on your schedule. I sure hope you're back here soon—we had a lot of fun."

"Fun?" Jack said. "Yeah, we did; but I was hoping there was more to our relationship than that."

"Jack, you're going to be a rock star. You don't have time for relationships. Besides, we spent a night together—that hardly constitutes a relationship. A person has to grab what pleasure he or she can get in life and then move on. I thought you knew that."

"So that's it," Jack was confused. "A night like that, and you move on."

"I need to experience everything, Jack. Food, dancing, books, movies, music. Last night I experienced you. Like I said, it was great. Listen Jack," she said, grabbing another piece of toast, "I gotta move. Let me hear from you next time you're in town." And she scurried out the door to get on with her life.

🍁　　　🍁　　　🍁

Jack was stunned at his treatment by Jenny; but luckily he didn't have time to dwell on it. It almost felt as if Chuck doubled his schedule as discipline for his slight insurrection. The interviews and appearances became so hectic that Jack lost track of where he was exactly. He learned to plaster just the right smile on his face, and he let others show him where to stand.

And then finally, just when Jack had all he could stand and was about to walk out, it was over.

"We're goin' home, boy," Chuck announced on the elevator up to their floor in the hotel.

Jack could hardly believe what he heard. "You mean it? We're really finished."

"A star is never finished," Chuck tried to sound profound.

"Yeah, but we're really going home!"

"There's a lot of work waiting for us back there," Chuck cautioned.

"Yeah? Like what?" Jack said, a real smile across his face.

"Like some more recording. You've got to get some new songs together."

"Chuck, I've put together a shitload of 'em. Being alone in hotel rooms doesn't hurt the old creativity."

"Good, good," Chuck said. "Then we have to start rehearsals for your first tour."

"Right away?" Jack's eyes pleaded for mercy.

"The first thing we'll have to do is to hire you a band. We'll hold auditions the Monday after we get back."

"But we've got a band, Chuck."

"A band? Oh, you mean those studio musicians?" Chuck said. "They can't go on the road with you."

"Why not? They're the best. You've got to admit."

"Oh, I admit they're the best," Chuck said. "That's why we use the same guys for most of our recording. But the band you take on the road has to be more than good."

"More than good? What do you mean?"

"The studio band laid down their best stuff…got some interesting chops in. They're pretty creative guys, you know."

"I *do* know," Jack confirmed.

"So now any mediocre professional can copy the stuff right off the recordings."

"You're confusing me, Chuck. Why would we want mediocre musicians when we can get the real thing?"

"Because they don't fit the image. A stage show needs window dressing. Can you imagine Sam up there in front of a bunch of teenagers with his stringy hair and beard and that country look. Hell, you'd probably have to wrestle that cowboy hat from him. And what about Snore Atkinson, with his sour puss and his funky cigars. Come on, Jack, you must be able to see that."

"I suppose it'd be okay if it was only about the music," Jack said dejectedly.

"Now you're starting to get it," Chuck said, unaware of Jack's point. "The music stops in the studio. From there on it's marketing."

"Well, at least we're going home for awhile."

"Don't worry Jack," Chuck said, realizing something was wrong for the first time. "We'll get good musicians. Hell, they've got to sing backup too. The objective is to duplicate the recording. We'll just make sure they know how to appear on stage."

"Yeah, okay," Jack sighed. "I got to get some sleep."

CHAPTER 23

❀

Colin was a young man of extremes. If he was to be the most hated columnist in town, he would throw himself into the role. He had always been like that. Nothing was ever middle of the road. Whether it be sports or hobbies or studies or music or whatever, Colin would read all the literature and totally drown himself in the subject.

And now he had made up his mind that he would not play the role that was asked of him by the *Boston Scroll*. No, he would be virtuous, honorable, noble—a man of integrity. Of course, he would throw himself into this just as he had done with everything else in his life. There were no gray areas for Colin. If his new objective was to be an upright principled man, he would dedicate every molecule of his being to it. He would be the most virtuous, most honorable, most noble.

Now, this would not be easy for even the best of us. How does one become righteous and ethical just because he decides to be? Colin was lucky; he had a pretty good head start. Down deep he had always had truth as his religion—that's why his short abandonment of it caused him so much pain. But Colin would do more to make himself authentic—he would pattern himself after what he considered the quintessential man of honesty. He would try to be like Doc.

Colin wasn't stupid or oblivious to his motivation. He realized that copying his idol would be a sincere form of flattery, but not a sincere individual. Still, a role model didn't hurt. Doc seemed to have a lot of the answers. He seemed to be true to himself. Above all, Doc didn't try to be something he was not.

Colin started by moving to a dumpy little apartment in the worst part of the city. Digs weren't important, he reasoned. Nothing but earnestness and authenticity were important. He would live simply, like Thoreau said. He would live only to discover the truths about himself and his environment. Any job would be only for survival purposes. His real objective would be far from the making of money.

Colin took a job as the cashier at the parking garage in the center of the city. He asked for the midnight shift so that he could be free to think and read. Seeing that nobody else liked this duty, Colin was easily accommodated by the city parking authority.

He was aware that a true individualist must have a center—in music or the arts. Colin knew he could not paint or sculpt like Doc. What he decided to do was to write. Yes, he would become a writer. He would write fiction that was full of truths—like Orwell, or Ayn Rand. He would help others to uncover their own thoughts—but he would make it in palatable story form.

Colin began taking his meals again at Fabulous Taco. The disappointment he felt his first time back was overwhelming. Naturally his intellect knew that his friends no longer had time to frequent their old haunt, but his emotional self expected them to all be sitting around, consumed with the newest topic.

Their absence didn't stop Colin from going, however. Somehow the hot dog stand spoke to him, drew him in. Even in its dirty loneliness, Colin felt grounded as he sat at the sticky table, staring at the traffic through the dingy window.

And then his imagination kicked in, and he saw Jack's form through the murky glass. But no, his mind wasn't playing tricks on him. When the heavy glass door opened, it was indeed Jack who entered.

"Son of a bitch!" Jack exclaimed. "Nothin' ever changes."

"Jack, what are you doing here?" Colin asked in astonishment.

"What am I doing here? Why, I'm here to eat the best damn hot dogs in the country, that's what."

"I thought you were on some kind of tour. Hell, Jack, I wasn't sure I'd ever see you again."

"I wasn't sure you would either, Colin," Jack said, putting Colin's head in a headlock so he could knuckle the top. "It's crazy out there, Colin. I mean, it's nothing like reality. Everything is for show or excitement. There's nothing genuine."

"Believe it or not, Jack, I think I know what you mean. Does Michelle know you're back?"

"No. I just can't call her right now for some reason. This is the first place I came when I got into town. I knew I had to, but I don't know why."

"Yeah, I know what you mean," Colin laughed. "It must be some drug or something they put in the hot dogs."

"It's like I'd rather sit in this dirty armpit of a fast food restaurant than be any place else in the world."

"Are you saying you don't want to keep going with your music?" Colin looked puzzled.

"Naw. First of all, this whole thing has got nothing to do with music. I guess I'm in for the trip, but I've got to take a breather once in a while. Everything's too fast, too flashy, too bright, and too lifeless. It's hard to explain."

"I remember when my family went to Disneyland when I was about twelve. Oh, my God, when I hit that Magic Kingdom, I was on overload. But then the assault never stopped. Music everywhere, pretty colors, activity, fantasy—I could hardly stand it after awhile. Even the hotel room kept with some type of theme. I wanted to escape. Imagine that—a twelve year old wanting to escape a dream world."

"It's kind of like that…except in wasn't all that exciting. I wasn't having much fun at all. And the loneliness—I don't know what I'm going to do when I go on tour."

"Have they got a tour planned for you already?"

Jack smiled somewhat sadly. "These guys don't wait for you do blink. Before I knew it, I was on the move—and I don't think I'm going to be stopping much until the whole trip is over."

"But it's what you want to do; it's who you are."

"It must be. I really can't think of myself as anything else. No…I think I'm *supposed* to go with it," Jack said as if trying to convince himself."

"You mean you think it's your destiny or something?"

"Something like that, Colin."

"I think that's bullshit."

"What?"

"I think people have choices," Colin said.

"I have alternatives," Jack said, "but I have no choice."

※ ※ ※

"So where do you want to eat tonight?" Sean said as he opened the door of his BMW for Sandra.

Sandra had been seeing Sean for a couple of weeks, and she had convinced herself that maybe this was the man for her. Everything seemed right about him—and he had a bright financial future. When they were out together, it was always a good time—Sean knew how to plan a date. And she was always proud to be seen with him. Yes, she thought, perhaps this was the right thing.

"I don't know. You're the one that knows all the interesting places to go," she said.

"Why don't we do things a little different tonight…Maybe stop for some hot dogs."

"No!" Sandra said abruptly.

Sean looked over at her in surprise. "Okay, Okay, don't get upset. You have something against pork by-products or something?"

"No," she forced a laugh, "I don't know why I said it that way. I guess hot dogs just don't appeal to me anymore."

"Anymore?"

"Yeah, I think I've had my fill for one lifetime," she said. "If it's all the same to you, I'd like to go to Armado's."

"Then Armado's it is," Sean said as they sped away.

CHAPTER 24

❈

Doc had a sudden urge to leave the darkness of his apartment. The only time this ever happened was when he was hungry or needed to visit the neighborhood brothel again. This time, though, he just had the need to walk.

It was early evening as he rounded the corner of the alley that lead from his door and headed for the main street sidewalk. He walked briskly—as if on a mission. He passed bars and poolrooms and secondhand stores. Doc looked in the window of a furniture and appliance rental shop and shook his head disapprovingly. Soon he found himself in a better part of town with trees and pleasant landscaping. He hadn't made it to the classy neighborhoods yet, or even lower middle class, but he was at a point in societal evolution where people cared about decorating their environments.

When Doc made a right at Buchanan, he unconsciously put his hand out to touch the bars of the big iron fence that surrounded Tarlington Place, a retirement building for seniors of meager means. Just before the corner of the block, the two big gates of Tarlington were opened. Behind the gates was a parking lot for the staff and the delivery area docks. A hot dog vendor was stationed intelligently by the staff entrance so that those workers who preferred to leave the building for their lunch break could add to his income. Apparently business was good because he had a waiting line. Those that had already received their food also stood around the little umbrella-topped stainless steel cart and talked and laughed as they enjoyed their food.

It was quite a busy little area. Truck after truck pulled in to make deliveries. A produce truck with "Sal's Fruits and Vegetables" painted on the side had just backed into the bay to begin unloading. A small blue Dodge station wagon with "Applecore Arrangements" printed on a magnetic sign on the door was pulled up near the back entrance. And then there was a late model Chevy Malibu dropping off a young girl, dressed in serving attire and a starched blue apron, who hurried up the walk to begin her shift. All the while, the people at the little hot dog kiosk were laughing and enjoying each other's company.

There was one more vehicle—but it was there to make a pickup rather than a delivery. A charcoal gray van with an unusual leatherette type of top and sides around the back window, reminiscent of an old Cadillac limousine, sat with its rear doors opened to the service sidewalk. It caught Doc's eye because it looked to be fashioned like the back end of the traditional hearse. On the door were the words "Grove Funeral Services."

Doc's first reaction was one of disgust. A representative of the funeral home was probably up there right now trying to sell an old person some kind of plan. Recently Doc had seen a commercial on the television over the bar advertising a funeral home, complete with a little jingle about peace of mind. Lawyers and hospitals had gone to these inappropriate lengths to attract customers, and now even the undertakers were partaking in the seedy side of capitalism.

And then the door to the back entrance opened, and two dark suited men rolling a gurney in front of them exited. The men had pleasant looks on their faces as they nodded to employees coming into work. When they got to the end of the walk, the men pushed the fully covered corpse into the back of the van. The older of the two men then closed the back doors and got into the driver's seat and waited for the other suit to run across the macadam and pick up a couple of hot dogs. He hurried back, dogs in one hand, two sodas held with his other arm against his stomach, handed the food through the driver's window, and trotted over to the other side. The van sped away with its load.

As Doc watched the scene, his stomach tightened into a hard knot. A man had just had his remains picked up as if an old refrigerator or television were being taken away for trade-in or repair. Obviously the socializing employees knew what was happening while they ate and talked, but not an iota of respect was shown. This was indeed a throw-away society. Buildings were torn down rather than renovated. Cars were junked at an early age. Even shoes were no longer taken to the cobbler for repair. And now, a person could be trashed without the blink of an eye.

People like Doc had spent a great deal of their lives wondering what our purpose here was all about. Cynically, some had deduced that there was no purpose. Others gave man a spiritual credit he probably did not deserve. But here was evidence that it all ended as a body bag being loaded into the back of a truck.

Doc was reminded of a poem by Emily Dickinson entitled "A Fly Buzzed When I died." It had always been a curious piece to Doc. He was never absolutely sure of Dickinson's intention—but he thought he might have an idea now.

CHAPTER 25

❦

When a girl is invited home to meet mother, something pretty serious is going on in a relationship. Sandra was so nervous that she couldn't touch a canvas the whole day of the dinner at the Brady house. Instead, she went out shopping for just the right dress and accessories. Then she spent hours in a beauty parlor, making sure her hair and nails were perfect.

When a girlfriend meets a mother, there's an immediate tension in the air. Any woman that a son brings home is a threat to the position of first woman in a man's life. Though the conversation may seem amiable and polite, and though the discourse may seem comfortable, both women know what's at stake. The young man is being pulled like a turkey wishbone, and he hasn't even got a clue.

Fathers, on the other hand, are excited when the "chip off the old block" brings home a pretty little thing. Not only does it show that one's testosterone has been genetically passed on to one's progeny; but there is a small hidden flirtation that goes on between the oldest male and the young female asking entrance into the tribe.

"She's lovely," Claudia Brady said, taking Sandra's hand at the door.

"Lovely? Hell she's a knockout!" Marcus Brady said, secure in the fact that nobody expected old men to be as dirty as they really were.

"Sandra's an artist," Sean announced proudly as they strolled into the parlor to await the servant's call for dinner.

The parlor was just what one would expect of a mansion. The furniture's design was from an elegant time around the century's turn, and it was punctuated by an abundance of expensive antiques.

"Our family has collected great art for generations," Claudia announced. "Since the family's collection has always been left to the Brady women," she said, giving her husband a mock look of disapproval, "I found early on that I needed to educate myself in great art."

"Then you two have much in common," Sean said, his smile aimed at mom.

"Yes," Claudia Brady said with just a minute hint of challenge.

"Tell me," Sandra said, "what kind of painting do you favor?"

"Well, there are different reasons we purchase art. What I like to do is combine the investment collectability with my appreciation for its aesthetic value. So naturally I'm looking for works of the great painters. We own a Monet, you know. It's hanging in the upstairs hall; I'll show it to you later."

"So you're not really interested in contemporary artists," Sandra said.

"Oh, on the contrary, my dear. I'm always on the lookout for great talent. Unfortunately, I have to admit that it's not that easy to find nowadays…or maybe my standards are just too high. How would you describe your painting, Sandra?"

"I hardly compare to the greats," Sandra said modestly.

"That's ridiculous," Sean broke in. "Sandra has impressed quite a few people with her pictures. She even spoke to the City Ladies' Club," Sean said proudly.

"Really?" Claudia seemed reluctantly impressed.

"When the hell are we going to eat!" Sean's father bellowed.

"Please, Marcus, try to control yourself," Claudia scolded. "There are more important things than food."

"You're right, Claudy," he said, knowing the irritation his wife had for his familiar name for her. "I'll just fix us all a drink."

"Now, you know better than to have anything too strong on an empty stomach."

"That's the best damned time to drink—you get a buzz faster. Come on, Sean, let's make ourselves a couple," he said heading for another room.

Now the two women were alone. Suddenly Sandra felt a cold fear in her bones. She didn't know why, but she was afraid that now that the men were gone, Claudia would use this opportunity to take the gloves off.

"You know, dear," Claudia said, "I think I do remember hearing your name mentioned at the Civics Society luncheon last month. A friend of mine mentioned that she bought something for the home she's building."

"Oh?" Sandra forced.

"Yes. Anita Gilesford, an old friend from college. Wonderful woman. She seems to have an obsession for Early American furnishings. She had her house designed after some place owned by one of the early merchants from Boston—very colonial. The middle class at that time tried so hard to feel like the gentry they left in the old country. Apparently your subject matter must appeal to Anita's tastes. What kind of subjects do you concern yourself with?"

"Oh, I've experimented with all styles," Sandra tried to avoid the conversation, "but my simple landscapes and still-lifes seem to be very popular lately."

"Yes, yes…now I remember seeing one of your things…very cute."

At that point the men came back into the room carrying clinking glasses. Sandra hoped her sigh of relief was not too noticeable. Sean handed Sandra a whiskey sour, her favorite drink, but nothing was brought for Claudia.

"Sean here tells me that you actually make a living as an artist. That's really something in this day and age," Marcus said.

"Well," Sandra said, sensitive to Claudia's judgment, "there are different kinds of artists."

"You do paint pictures, don't you?"

"Well, yes."

"Then I'd like you to paint one for me. Yeah…I want to commission a painting."

"That's very nice, Mr. Brady," Sandra said nervously, "but you've never even seen my work."

"First of all," Brady boomed, "I expect you to call me Marcus. Hell, I'm an old man, but I don't like to be reminded of it. Secondly, I have a lot of faith in my son's taste. If Sean says you're good, you're good."

"Thank you, but—"

"Now, what I want is something for over our bed."

"Our bed! We have a four hundred thousand dollar DeAngelico over our bed, Marcus!" Claudia exclaimed.

"And I've never liked it. It's kind of creepy, you know? Like being in a church at night or something."

"Mr.—Marcus," Sandra said, "my painting is hardly a replacement for a DeAngelico."

"Why the hell not! This DeAngelico guy was not some kind of god or something; he was just human like everybody else. In fact, I'll bet the people of his time period were creeped out by his stuff too. A lot of people think things are good because they're *supposed* to think things are good."

"I believe you've got a point, dad," Sean said, oblivious to his mother's irritation. "Take Bach, and Beethoven, and all those musical geniuses of old. Was there something that limited the greats to the past? I mean, in all those years, hasn't there been one contemporary composer that measures up? Maybe if McCartney or Paul Simon lived in those days, we'd be celebrating their works today."

"There's a big difference between classical composers and pop songwriters," Claudia said indignantly.

"Oh, I don't know, Mother," Sean said. "I think we give those guys a lot of credit. Let's face it, people should know much more about musical theory and harmony and whatever now than they did then. Shouldn't music be better? Besides, ordinary people liked Beethoven. He was the Pink Floyd of his time. Why do we venerate art from the past at the expense of great creations today?"

"Because they were more than just *tunes*," Claudia tried to stay calm.

"If classical music and ballet and old art is all that great, why is there such a limited audience? Because we're less sophisticated? Hardly. If anything, we're more sophisticated. A commercial for Jello probably takes more work for its background jingle than any classical symphony. Today's power chords are just yesterday's orchestras."

"Bravo," Claudia said. "You've just reduced the best that civilization has ever had to offer to Led Zeppelin."

Sandra smiled and made small talk all through dinner, but she didn't taste a thing. The whole experience was like a dream—a dream that she wanted to wake from. Of course, it was not Sean's fault that she was so uncomfortable, and it seemed to mean so much to him that they spend the evening with his parents. Her only hope was that Claudia would get an early migraine or something so that this night could end.

But Sean may have been more sensitive to the mood than he let on. They did stay for coffee, but he made the excuse that he had an early plane to catch the next morning and would have to take Sandra home. Of course, Sandra knew this was untrue—they had planned a trip to the mountains for a picnic. Apparently Sean's mother wasn't privy to her husband's business dealings.

"So what did you think?" Sean said once they were safely in the car.

"I thought your parents were quite charming."

Sean only laughed.

❋ ❋ ❋

"Awesome sound you've got," the young guitarist with the Hawaiian shirt and the moussed spiky hair said.

"Well, thank you," Jack said, never able to take the word *awesome* seriously.

"I guess you're going to ask me a lot of questions."

"Questions?"

"Yeah. Chuck said that this was going to be a pre-audition interview."

"I think Chuck is interested in the kind of person you are—whether you would project the right image."

"That's cool."

"I'm more concerned about how my music sounds."

"Whether the gig goes off."

"Yeah…something like that."

"Dude, you can rest assured—I don't do drugs."

"Good—but what kind of *guitar player* are you?" Jack was getting a little annoyed.

"I like to have an instrument with lots of mass—for sustain, you know—although you can get that synthetically. I've got this old Les Paul with screamin' hot pickups, but it just doesn't look good on stage. As far as effects—"

"How do you play? Are you any good?' Jack interrupted.

"I can copy any lick recorded," the young man said proudly.

"And your interest in music?"

"What do you mean?"

"I mean, what got you started?"

"Oh, you know. Played a lot of air guitar as a kid. Wanted to rock and roll."

"So, music is not a real serious activity for you."

"Dude," the young man said with the sincerest expression, "music is my life."

Unfortunately, all candidates for the band tended to be the same type of individual. They would be, naturally, because they went through a screening by Chuck before Jack could even talk to them. After a few hours of this, Jack just left—without telling anyone.

There was an old pump house by the little river that ran through the bottom of town. It was not the nicest area. The river was one of those waterways that regrettably runs through an area where it is not enjoyed but used as a sewer. Everything from discarded motor oil to shopping carts from the grocery over the bridge was thrown into the little stream. Fish had died out long ago.

But Jack had always gravitated to the old pump house as an adolescent. There was something about sitting in solitude—no one ever visited the banks of this polluted stream—and watching even the worst of some natural waterway. Though the odor was sometimes overpowering, Jack would sit for hours and hours as a kid, trying to make some sense out of things.

Jack had been home a week now. Home. He hadn't been able to wait until Chuck announced their return. But it was like an extension of Chuck's twisted world had come home with them. The people and the values he had to deal with were about the same. Except for his fortunate meeting at Fabulous Taco with Colin, life was just about as frustrating as the road.

He hadn't called Michelle yet. He thought it might be guilt because of the night with Jennifer—but down deep he knew better. It was guilt, all right, but not because of another woman. Michelle made Jack feel phony and ridiculous about his new career. He so wanted her to be as excited about who he would become as everyone else, but it wasn't in her. No matter what image Chuck would create and no matter how Jack would come to perceive himself after his new fame and success, Michelle would always know the real man. Somehow this was frightening and intimidating to him rather than comforting.

Michelle had to know that Jack was back in town. Of course, she was not the kind to investigate these things herself, but someone must have told her. Apparently she was just giving Jack his space like she always did. Many men would kill for a woman like this, but Jack wanted just the opposite. He wanted her to be impatient and jealous. He wanted her to be selfish about his time. And somehow her cool wisdom and maturity was so unnerving to Jack at this point, he just couldn't face her yet.

Unlike Michelle, however, Chuck could not wait for Jack's time. As soon as he found him missing, he sent a couple of his "rock lackeys" out to find Jack. Somehow, by asking questions and following whatever leads they could, they located him.

"Jack, where've you been?" Denny Sorenson said, whining through his multiply pierced nostrils. "We've been looking for you everywhere!"

"Wha—! How did you find me here!" Jack said, upset that his sanctum had been violated—especially by such disgusting characters.

"That's our job, man," Jase Timmons grinned from under his platinum-spiked hair. "We're always huntin' down musicians for Chuck. We drag 'em out of bed, sober 'em up—everything."

"Well, I don't want you here. You tell Chuck I'll be back to interview his imitation musicians tomorrow."

"No can do," Denny said, scratching his skinny tattooed arms. "Chuck will have our heads if we come back without you. Come on, man, the bugs up here are driving me crazy."

"I got Chuck's car," Jase said proudly, "parked just over the bank."

Of course, Jack had a choice. These were not tough thugs who would force him to go back. He could just walk over to Fabulous Taco or see what Colin was up to or…see Michelle.

"Okay," Jack said. "Let's get this circus over with."

CHAPTER 26

❈

"I'm about a hundred pages into my first book," Colin said as he sat in Doc's old chair, starting the six pack of Coors Original he had brought.

"That's great, Colin. You know, this is only the second time you've stopped by my place in all the time we've known each other. I wasn't even aware that you knew where I lived."

"I hope it's no problem, Doc. It's just that I feel we're kindred spirits and that you're some kind of a guru or advisor or mentor to me now."

"Guru?"

"It's just that you got my mind on the right track after my first visit. I think you pointed me in the right direction."

"Well, that's good, I guess," Doc said, "but that's all I did—point you. The rest is up to you, Colin. I'm in no position to be a mentor about life. Look at the way I live!"

"That's just it," Colin said enthusiastically. "You live the life of a true intellectual—a true artist. Everything about you is true. You're a real person, Doc—hard to find nowadays."

"I don't know how 'real' I am, Colin, but I do know that if truth is what you want, you can't find it by emulating anyone else—least of all, me."

"I've thought that through also," Colin said. "I knew that would be your attitude. It's just that now I need some direction. Maybe talking to you about some of my ideas and getting your perspective will help me to focus on my own truths."

Doc turned and walked a few steps, scratching his fingernails roughly against the top of his scalp. "What if...what if there *aren't* any truths."

"How could there not be!"

"Why does there have to be? There may not be any meaning whatsoever, let alone principles."

"No...we've had this discussion many times at Fabulous Taco. There's too much order to things for there not to be some kind of divine purpose. I know what you're trying to say though, Doc. You're trying to tell me that you're still looking for answers. Don't worry; I understand that. It's just that you've been at it longer than I have, so I'm looking to you for approach. Maybe we'll find the answers together."

When Colin left, Doc had an uneasy feeling. Not because he might be leading a young person down the wrong path or that someone was looking to him for guidance—though these things were not comfortable for him. Doc had been alone for a long time—desperately alone. For many years he had suffered because of it. He still suffered terribly from it. But loneliness had become like an old friend. It was something familiar and permanent for him. Like smoking a cigarette or having a regular drink by oneself, his constant unwavering loneliness brought a perverse assurance to his life.

Colin, on the other hand, would provide a disruption to Doc's melancholy routine. His set ways would be intruded upon. Though company should be welcome to the companionless, any change in routine, including habitual mood, brought anxiety. When Colin finally left, Doc found himself in a state of disquiet; and his usual sorrow offered no immediate stability.

Luckily, he didn't have too much time to think. He had to be at work in a half-hour, so he quickly grabbed his jacket and headed out the door.

It was a Tuesday night, and the bar was quiet. With all that was on Doc's mind, he would have preferred noise and confusion. What he had were three drunks slumped over their glasses and an aging slut nursing a beer at the table across the dingy room.

One of the men at the bar was not someone Doc recognized. That wasn't too surprising, even for a neighborhood bar. The draw of the corner saloon transcends time and space, and the occasional alumnus would return after a new life had failed or a career had gone belly up. We're often drawn to our self-destructive vices when life takes a bad turn.

"Fill her again, friend," the man addressed Doc.

Doc, without a word, presented the man with another bourbon.

"This place never changes," the man said, obviously wanting conversation.

"That's why it's so popular," Doc said, washing glasses below the bar.

"Yeah…you're right," the man drawled drunkenly. "There's so little in life that stays the same. Buildings, streets, taxes—they usually stay the same. And the things that are bad for you. How come only the good things change so much?"

"I don't know," Doc said. "Maybe it's because we began to expect so much from them. Maybe we just can't take them for what they are—we want more from them, for some reason. The bad things in life? We just kind of accept them for what they are."

The man fumbled in his breast pocket for a pack of cigarettes. "Yeah. I can always depend on a cigarette when I'm feeling down. What kind of shit is that when you light up a cancer stick to feel better!"

"Don't know," Doc said, trying to end the conversation.

"I'm happy here," the man said. "I could stay in this little cave, drinking and smoking and listening to the crappy songs on that juke box forever. I think I'd rather die on this bar stool than to go back into the world out there again."

"Unfortunately closing time's at two," Doc said, wiping the bar.

"Listen," the man said in an inebriated sudden change of direction, "You ever see a young girl here named Debra Dunlevy? How 'bout Charlie Lewinski? Burt Parker?"

"Sorry," Doc said, "never heard of 'em."

"But they're regulars here, buddy. They used to open and shut this place twenty years ago."

Doc stopped appearing busy and looked the man in his red eyes. "That's the thing," he said. "The places don't change, but the life that travels through them does. After a place like this does its job on a generation, it begins to feed on a whole new group. Some make it, some lead lives of disaster. All of them pass on."

"Yeah," the man said, stumbling to get off his barstool while throwing a wad of bills at the bar, "and my time here is finished."

Doc closed his eyes in a wince as the man staggered toward the door.

CHAPTER 27

There are some scientists that feel that everything about us is chemical—that we're just millions of human shaped beakers sloshing around one another, trying to make some sense of it all. Everything about us seems to be able to be boiled down to some substance in our system. Some men of science claim that even love is merely an element of some type in our system—which dogs, incidentally, possess also.

So when a man and a woman have good chemistry together, that may be exactly what they have. Some don't want to hear this. They claim that there's physical attraction—which may be attributed to biology—and then there something on a higher level. To think that something like love could be an ingredient in the recipe for humanity is a repulsive idea.

But the fact remains, two people that seem so perfect together with everything in common often find no attraction. On the other hand, a couple that should not be is frequently a fact. Maybe one cannot account for taste, but surely one can understand how some chemicals mix better than others. Perhaps pheromones signal more than we know.

Sandra and Sean were the prefect couple. Sandra was the pretty blond girl with the interesting career. Sean, the clean cut, good-looking young businessman with a fabulous future before him. They looked so good together that people would often remark about the fact. Sometimes strangers would actually approach them to comment on the attractive couple. And friends...well, friends made it clear that the two should pair up legally. What were they waiting for? Never had they known a couple that was so meant for each other.

Eventually both Sandra and Sean began to believe what they heard. Ideas of marriage were going through both heads on a regular basis. Of course, there's a protocol for an All-American couple that has to be followed. Everything has to be just right.

It was a French restaurant in the country that Sean chose for their special night. Everything about the place was perfect—and expensive. Though Sandra was beginning to get used to dining in the best of places, she was more than impressed by LeCorde's. A field stone fireplace on the back wall and candles provided the only lighting—lighting that was reflected on the best of glassware and silver. It was a magical room.

During dinner, Sean did the expected. He reached across the little table and took Sandra's hand in his—staring deeply into her shiny blue eyes.

"Will you marry me?" he said as sincerely and deeply as any soap opera actor asking the same question.

"Of course," Sandra answered, one of the stock answers she had been rehearsing in her head while she picked at her squash.

When Sean took her to her door that night, they walked in silence, hand in hand. A perfect gentle kiss was the only communication between the two before Sandra scurried into the house.

"I've been waiting for hours," Sandra's mother said from the loveseat by the window of the dark living room.

"Oh, mother," Sandra chastised.

"We knew it would be tonight. Your father went ahead to bed—he needs his sleep. But me? Well, I just had to talk to you."

"Well…he asked me," Sandra almost whispered as she displayed the rock on her ring finger.

"Oh, my God!" her mother exclaimed. "I didn't know they made diamonds that big."

"I always expect this kind of thing from Sean," Sandra said evenly.

"Tell me all about it," her mother said.

"There's really not much that was unexpected. The restaurant was beautiful…and the food was good. It was like being in a movie or something. Everything was wonderful."

"You don't *seem* very excited," her mother commented.

"Oh, I'm very happy…I'm just tired," Sandra said.

"I remember when your dad and I got engaged. He took me to a baseball game that day—the Cubs were in town. He gave me the ring, all wrapped and beautiful, in the parking lot of the stadium. Then afterwards, we stopped at a liquor store and got some Cold Duck to take to the drive-in with us. Your dad went into the concession stand and bought two large buttered popcorns and a couple of empty cups. We didn't watch much of the movie—I can tell you that."

"You make it sound like you thought it was wonderful."

"Oh yes," her mother said dreamlike, "it was. I'll never forget a moment of that night."

"But it wasn't exactly romantic."

"It was the most romantic evening I could have imagined…Well," she said, waking abruptly from her reverie, "I'll bet your evening was just as perfect."

Sandra stared blankly before answering, "Yes. It was perfect."

❦   ❦   ❦

Colin's apartment was in the worst possible part of the city. He planned it that way. What he didn't take into consideration was what went along with the grimy little place. Because Colin no longer kept a car, he walked everywhere he went. In his new environment, it was the custom for the residents to sit on their door stoops and talk before retiring to their hot little hovels. Colin, unaware at first that his presence stirred some hatred in the neighborhood, tried greeting the people as he passed, only to be given quiet cold stares. Of course, this didn't stop Colin. He was bound and determined to live this new life of his, and he would work on making a more friendly environment too.

One evening, just after being rebuffed by a large woman leaning against a rusted steel stair rail, Colin was grabbed roughly as he turned the corner of the street. The hands took him by the front of his jacket and slammed him against a brick wall just inside the alley.

"What you got for us, man?" the venom filled voice spat at him.

"I've got nothing," Colin answered.

"Don't you fuck with me boy!" the voice said. Suddenly two others joined his assailant.

"I'm telling you the truth—I've got nothing."

"What you doin' in this neighborhood?" the first man demanded.

"I live here."

"Live here!" the man laughed. "Man, what are you doin', research for some book or somethin'?"

"As a matter of fact, I am a writer," Colin announced somewhat proudly, considering the circumstances.

"And you want to feel what it's like to live with just the basics, that right? You think if you live in some rat hole, you'll get some kind of inspiration?"

"Not exactly—"

"Well, I've lived here all my life, and I got plenty of inspiration. I'm inspired to steal and do drugs and get violent. How's that for inspiration?"

"I'm not here to hurt anyone," Colin promised.

"We know you ain't gonna hurt anyone," the man said to the whoops and guffaws of the other two. We're gonna be the ones who does the hurting."

"Why would you want to do that?" Colin asked. "I've got nothing—really. I just want to live and let live. Why is that so much to ask?"

Colin's attacker had a moment of confusion on his face. "We don't like you in our neighborhood—you understand that? You don't belong."

"That's my problem," Colin said more to himself. "I don't belong anywhere."

Another look of uncertainty crossed the man's face. "We'll be watchin' you," he said, giving Colin one last push against the wall. Then the three strutted away, leaving Colin shaking in his shoes in the damp dark alley.

Colin made his way back to his building and up the dim creaky stairs that led to his door. When he went to put his key into the lock, the door opened inward with the pressure. Once inside, Colin discovered what he feared. Everything of any value was gone—his stereo, his small television, and, worst of all, his computer. The cabinets above the sink were all opened, and the drawers in his desk and dresser were pulled out in the search for something of worth. That meant his prized 35 millimeter camera was also gone.

Because Colin was now living the life of a true artist, he did not have renter's insurance—not that any company would have given it to anyone living in this part of town. Now he really had nothing. Now was the true test of character.

Colin didn't get emotional. He didn't call the police. What he did was reach into his opened bottom desk drawer and pull out one of the many legal pads he had stored there. Then he reached up and grabbed a pencil from the jar on the desktop. For the rest of the night, he sat on the hard wooden floor and wrote the next twelve chapters of his book in longhand.

❧   ❧   ❧

It took another two weeks of auditions and interviews before Jack's backup band was finally hired for his first road trip. In all that time, he hadn't as much as given Michelle a call. Now, since so much time had passed, he was afraid to. She certainly had heard he was in town, so she was probably waiting for his move. At this point she was probably hurt or very, very angry. Jack had used the band as an excuse to himself that he was just too involved in his work to have time to see Michelle; so when the band was finalized, he felt he had to make the call.

"Jack," Michelle said pleasantly on the other end of the phone. "I was hoping I'd hear from you soon."

"Well, as you probably heard, I've been back awhile."

"No, I hadn't heard. I've been really busy at work, so I haven't seen anyone in a while."

"Oh," Jack said, a bit disappointed. "Well, I didn't call right away because I've been bogged down with getting the tour band together. I'm sorry…It's just that it's been so much work that I—"

"That's okay, Jack. I know how musicians are. I'm just glad you have some time now."

"Yeah…well…I'll be pretty tied up with rehearsals…but maybe we could get together."

"Oh, I hope so," Michelle said cheerfully. "I've missed you, Jack."

"Really?"

"Of course, I have. I just try to keep real busy."

"Maybe I could stop by tonight," Jack said hopefully.

"Sure, Jack. I'll make some coffee, and we can talk."

When he hung up the phone, a wave of anger flashed over Jack. Was Michelle really glad he was back? She hadn't seemed the least bit upset about his not calling her right away. How could she be so damned sure of her relationship with him anyway. After all, he was becoming a star. He met lots of people—lots of *women*. How dare she not be concerned. Jack got himself in such a frenzy, he almost decided not to see Michelle after all.

When he got to Michelle's apartment, Jack hesitated before he knocked. Finally, after gently clapping the doorknocker once, Michelle opened the door. She was beautiful. More beautiful than he remembered. And it wasn't because she took pains in preparation for Jack's visit. No, Michelle greeted him in blue jeans and an oversized gray sweatshirt with "Temple" printed across the front. Her hair was kind of pushed back out of her face, and she had very little makeup on. She was, however, stunning.

"Oh, Jack, I really did miss you," she said, falling into his arms.

Jack smelled her wonderful hair and felt her form melt into his. He thought of her fresh face and her genuine smile as he closed his eyes during their embrace. Her smooth voice echoed through his head as he squeezed her tighter. And he knew he was with the one person in the world he was meant to be with. He also knew at that moment that he was with the one person in the world who truly understood who he was; and though this was what frightened him most about Michelle, he wanted to be no other place than with her right now.

Then, his face now buried in Michelle's smooth neck, Jack began to cry. At first his tears were silent. Then real emotion tried to break through as his body jerked to try to hold in. Finally he let go and sobbed like a little child as Michelle kissed his wet face.

It was a while before Jack recovered himself, and then he was embarrassed.

"I'm sorry," he said, wiping his eyes with the bottom of his T-shirt. I don't know why I did that."

"It's okay," Michelle said, petting his hair as they sat together on the couch.

"No…I really don't know why I did that," Jack said.

"Yes you do, Jack," she said, looking him straight in his wet eyes.

"What?" Jack said, a little surprised.

"I said that you know why you did that," she said a little too firmly.

"Oh, yeah?" Jack asked, starting to become defensive. "Why?"

"Because now you're really home, Jack. You're really home."

CHAPTER 28

❁

Doc had a day off. A free day. The thought struck fear in the very depths of his soul. Most of his time off from the bar was spent sculpting, but he had just finished a big piece that he had spent months on. Starting something new was like a writer before a blank piece of paper—oh, the terror. Of course, Doc had down times during his days, but these were usually spent reading or drinking (he had tried to do them both at the same time, but then he enjoyed neither activity). Reading and drinking were fine, but he had 24 hours of space ahead of him to fill.

Now most people live for their time off. Doc, on the other hand, had no reason whatsoever to live. There was no purpose to his continued existence—and too much time on his hands reminded him of the fact. Tortured souls never stop agonizing, but the agonizing can be alleviated by focusing as much attention as possible on something external.

People frightened Doc. He was not shy or intimidated by them; he was disgusted at what God had wrought—so he just couldn't spend any time around other members of his species. The thing that really bothered Doc about his fellow men was the fact that they didn't have a clue as to their ridiculous lives and thoughts and inane communication. Most people just lived—they took things as they were handed to them. They played roles that were expected. Even their goals and disappointments involved the artificial—the American dream, status, money. Since Doc was cursed with a horribly contemplative nature, he couldn't stand to be around them. And Doc was honest enough with himself to understand that his misanthropy might be jealousy.

Some people seek solace in nature. A walk in the park, a trip to the country, or a fishing trip revitalized them—relieved stress and helped with positive perspective. Though Doc loved nature, a quiet wooded area or a bubbling stream exacerbated his loneliness and didn't take him away from his thoughts.

A lonely man who couldn't stand people is the ultimate paradox. Most people are gregarious by nature. They like to go places where there are lots of people and excitement. They live in houses where one is expected to strike up relationships with one's neighbors—even have a block party once a year. The noise and stimulation that crowds generate makes a location popular with the majority of humans. Others, those who appreciate nature, connect with its calm. Doc could do neither.

To make matters worse, Doc awoke that Tuesday morning at 5:30 a.m. One way of coping with life for those with a touch of gloom is to sleep through some of the miserable hours. Lots of depressed people become very adept at napping. Doc, on the other hand, never found sleep easy. If he got four or five hours of sleep in a 24-hour period, he considered himself lucky. So here he was, facing a day of angst at its very beginning.

Suddenly Doc knew what he would do. It was the perfect combination of people and quiet. He would spend some time in the public library. Here he could occupy his brain with book searches and magazine articles. Here he would lose himself amid the friendly tomes, many written by tormented individuals much like himself. Here he could lose himself in the stacks, but he would feel close enough to a societal structure so that he couldn't fall apart.

Libraries have always been special places for special people. Unlike bookstores where pretentious people can have designer coffee and a croissant before browsing for whatever book has been discussed by Oprah or National Public Radio—before buying the newest volume of Maya Angelou's poetry or the witticisms of Garrison Keeler—the library is a place for true lovers of the printed word. The faces one saw in these institutions were of happy purpose—voracious cerebral appetites. And the patrons of the library were of no specific social class. One would see professionals and laborers, L.L. Bean and work shoes. Often there would be a homeless person reading a free newspaper or gazing through a picture book at what the world offered.

Doc felt a warm camaraderie with his fellow book lovers as he stood with them in the shelf aisles. He was not anxious at the thought of being crowded. He did not fear bogus conversation. The people at the library were not there for each other. All they shared was the same obsession—and somehow that little bit of shared humanity made Doc feel good.

For awhile Doc had gone through a period of reading only biographies. It seemed to do him good to note the complications involved in people's lives. Then he spent a time where everything was politics and history. Recently, though, he was going through the great classics. He considered this his philosophy stage because the great writers were simply deep thinkers who conveyed their ideas in story form. Doc would pick an author—Faulkner, for instance—and read everything the library had. Soon he would get used to the writer's style. Then when he exhausted every work of that individual, he would go to the next. His only fear was that he would read them all and have nothing left.

As Doc sat at a little table at the end of the long thin room full of fiction, perusing a volume of Dostoyevsky, two young boys appeared from what seemed like nowhere and began chasing each other around his table. Doc was startled by the foreign movement in this cathedral of thought and looked up and around his back to see what the commotion was. The boys, undaunted by the presence of a disapproving adult, continued the chase—knocking over the chair across from Doc, running up and down the aisle perpendicular to the stacks and then back again.

Doc had not always hated children, but lately he found them harder and harder to take. It got to the point where he wondered why mothers did not all destroy their young at birth. But what upset Doc the most about these hyperactive monsters was that they never seemed to have any supervision—even in the rare cases where there was a parent present. Somehow, people had recently come to the conclusion that the wildness and inconsideration for others was only natural; and that one had to let kids be kids. Besides, it took so much effort to tame them. And what was even more disconcerting was that the parents assumed that the intrusion of their youngsters on someone else was a welcome, happy event—that all people loved and understood all children.

Finally a stout woman of about thirty came walking up to Doc's area, a smile on her face.

"Okay, boys," she said as they continued to race around, her presence seemingly ignored, "we're about ready to go now."

Doc looked up at the grinning face. "Lady, what are you doing in this place?"

"Excuse me," she said, indignantly confused.

"What..." Doc started as one of the boys darted behind his chair, "are you doing in a library?"

"What does anyone do in a library?" her tone now became prickly.

"If you're here to get reading material—to expand your mind—I applaud you," Doc said. "But does your presence here have to be a disturbance to others?"

"Oh, I see," she said, folding her arms in front of her. "You're one of those child haters."

"With custodians such as yourself, lady, I can't imagine anyone liking them."

"It's people like you who take the sunshine out of life for others—bitter, bitter people like you." And now she actually collared a youngster in each hand and pushed them toward the exit.

It was times like this that Doc questioned himself. Was he really such an ogre? Were people actually as thoughtless and selfish as he perceived them, or was he unusually critical. What kind of monster had he become! It was so unnatural for a human being to have disgust for his own kind. Yet he couldn't help thinking that people were, in fact, abhorrent—but why was he the only one cursed with this recognition.

Life had become a hair shirt for Doc. To see others actually reveling in what one feels to be torment was so confusing that he often wondered if he had indeed lost his mind. After all, "insanity is a minority of one," as Orwell very aptly said. If a person is so different and so intolerant of the norm, the onus, of course, is on him to conform. Thoughts about the universe so different from others was what psychosis was all about, wasn't it?

Doc was no longer able to enjoy the solitude that was left to him now that the brats were gone. All he could do was sit there shaking, contemplating his own abject presence in this world. Maybe he was an abnormality, an unacceptable mutation among his own species. Why had he come this far in the first place? Weren't such oddities in nature naturally destroyed—wasn't that the way of all living things? Why had he survived? Should he have bowed out much earlier in his life and saved himself and others the misery of his existence?

After awhile Doc calmed himself and began smiling at the many Russian name variations he saw in the pages before him. Just as he was about to settle back and enjoy his book again, Doc heard a young girl's voice.

"I wanna go to get pizza *now*!" the voice demanded from just outside the door to the next room.

Doc immediately gathered up his books and headed for checkout. He could not hide here any longer.

CHAPTER 29

❀

Sandra and Sean planned the perfect wedding. It would be a big affair, and it would be held at the exclusive Woods Edge Country Club of which Sean's family had been members since its inception. But that was only the beginning. Like many young brides-to-be, Sandra found herself carrying around magazines, through which she would pour whenever there was a free moment, dedicated to dream weddings.

Sometimes it seems like the wedding event is far more important to women than the contract between two people that will be taking place. Like a high school prom, dresses have to be considered for her and her bridesmaids—not to mention just the right tuxedos for the men. The cake. Decorations. Announcements. Entertainment. Food. Drink. Speeches. Everything had to be out of some dream that society has somehow placed in the brains of its female half.

In seems, in fact, that women are in love with the *idea* of weddings and marriage. The idea is so strong in them that they sometimes place the priority of choosing the proper partner behind who will be singing during the ceremony. Just the thought of standing there as the white clad center of attention must be all that some girls have ever wished for. The threat of the divorce rate statistics predicting an early end to the union doesn't seem to cross their minds. It's the memories that will be made on that special day that are most important.

But the wedding can also act as a diversion. A diversion from the struggle ahead that any household has to endure. A diversion from the pressures of job and finances that a couple must go through. Even a diversion from the denial each partner in the coming contract has been undergoing about the deficiencies and incompatibility each has sensed in the other. Maybe a diversion from the fact that there is no basis for the marriage whatsoever besides established role-playing.

Of course, Sandra was not conscious of anything but planning the upcoming occasion. Not only was it important that the wedding replicate her childhood fantasies, she now had the expectations of a high society future mother-in-law who would be insisting on the very best. After all, this was her only son, and a quality show must be planned and performed.

The list of guests would include some of the most prominent and influential people in the city—not to mention Sean's wealthy, successful relatives from across the country. Sandra's list, on the other hand, dulled in comparison. Her family were all simple people—not poor, but simple. And her friends—well, they had always been somewhat peculiar. In fact, though she fought not to recognize it, there were stabs of guilty embarrassment as she sat and listed her people on the long pink legal pad.

How would her friends act at the reception? Would they drink too much? Would their drilling honesty offend Sean's guests? And would she invite everyone? Surely, Doc would not attend, she thought with abashed relief. And Colin—what about Colin?

There wasn't a time in her life after she met Colin when she didn't recognize an unusual bond—even when they stopped dating and became bickering friends. For a long time she could not make a decision in her life without wondering what Colin would think—not whether he would approve, necessarily, but what he would think.

Actually, her relationship with Sean had enabled her to put Colin out of her mind for awhile; but now his strong presence was back as she poised her pen over the tablet.

Surely Colin would do nothing to upset the proceedings. Inaction, in fact, would be Colin's most diabolical method of showing his non-endorsement. The man could act infuriatingly cool and indifferent while all the time making Sandra examine the depths of her every intention. But he would have to be there—he was an important part of her life. But her new life was so very different—as if what had come before was an unfortunate journey that need not be celebrated, or even acknowledged.

She would invite every one of her friends, she determined. If her marriage was real and truly her destiny, the presence of those representing different values should not disturb her; and the worst thing she could do would be to eliminate that "growing time" from what she was becoming. She would use it as a test—though she did not admit this to herself.

It's interesting how things happen just when we're thinking about them. A song on the radio, for instance, comes on just after we've been thinking of it or singing it. Or a person calls whom you have just been talking about. Coincidence? Maybe. But just about everyone you know will have examples of these same phenomena, and that's too much for coincidence.

Anyway, just as Sandra bravely and boldly printed Colin's name on her list, her mother knocked on her bedroom door.

"You have a visitor," she said joylessly.

"Who?" Sandra asked, noting the disappointed tone in her mother's voice.

"What bad penny keeps coming up?" her mother said with irritation.

"Colin?" Sandra was surprised at the excitement she felt.

"The one and only. Make sure you tell him that you're getting married. Maybe he'll take the hint."

Colin sat sprawled on the couch as Sandra walked in. Upon seeing her, he straightened up.

"Colin, what are you doing here?" she asked.

"What am I doing here? You've never asked me that before, no matter how long between visits."

"I'm sorry. That was a silly question. It's...just that you usually have a reason..."

"That's true," Colin said enthusiastically. We have kind of a tradition—you and I—of sharing big steps in our lives."

"Yes...I guess we have," Sandra said uncomfortably.

"Well, I've got news about my book. I sent the first few chapters to some obscure publisher in Connecticut, and he's interested. He's even going to give me an advance."

"Oh, Colin, that's wonderful news!" Sandra said with genuine interest. "So, you're in the money."

"Not exactly," Colin said. "It's just $500, but it's a start."

"I'm so happy for you. I wasn't even aware that you were writing books," she said, suddenly aware of Colin's dirty clothes and scruffy appearance.

"And it's my first one! Finally I'm on my way with something that's really me."

"That's good. I was never sure that those columns were your thing."

"Yeah...I had a long talk with Doc," Colin said with a not of deference. "He gave me a better perspective on things."

"I'm so proud of you."

"Thanks."

After a short but awkward silence, Sandra said sheepishly, "Colin...uh...I've got some news in my life too."

"Oh yeah? That's great!" Colin said. "Did you sell one of your paintings for a lot or something?"

"Actually…I haven't been painting much," Sandra said with a slight look of puzzlement at her own revelation.

"You haven't! I thought you never stopped."

"Colin," she said quickly, as if she were delivering extremely bad news to someone, "I'm getting married."

The stunned silence that followed brought unwelcome tears to Sandra's eyes. And try as she might, she could not think of anything to fill the void.

"You're going to marry someone?" Colin delivered in an incredulous voice.

"Sure…" she forced a smile. "People usually marry *someone*."

"Yeah…right…I just…I mean…"

"We're perfect for each other—everyone says so," she said, almost defensively.

"Not everyone. You didn't ask me."

"Colin," she laughed nervously, "you don't even know Sean."

"*Sean*? Typical."

"I thought you'd be happy for me."

"I'm sorry," Colin said, closing his eyes and shaking his head as if to remove the cobwebs. "Of course I'm happy for you."

"I've been so busy," she exhaled in relief. "There's so much to do before getting married."

"You mean like the blood tests?"

"No, no," she laughed. "I mean for the ceremony and the reception. Everything has to be just right."

"I thought you just said you were perfect for each other."

"I did."

"Then everything is *already* just right."

"Now you're being silly."

"*Silly*?" he asked, having never heard that word from Sandra's lips.

"And of course I want you to be there."

"Sure...yeah, I'll be there."
"I'm so excited," she grinned.
"Are you *happy*?" he said, looking her straight in the eyes.
"Why wouldn't I be?"
"I don't know...That's why I asked."
"You just don't understand girls and weddings," she smiled.
"Can I ask you a question?"
"Of course."
"You're not going to stop painting, are you?"
"No. Why would you even ask?"
"Because painting is who you are. Not a bride or a wife—you're a painter."
"A person is many different things, Colin. You must realize that."
"No," he said stubbornly. "If I get married, I'll be a writer with a wife. If Jack gets married, he'll be a musician with a wife. And you...you'll always be a painter first."
"As one grows up," she said with a trace of condescension, "one finds that things are not as simple as that."
"Then I don't want to 'grow up,' as you put it."
"Tell me more about your book," she said, abruptly trying to switch gears.

When Colin left, Sandra sat for over an hour, staring blankly out the front picture window at the empty street. It was late, and many of the houses had turned off lights for the evening. Sandra's house was dark too—she had talked to Colin in the kitchen and hadn't bothered to switch on the lamp in the front room. Her parents had turned in long before after waiting impatiently for Colin to go, so she was alone with her thoughts. Finally, as if being beckoned by some spirit, Sandra arose from the couch and walked trancelike through the kitchen toward the basement door. After walking zombie-like down the first two steps, she unconsciously flipped on the light, illuminating her studio. As soon as she saw her easel and canvases, her step quickened. In unconscious motion, she donned the blue smock she had thrown over her stool, and picked up a brush that had been resting on the easel tray. And then Sandra painted. She painted like she hadn't ever painted before. Sandra painted with passion—with aggression—with anger—with obsession. She painted all night, her fervor uninterrupted by fatigue.

In the morning, as the sun shone through the small basement window, she dropped her brush, turned, and fell limply onto the little floor rug where she slept until noon. Her appointment with the people who would be decorating the hall at the country club was at ten.

CHAPTER 30

❀

One of the most difficult parts of being a musician—successful or not—is being on the road. Young rock stars will initially find it exciting with the decadence that accompanies their first time out, but the veterans lose some of their enthusiasm after a few tours.

That doesn't mean, however, that there is not something in every entertainer that actually finds the road attractive. It's kind of a love/hate thing. Though every troubadour claims at the end of his travels that he will never leave home again, there comes a time when the nature of this kind of man yearns to be on the road again. That sense of freedom with the long highway ahead is a draw that keeps many coming back for more, regardless of the trials of the last venture.

After a little over a month of rehearsals, Jack was itching to get things started. They had gone over everything—music, stage presentation, lighting—and were fine-tuned and ready to try things out in front of an audience. Live rock crowds can energize an act that has been beaten into perfection to form the perfect concert experience. Now they were ready.

The band would be traveling in a convoy of trucks and buses full of equipment and road personnel. The lead bus, of course, would contain the members of the band. The vehicle was a plush traveling hotel with anything a person could ask for but privacy. Though Jack would be given his own quarters in the back, the room was small, and he would be doing a lot of socializing with the other band members. Chuck had told him that this was an integral part of the preparation for the show. The musicians must live together and get to know each other's minds, he said, so that there was communication during a performance. Not only would this communication help with executing the music and stage movement, Chuck had emphasized, but the audience would pick up on the camaraderie of the entertainers.

Jack's goodbye to Michelle was an emotional one. Michelle, though she would be fine and have it no other way for Jack, was tearful as she embraced him one last time before he turned and ascended the stairs of the bus. Jack was affected also, but things changed as they got underway. All of a sudden he felt free, like an animal just let out of a cage. Starting now he would take on a new persona, unshackled by truth and guilt and realism. Now he would be in that artificial world he had hated so much his last time out—but this time it was an escape. He would be whom he wanted because out there nothing was real anyway.

Jack sat up in front, looking out the large side window at the scenery for the first few hours on the road. Eli Evans, the drummer, nervously rapped on the sofa handle on the other side, chewing his gum in a counter rhythm. Neither had said a word for miles.
Hale Biggs—keyboards, guitar, harmonica, and background vocals—was the oldest of the group (about thirty-six) and was a veteran of the road. The minute he sat down in the common room, he opened one of the pile of thick books he brought with him and buried himself in the story. He had also been silent for a long time.
The other two members of the group were youngsters. Billy Wharton was a killer guitar player whose lightening riffs produced a blur on the neck of his modified Les Paul. Without the instrument in

hand, however, Billy was a ball of nervous energy without an outlet. To fill the time, he sat in one of the two chairs on either side of the door to the next section and bent the ear of poor Garth Barton.

Garth was the bass player—and not much else. But he was a hell of a bass player. He moved up and down the electric bass with the speed and dexterity that would be more characteristic of a guitar player. But Garth had never played the guitar. The man began his musical career with the deep booming of a background instrument that always traveled with the pack but never led. And like his instrument, Garth never stood out; but when he did say something, it was a profound communication that made all the difference in the mood.

Chuck had given Garth the thumbs down during the auditions.

"He's the best damn bass player I've ever heard!" Jack had protested.

"But that dour personality. He's going to depress people."

"I don't know if you've noticed, Chuck, but a lot of bass players are like that," Jack said.

"The stage requires energy, Jack. Garth shows very little."

"If you close your eyes and listen to him," Jack said, "you'll discover that the group's whole momentum is carried on his lines. Come on, Chuck, let me have at least one pure musician in the group."

"Then he'll have to sing."

"He can sing," Jack said.

"He's got to look like he's opening his mouth then."

When Garth was told that he made the band, he had the same dull response on his face as if someone at a garage had told him his car was ready. But Jack could see that something—just a flicker of enthusiasm. Jack knew he had made the right choice.

Nights aboard the mammoth vehicle were a little livelier. After stopping somewhere for dinner, everybody's mood improved. All of a sudden the musicians seemed to be energized. After all, entertainers are night people—that's when they come alive—so it was only natural that a new spirit pervaded the coach. And, of course, that spirit would eventually show itself in music.

About eight o'clock, the instruments started coming out of nowhere. It began when Hale pulled out an old beat up Martin flat top from the storage compartment under one of the couches. Soon Billy was plugging in a tiny Peavy practice amp, and Garth brought a big acoustic bass guitar from over his bunk. Eli simply added sticks to his previous drumming on the sofa handle, and added a small suitcase and an empty Coors Original bottle for variety.

Of course, the jamming required a bit of stimulation; so the next things to appear were little bottles of various kinds of whiskey.

"Nothin' like Lord Calvert and weed," Hale said, as he pulled items from the Martin's guitar case.

The singing and playing went on all night long. The band did anything they had ever known for music. They played country and bluegrass, blues, even a polka or two. Jack was pretty impressed at the range of tastes. He began to think that these individuals were more than simply showmen.

The bus reached Sandford, Connecticut at 6:45 the next morning. Jack, who had expected the gang to find some place to have a big breakfast together, was surprised as the faces collapsed into weariness as they carried their belongings from the bus to the motel room. Like vampires, this was the time for these men to sleep. They would wait till darkness to come to life again.

Jack, on the other hand, had a body clock that was a bit more normal; so he set off down the street until he found a little diner where he could get the greasiest eggs and bacon he could find. He sat in a booth on a ragged plastic-covered seat, drinking his coffee late into the morning, a look of happy wonder on his face at the life he was just beginning.

Colin too awoke to an interesting morning. Just after 7 o'clock he received a call from his literary agent.

"Colin," an excited voice said over the line, "I'm calling you from New York. I waited as long as I could, but I just had to call with the news."

"What is it, Steve?" Colin said, still a little sleepy.

"Your book—we just finagled a deal where your book will now be published in hardback by Double House!"

"But how can that be?" Colin asked. "We already made a deal—"

"We made a better one. We're going places Colin—both of us."

※　　　　　※　　　　　※

With a lot of work by Steve Gretski, his agent, Colin's book *Smoke and Mirrors* had gotten the attention of some big shots in the publishing business. This was not a small feat, considering the millions of submissions rejected every year by the elite group of individuals who fancy themselves judges of not only the public's present tastes, but good literature as well. Unfortunately, some of the best have never seen print because of the whim of some liberally educated sweater and Docker-wearing yuppie. But that's the way of the art world.

"And there's a big, big advance this time," Steve hyperventilated.

"I don't have to give the last one back, do I?" Colin asked.

"Naw. We're headed for the big time, guy. *Smoke and Mirrors* is scheduled to be in the front display of the major bookstores in the country in a couple of months."

"That soon? In a display!"

"The people at Double House don't fart around when it comes to marketing. They know what power they have when it comes to pushing something they believe in. As far as print time—we're living in a brave new technologically advanced world, my man."

"Wow!" Colin said. "It's all happening so fast. One day I couldn't even get a good position on a newspaper, and the next day my book is going to be published by a major player."

"We got lucky, Colin. I was in the right place at the right time. Most agents wait years before a deal like this."

"Don't worry, Steve," Colin said. "I've got a lot of books left in me."

❦   ❦   ❦

Sandra was never happier with her own work. Though she wouldn't admit the fact, her current success was based on painting to please others. Her last painting, however, was right from the center of her being. It had taken her all night—the night after speaking with Colin—but she was satisfied with the results. There was no more to do.

This time she took the painting to an art dealer in Boston, a man who had called her earlier after hearing her name and reading about her success. Before, after talking about her paintings, he had seemed more and more disinterested; and she never heard from him again. Funny how this man popped into her head when she was ready to sell the recent piece. Why did she feel he would be interested? Was it that she finally produced something she knew was worthy of praise? Could this possibly be her very first "big league" painting?

She drove into Boston alone. She didn't even mention her mission to Sean. Oddly, she didn't want him to be a part of this aspect of her world. How could your future spouse not be involved in the most important thing in your life! Of course, she assured herself that Sean would have taken a big interest if she had told him—at least he would have acted that way.

The little shop should have been difficult to find. After all, anyone unfamiliar with the layout of a metropolitan area has nightmares finding his way—especially an old city where the streets follow the idiosyncrasies of time. Strangely, Sandra didn't have the least bit of trouble finding the little street. It was as if her car knew where to go—as if something were pulling her to this part of her destiny.

A chubby bald man looked up as the bell rang over the door, announcing Sandra's entrance.

"Yes," the man said very businesslike, "can I help you?"

Sandra who was carrying a large painting simply held the covered square up and smiled.

"You're Sandra, aren't you?" the man said.

"Yes…but how did you know? I didn't tell you what day I'd be stopping in."

"Because you *look* like Sandra," the man said, as if that was the most natural deduction in the world.

"Now I know you weren't interested in my work before—"

"I've never seen your work, Sandra," the man said, looking her squarely in the eyes. "But you're right—I wasn't interested."

Sandra paused before going on. "Yes…well, I think you might be interested in this."

"I know I will be," the man said matter-of-factly.

"How could you—?"

"Come on, open it up."

Sandra ripped the brown paper from the painting like a child impatiently opening a Christmas gift.

"See?" the man said. "I know what I'm talking about."

"It's so different from anything else anyone has liked."

"That's the point, isn't it? It's easy to provide them with what *they* want—lucrative too sometimes. But presenting them with *what you do* and having it hit them right between the eyes—that's what it's all about."

"So you think this will sell?"

"You just ruined it," the man said shaking his head disgustedly.

"I just—"

"You just turned it all into a business venture. Artists are not salesmen. Artists survive on the sales of their work in spite of the fact that they don't care if it sells. It's a hard concept to grasp if you're not a true painter."

"I want to be," Sandra said a little pleadingly.

"You mean 'wanna be.' Artists are not 'wanna be's'—they just are."

Sandra's head went down in defeat.

"But you have hope," the man said, lifting her chin. "At least for the creation of the work you have just brought me, you have been a real painter."

🍁   🍁   🍁

Doc's new project was his most ambitious. He would be sculpting three full characters of homeless people. His inspiration came from some life forms he saw on the street daily when he ventured from his cave-like presidio. Of course, most of the poor souls he passed on the sidewalks of this part of town were men, usually down on their luck. But there was a woman who was living on these mean streets, and he was especially moved by her will to survive. It was hard enough to understand why individuals at the bottom of life's toilet could find any reason to want to live through the next day. But a woman! What made her cling to life?

He would have to do his new work in pieces, considering the size of the end product, so that he could get it out the door. However, what he would do once he removed it from his apartment, he did not know. His sales were few and far between, and a work as depressing as this was not attractive to buyers.

When Doc was working at his art, he was totally consumed. It was the best part of his life. Tortuous thoughts, gut wrenching regrets, and philosophical arguments about the meaning of existence had no place when he was creating. Everything was for the work. Later he would wonder why his art was so subjugating, considering its ridiculousness in helping to define the purpose of the universe—its uselessness it everyday survival—its confused expression of a race of mutant life forms. But it was the one thing that drove him that he could not come close to explaining.

Once, when he fell exhausted into to his dirty over-stuffed chair after a particularly long session of work, he was reminded of a movie he had seen where a man was driven to create—*Close Encounters of a Third Kind*. It seems that the man had to recreate a natural land formation out of everything in the house. He couldn't stop himself. Of course, the audience knew that he was influenced by extraterrestrials—but his family and neighbors were convinced of his insanity.

This got Doc thinking. Was there such a thing as madness, or were the reasons for one's behavior just misunderstood? Was his overwhelming dedication to his own work some kind of crazy psychotic obsession, or did art have some kind of purpose? If it did, what could it possibly be? It contributed nothing to survival—yet earliest man had found it important enough to allot valuable hours, otherwise used for hunting or sleeping, to it. Was it truly an expression of our humanity or our insanity? And how could insanity be the core of one's existence—the reason for going on?

CHAPTER 31

❁

A giant red foam phone rang as Sandra sat waist deep in colored plastic balls. She was not alone—there were children all around her, diving into the safe multicolored orbs, burying themselves and then popping up to show how invulnerable they were. But none of the kids seemed to hear the phone. Perhaps that was because children blocked out such things that did not concern them. It was an adult's job to answer the call.

After about the tenth ring, Sandra could not stand it any longer. She was the grown-up here, so it was her job to respond to the ringing. Slowly she waded through the pit toward the wall where the telephone hung. When she arrived, she stood as tall as she could so that she could reach a receiver that was half her size. To her frustration, the wall phone was mounted just a bit too high. But it continued to ring, and Sandra was compelled to put an end to it. Finally she was able to stand precariously on a foundation of plastic balls just high enough so that the tip of her finger could push up on the receiver and release it from its hook. The phone then fell on top of her, pinning her between plastic and foam rubber to where she thought she could not breathe. And the ringing continued.

"Sandra," her mother said, removing the pillow from over her head. "Get out of bed. You've got a phone call."

"Wha—?"

"I think it's Sean's mother."

Sandra sprang up, shaking her head to take in reality. Then she hit the cold floor and padded to the kitchen phone, still a bit woozy and confused.

"Hello," she said hoarsely.

"Sandra, this is Claudia Brady."

"Oh, hi," Sandra said a little clearer.

"I was working on our guest list, and I thought we might get together and see what we have as far as possible guests. Have you completed your list yet?"

"Oh…uh…almost," she lied. "I still want to talk to my parents about who else they may want to invite."

"Well, bring what you can," Mrs. Brady said curtly, with obvious irritation at Sandra's laziness. "I think it's important that we both know who will be there."

"Sure…yes…of course."

"In an hour then? At my home?"

"Yes…I'll be right over," Sandra said.

It took Sandra a few minutes before she moved for the shower. It never occurred to her to tell her future mother-in-law that she would need more time.

As she adjusted the temperature of the water with the round handle over the tub's faucet, Sandra's mind wandered back to her dream. Such a silly one—but she couldn't help feeling disconcerted by it. Why would such a ridiculous bit of fantasy affect her in such a negative way? And why could she not dismiss and forget this dream like the thousands of others she had had?

Mrs. Brady did not meet Sandra at the door of the stately old mansion. A servant dressed in maid's livery did the honors. She was then shown through the dark wood paneled rooms to a little parlor where Mrs. Brady sat drinking tea, perusing the contents of a sheet of beige paper. She didn't look up as Sandra entered.

"Sit down, dear," she said, still looking down. "That will be all, Delia," she said coldly to the maid. "So did you bring what I asked?"

"My list is far from complete," Sandra said.

"My dear," Mrs. Brady said, looking at Sandra over her glasses for the first time, "what have you been doing with your time?"

Sandra managed a weak smile. "I know I should have had more of this finished by now, but I've been very involved in my work?"

"Your work? I wasn't aware you took a job?"

"My painting," Sandra said.

"Oh that. I hardly consider that work. That's more of a…hobby, isn't it?"

"No, Mrs. Brady—it's my life."

"I guess you'll be making some big changes then—in your 'life.'"

"Changes?" Sandra said with a little more strength in her voice.

"Would you care for some tea, dear," Mrs. Brady said, readying a cup.

"What kind of changes?" Sandra pursued.

"Why, changes in the meaning of your life, of course," Sean's mother said, filling Sandra's cup. "You'll be Sean's wife. He will be the center of your universe. Oh, don't worry, I'm sure they'll be plenty of time in your days for your…pastimes."

"Mrs. Brady, my art is hardly a pastime," Sandra said, with surprising defensiveness.

"Come now, Sandra, you don't really consider your little decorative pictures to be great art, do you?"

"Great art? I don't know. What I do know is that what I do is part of who I am. I don't plan to change who I am because I've become a wife."

"But that's exactly what you'll do," Mrs. Brady said. "Your husband will be the focus of your existence. You will be there for affection and support. You'll entertain his friends at dinner parties. You'll even be well read enough to offer intelligent conversation. But first and foremost you'll be a wife."

"I don't want to argue, Mrs. Brady—"

"Nor do I," Mrs. Brady said innocently.

"Well, then let's do what we came here for."

"Yes…yes," Mrs. Brady said with a large grin. "Let's see your list, dear."

Sandra's list was written on lined paper that had been torn from a notebook. The uneven tear holes looked wildly ruffled as Mrs. Brady held them tentatively, like they were unclean.

"We must get you some stationery," she said.

Though offended by Mrs. Brady's attitude, Sandra held her tongue.

"Who are these people you have added at the end?" Mrs. Brady said. "It looks like you have crossed them out and then added them again."

"Those are my friends," Sandra said.

"Your friends? Three men?"

"What's so unusual about that?"

"Will they be bringing wives or dates?"

"I'm not sure."

"What kind of people are they?"

"Why?" Sandra asked. "They're my guests, not yours."

"My dear, are you aware of the kind of people that will be attending this event? Some of the country's most prominent and influential individuals will be my guests. We do not want the Governor or a senator or someone from higher society to be forced to associate with riff raff."

"Riff raff? I told you that these people were my friends. Why is it that you assume they're riff raff?"

"But that's why I asked," Mrs. Marcus Brady said gently, as if surprised by Sandra's slight outburst. "They may be quite wonderful people."

"I assure you, Mrs. Brady, my friends are extraordinary people. And the point is—they're my friends." Sandra stood and took the list from Mrs. Brady's hand. "There's no reason to go over our lists together. I'll make mine, and you can make yours. And I promise you, my friends will be no problem for yours—no matter how rude your guests might be to them."

At this point, Sandra walked out indignantly. She was sure that when she reached the confines of her car, she would burst into tears—but she did not. Instead, a peaceful feeling of liberation came over her, as if she had just been released from incarceration, or a great problem had been solved. The next list she showed anyone would have Colin, Jack, and Doc at the top.

❦   ❦   ❦

Colin rarely received mail at his new place, let alone a large package delivered via UPS. What could someone possibly be sending him? he thought, as he ripped open the outer box. Inside was a copy of *Smoke and Mirrors*, the way it had been published by Overland Publishers. Strange that someone would be sending him his own book. Underneath the book was an envelope, obviously explaining the strange parcel.

Dear Colin, it read.

> We are so pleased that your wonderful novel will be part of the Double House family. Now that we will be working together, we have decided to make the very best of your book by having our editors work some changes. While our suggestions may be quite extensive, rest assured that they will not in any way jeopardize the integrity of the book.

Sincerely,

Wallace A. Bernard
Executive Editor, Double House Publishing Company

There probably isn't a writer alive who is really comfortable with criticism. Sure, it's okay if some grammar or usage problems are dealt with—this prevents embarrassment. But the actual wording—that's part of the art. Would a painter respond well to someone telling him to use a different stroke here and there; or, worse yet, paint a whole section over?

There's a story about a famous novelist who accidentally used different names for two of his characters in the last part of the book than what they were called in the first part. When his editor pointed this out, the writer told him to leave it the way it was. Because the author was celebrated, the editor backed down and reluctantly let him have his way. The novel became a best seller.

Smoke and Mirrors was not fresh from Colin's pen. It had already been edited for errors and actually published. Now this big shot book company wanted him to change his completed work. Who did this Wallace A Bernard think he was, anyway? Had he ever written a book?

Incensed, Colin got Steve on the phone.

"What the hell is this, Steve?" he asked angrily.

"Calm down, Colin. I knew this would be upsetting to you—"

"You knew! And you let them get away with it?"

"Listen, Colin," Steve said calmly, "you're breaking into the big time here. Sometimes you have to give a little. Did you know, for instance, that Stephen King had to cut *The Stand* down?"

"But he came out with the full version later."

"Exactly. When he was famous. All of the big ones have to give a little to get where they want to go."

"You mean, sell out!"

"I mean 'give a little,' like I said. Later, after you've proven yourself, you can call *all* the shots."

Slightly mollified, Colin's tone changed. "What was so bad about the original?"

"Did you read their comments?"

"Not exactly. But the book is marked up in red from cover to cover."

"Colin, these guys like to think they know all there is to know about literature," Steve said. "They can't let anybody think he's so great that his work is perfect. What kind of bargaining position would they be in then? Trust me, it's best to go along now so you don't have to go along later."

"I'll think about it," Colin said.

"Good," Steve was relieved, "that's all I ask. We'll talk later in the week."

🍁 🍁 🍁

"I've got to admit," Jack said to Chuck over coffee at the little hotel restaurant, "I was wrong about these guys."

"What guys?" Chuck said distractedly.

"The musicians we hired. I thought they were all phony sellouts who had traded their music for a turn on stage. I was wrong."

"And how did you discover this?" Chuck said with an uncomfortable surprise.

"On the bus. You were right. The time we spend on the bus is very valuable. These guys really showed me that they loved music—all kinds of music. I mean, even old school country! You should hear Hale doing his Ferlin Husky medley."

"We'll put an end to that type of thing right away!"

"No," Jack said. "You don't understand. It's great!"

"Great? What if some of your young fans found out that you guys really liked that cornball shit? They wouldn't understand. We're dealing with more than music here, Jack. We're dealing with an attitude, a subculture."

"But a real musician can enjoy a polka as well as a pop tune," Jack explained.

"They were playing polkas? Who are we traveling with here, Lawrence Welk! This has to stop!"

"It's just fun," Jack said. "It's a pressure release. You can't cause trouble over it."

"I can, and I will," Chuck asserted.

"Then I'll put a stop to the whole thing right now!"

"You're kidding. You'd put a career on the line for something like this?"

"I'll tell you what, Chuck, I'll make sure nothing like this ever leaves the bus. How's that?"

"I'll need your solemn promise on that," Chuck said. "You know, the potential—"

"I promise."

CHAPTER 32

❀

Nobody walks anymore in America. Other nations have extensive public transportation systems where one could live out his life without the purchase of a car; but not in the United States. Even to go down the block, many Americans don't think twice about using the automobile.

It may be a safety thing. After all, no one can get to you in your little moving fortress. One has his music and his air conditioning. It's possible to travel through even the most alien of environments without feeling uneasy if you can take yours along with you.

And for anyone who has tried the old fashion method of movement, the rewards are few. One finds the noise and pollution almost unbearable. And there are no sidewalks built anymore, so an individual finds himself walking precariously on a small strip along a busy road or on the road itself. Traffic no longer recognizes the pedestrian. A walker is an irritant to drivers who believe that a vehicle has the right of way in every case. But worst of all is the abuse the vulnerable walker takes: the cat calls and near accidents and garbage thrown out car windows.

But Doc had no car. It didn't matter much since he hardly left his place. On this particular day, however, he needed a break from his new project. Sometimes, he found, the intensity would become so great that he would lose his perspective, so he would need a change of scenery. Since he had no automobile, Doc took walks to clear his head.

Doc preferred to walk at night—in the protection and security of the darkness. But he needed some fresh air now, so he was willing to brave the aggravation. And aggravation he got. Naturally one would expect to hear road noise, horns honking, and an occasional siren or two. These were city sounds. And, of course, some shrill fishwife voice had to cut the air from some fire escape window—not pleasant, but expected.

What really got to Doc was the manufactured noise. It seemed that humans could not be anywhere without their music. Blaring music came from everywhere! Every greasy spoon, every mom and pop store front, every seedy bar, every packaged liquor store. There was no place you could escape it. Even if you went down a residential street, the cheap stereos were throwing some repetitive clamor that these people called music.

Was it that music was kind of a security blanket? Was that why the beaches and campgrounds and parks and playgrounds always had some boom box providing an aural background. Was there no haven of quiet anymore?

Finally Doc found himself on a short, shady back street that seemed relatively peaceful. Just when he sighed in comfort, however, he experienced the sidewalk-shaking earthquake-like bass tones of one of the new killer automobile sound systems. There was nothing to hear but the pounding simpleton bass line. How could someone stand to actually be in that car for any period of time? Doc had heard that they had decibel contests to see which car was the loudest—and that, for health reasons, some of these contests required that the owner would not sit in the car during competition.

It wasn't just the assault to the ears that drove Doc crazy. Everywhere there were signs and colors and lights and movement. No wonder people today could not concentrate; they were over stimulated. Perhaps this was behind the sudden outbreak of attention deficit syndrome in so many children.

Doc cut through Lafayette High School's back lot by the practice football field and made his way around the old building, with its many orange security lights. This put him on Hanover Street by the riverbank. Doc cut across the street, nearly hit by a car which seemed to come out of nowhere—the driver sitting so low, it almost looked unoccupied. Now he walked along the riverbank through the overgrown weeds and bushes, imagining himself in the country.

Suddenly Doc's big feet hit something, and he went tumbling, head over heals. He just lay there in the cool grass for a moment before lifting himself up, beginning to build a line of powerful epithets. But like most of us, the first thing he did was go back to what tripped him. People do this even when they know it was their own clumsiness that caused the accident—our nature always looks for someone or something else to blame for our looking ridiculous. In this case, however, there was something in Doc's path that should not have been there.

The clump of weeds where the object lay was thick, so Doc had to push the feral plants aside to get a glimpse of the object of his annoyance. At first it looked like someone had dumped old rags and other trash on the bank and that this had kind of hardened into a lump. Then upon kicking at it, Doc realized that the mass yielded in a strange way. Doc wasn't sure why, but he knew that the feel of the object signaled something both shocking and repulsive to his brain. When he looked closer, Doc caught a strange odor that also signaled something to him subconsciously. And then his mind allowed him to put the pieces together. A man lay before him—a man that had been there a very long time.

Doc wedged one of his large boots under the man's back and lifted up, turning the man over and out of the weeds that had hidden him. Then he rolled the corpse again. By the look of his clothes, the man had been fairly wealthy. What was left of an expensive looking suit, complete with vest, was exposed behind a pricey dark overcoat. The man's shoes were that slipper type that only the classiest had the guts to wear.

The dead man was not dressed to be walking the riverbank in this part of town. Logic said that he was killed and then dumped here—maybe for his money. Doc began a search of the man's inner suit jacket pocket. Surprisingly the man's black leather billfold was still there. More astoundingly, as Doc searched for some type of identification, he found a wad of bills in the back. Apparently it was not money that contributed to this individual's end.

The cash came to about five hundred dollars in fairly large bills. Doc, who had originally picked up the wallet to be able to inform authorities about his find, dropped the billfold unconsciously while staring transfixed at the money he retained in his right hand.

To say that Doc lived modestly would be a great understatement. The truth was, Doc had not seen that much money in one place in over ten years. The man who had chosen not to make the almighty greenback the focus of his life was now as spellbound by his discovery as the men he abhorred. It was if he were a seaman caught up in the Sirens' songs—he knew he must move away, but he could not.

A blank look of possession on his face, Doc shoved the bills into his coat pocket. Then he dragged the body up the bank and halfway down the other side. Here he found a bare spot where he could give the corpse one last push with his foot, and it would roll into the polluted water. After he heard the splash, Doc continued to stand zombie-like for an entire minute before he turned and headed back up the bank.

CHAPTER 33

❁

"What did you do to upset my mother?" Sean asked when he picked Sandra up for dinner.

"Why do you think I did anything to your mother?"

"When I stopped over there this afternoon, she was crying like a baby. She said you acted like you didn't like her."

"How so?" Sandra worried.

"She said you were rude. She said that you became really defensive when she asked about your friends. That you insulted the people she was inviting."

"Do you believe that, Sean?" Sandra asked, looking into his eyes.

Sean looked away. "I don't know what to believe. Maybe mother was just being too sensitive. I can't conceive of you ever being intentionally mean."

"Sean," Sandra said, "your mother—"

"Yes?"

"Nothing. I'm sure we just got our wires of communication crossed. I'll call her and straighten things out."

"That's my girl," Sean said, giving her a sideways hug.

"Sean...?"

"Yes, Sandra?"

"Sean…you know how important my painting is to me, don't you?"

"Of course I do," Sean said emphatically. "Why do you even have to ask?"

"It's not a hobby."

"A hobby? Not with as much time as you put into it. Why?"

"No reason."

"What do you say we stop by the country club later on for a drink. I've got some friends I'd like you to meet."

"Friends?"

"Yeah. It's about time you met them," Sean smiled. "And when am I going to meet some of yours?"

"Mine…?"

"Your friends. When will I meet your friends?"

"Oh…I never had much time for friends," Sandra said.

🍁   🍁   🍁

At Addison Park Arena the dressing rooms were trailers pulled up to the side of the building next to the stage door. This is where the star of the show was separated from his backup band. Jack sat alone on a chair staring at the shiny red silk shirt and black leather pants he was to wear for his first public performance. These items had been selected for him by a woman who traveled with them, a Nancy Marsdon. She was responsible for everyone's wardrobe, from purchase to repair. Of course, Jack's clothes had been presented to him for a perfunctory okay; but unless he had a very good argument, his stage outfit was a done deal.

Finally, because time was short, he forced himself to don the foreign raiment. This was definitely not who he was. The question was, Was it whom he wanted to be? Chuck seemed to think that the image they were trying to make was vital for his success. All Jack could think of were the times he had seen old established stars trying to look "happening" by dressing in these types of outfits. The clothes felt as alien to Jack as they must have felt to those old-timers—the point being that people looked ridiculous when they were trying to be what they definitely were not.

Jack had always avoided extreme clothing. He was never comfortable being the center of attention. When one tried too hard at appearance, it felt like wearing a costume of some kind. Instead, Jack wore natural colors, blue jeans, work shirts, and casual brown leather shoes or boots. Strutting like a peacock in full plumage was not his cup of tea.

When he finally got enough courage to leave the security of his dressing room, he stepped awkwardly down the metal stairs, almost wincing at the ribbing he was sure to get. The rest of the band was already out there waiting for him, and they were in no state to hand out criticism. As Jack scanned the group, each seemed to be dressed in a more outlandish set of clothes than the one next to him. All, it turned out, were more ostentatiously attired than Jack. That was Chuck's plan. Jack would be the most "normal," of the group. Though his wild clothing would denote the presence of a professional entertainer, he was not to come off as some eccentric or weirdo.

The strangest thing, though, was how relaxed the other musicians seemed. It was as if they were standing there in blue jeans and sweatshirts. Jack guessed that they had become inured to the ridiculousness of their stage garments. It was like wearing a shirt and tie to school on picture day. You felt odd and uncomfortable, but the teachers who wore the attire daily never thought twice about it.

The stage was pitch when they took their places. Chuck stood in front of them all, his large dark figure silhouetted against a charcoal gray sky.

"Okay, everyone," he said. "It's all attitude now. You're a group with a hit recording. The people out there have paid a small fortune for their tickets. They want to see performers with lots of confidence—hell, they want you to be damn near egotistical. They'd rather have you spit on them than to look tentative. You're heroes to a rebellious age—now you have to show it. And energy is everything. Don't worry about the music. You've got that down cold. Give every bit of emotion your souls have to this show. It doesn't matter how you feel or what you're thinking about. These people only get one chance to see you, and they have to see you at your best. Now play with force, with drive, with perceived abandon. You are touched by God for the next two hours. You're worthy of worship and adoration. Fuck, your shit doesn't smell! Now make this an experience that crowd will be talking about for years!"

And for some perverted reason, that pep talk worked. Jack and the band were able to take something over-rehearsed that had had the heart kicked out of it a month before and transform it into a spirit-packed dynamo of a stage show. The people, who were just as worn from the constant hammering of plastic media and commercial hype, involved themselves totally, as if Jack were offering them a religious experience.

Now it must be noted here that neither the music nor the audience was based on any real meaning or true connection; but the fact that all parties involved allowed themselves to believe—for the duration of the concert—that something unworldly was happening, the result was the same—and all participants would talk of it as if they had experienced something holy.

Coming off stage, Jack was exhilarated like no other performance in his life.

"Damn," he said, as hyper as a little boy at Christmas, "what a rush! We really touched them with the music out there. It's like I always say—it's all about the music. It's the ultimate form of communication. I mean, I shared myself out there with thousands. We were like one soul."

"It was a pretty good night," a fairly subdued Hale said.

"A good night!" Jack said. "It was magic! It was mystical! It was the ultimate expression of out humanity! We all showed each other out there that there's more to us than survival in this world. We have a spiritual connection, we humans; and if we can allow ourselves to let go, we can experience it."

"Man, you're going to have to put this in some kind of perspective before the end of the tour, or you're gonna have a stroke," Garth said, as he wiped off the strings of his Rickenbacker fretless bass before placing it gingerly into its protective case.

"What are you talking about!" Jack was incredulous. "Didn't you feel what I felt."

"Sure we did," Hale said gently. "But it's part of the act."

"Part of the act? You mean you were only acting?"

"I mean," Hale said calmly, "that you have to throw yourself into the show—but then you have to leave it there. It's like being a stage actor. You have to feel the emotions of the moment, of course; but you are still only acting."

Jack was stunned. He walked into his trailer and sat on the small sofa, his eyes wide saucers of shock. Was this really just a manufactured experience to exploit the emotions of a vulnerable crowd? How could it be? His songs were part of his very core. Wasn't he truly sharing this with strangers? Wasn't this why they had all joined in communal celebration?

A knock came on the dressing room door. It took Jack a moment to acknowledge the sound.

"Yes," he said dully.

"Jack. It's Chuck."

"Go away, Chuck."

"Jack, I know what's bothering you. Let me in—we need to talk."

Reluctantly Jack rose from the sofa, and in slow motion he made his way to the door.

"Jack, I was just talking to Hale, and he thought it might be a good idea for me to stop by."

"Why? So you can explain to me that what happened out there wasn't real?"

"Oh, it was real alright. At least as real as anything can be."

"It was fucking religious!" Jack protested.

"All right, all right," Chuck said to appease. "But even those evangelical religious events where thousands of people raise their hands and sway in the Holy Spirit—even they are contrived. Everything about our lives is contrived."

"You have to be the most cynical son of a bitch I've ever met," Jack spat.

"Or the most realistic."

Jack sat on the couch and put his head in his hands.

"Listen, Jack, you're not the first entertainer to go through this. It's a fucking rush to have that many people in the palm of your hand. You get to think that it's something on a much higher level. It's just that you have to separate yourself from the show now, or you'll burn out."

"Don't worry," Jack said tersely, "I'm just fine."

"At least your material still has a part of you in it," Chuck said uncharacteristically. "I mean, what about these acts that have been put together by business people—like the Monkeys or O-Town. Those guys get out there on stage and really believe that they are more than some type of synthetic artists. You, at least, had a core of reality."

"A *core* of reality?"

"Jack, a lot of guys have a tough time coming down from a concert. Sometimes you have to help yourself a little—artificially."

"What are you talking about?"

Chuck reached into his pale blue sports jacket and pulled out what looked like a prescription bottle from some pharmacy.

"Take one of these. It will settle you down—put things in perspective."

"You're giving me drugs!" Jack exclaimed. "This is like a bad movie."

"People take sedatives all the time, Jack," Chuck said coolly. "Besides, these are prescription."

"Prescription? Whose prescription?"

"Just take one," Chuck urged. "You'll feel a lot better."

"I know I sound like Nancy Reagan or something, but I'll just have to say, 'No, I can live without it.'"

"Suit yourself," Chuck shrugged. "I'll check on you a little later."

❦ ❦ ❦

Colin couldn't believe the number of changes they wanted him to make in *Smoke and Mirrors*. Wasn't it ironic, he thought, that the world could take art—the very essence of humanity—and peddle it like cornflakes? Well, he had a simple choice to make: either play the publisher's game, or remain one of those nameless authors who, though true to his or her craft, go unread.

Slowly, but surely, Colin went page by page and made his changes. This was extremely time consuming because of the emotional toll it took. Colin would occasionally jump from his desk in a rage, sometimes calling Steve and telling him he would not do it. After the rage would pass, or when Steve would calm him down and remind him of the ultimate rewards, Colin would begin again. The process took weeks.

When Colin was finally finished, he called Steve Gretski.

"Come and get it," he said sourly.

"You finished?"

"Just come and get it, and take it to the butchers. I don't want to hear about it again. I'm just going to think of this first book as a means to an end."

"You won't be sorry, Colin. In the end you'll have a great career," Steve said in his never-ending cheerfulness.

"Yeah...well I'll be working on my *real* novel now."

"Good...Good! You're on your way to greatness, Colin."

❦   ❦   ❦

Five hundred dollars is not a great deal of money. Why, then, had Doc done what he had done? Doc had never as much as stolen a grape from a grocery store before. For some reason, though, this was different. The wealthy corpse symbolized something to him. It was all about his frustration with those who sacrificed scruples to have the comfort in life that those with principles did without.

As usual, as soon as Doc recovered from the state that had carried him through this uncharacteristic act, he began to analyze the motivations behind his actions. His deductions were somewhat frightening to him. Basically, he was tired of being the sucker. He wanted his share of the pie. The man he had kicked into the water represented everything that Doc had been battling in this world, and he was tired of being beaten—at least momentarily.

The problem was that one could not allow himself even one act of selfishness and continue to tout his own integrity. That was the difficulty with integrity—it had to be all or nothing. It was a form of self-punishment. It was the penance of existence. And maybe, just maybe, it was a "holier than thou" attitude that was just as self-serving as society's game. Perhaps it was an attitude that was just as phony and pompous as any politician or plastic messiah.

No one was pure of soul, he reasoned; and aspiring to be—or worse, pretending to be—was the same as what he thought of as his antithesis. Doc had always despised haughty arrogance, but isn't this just what he himself was displaying in his self-righteousness? Any extreme was just as bad as the other. He had only been deluding himself that he was any better than anyone else. Who did he think he was?

Of course, this argument was no rationalization for what Doc had done. He still felt horribly dirty and guilty—yet, he felt good about the money. It was exciting to have that much to spend at one time.

Things…things he could buy went through his head. Suddenly the material world invaded his sanctuary. There was no going back now.

That evening—the evening after he had found the money—Doc took a shower and dressed in his cleanest clothes. He then headed for the Gables Cinema, the new movie complex in the strip mall on Worthington Avenue that boasted ten separate theaters.

It had been close to 20 years since Doc had been to a movie, so he was not prepared for the exorbitant ticket price; but he paid it without so much as a twitch. Then he headed to the refreshment counter and purchased a box of popcorn and a coke for an amount that would have fed him dinner for three days. This he also did without blinking. Tonight he would experience the decadence and waste of the world he had spent so many years rejecting. And he planned to enjoy himself.

CHAPTER 34

❀

Sandra had been to the Woods Edge Country Club before, but the people that Sean had introduced her to on these occasions were older friends of his parents. This night he had planned an evening with the younger generation of "clubbers"—those who had inherited a special, uncommon lifestyle along with their parents' money and influence.

There's nothing inherently evil about the "haves" of the world. Living with advantages is something fortunate and cannot really be characterized as wicked or sinful. After all, what self-respecting person who struggles for his daily bread wouldn't trade places in a heartbeat?

It's obvious that those who want to "share the wealth" are always those without it (or those with it, but confident that things will never change no matter the volume of their idealism). So basically, the whole thing boils down to jealousy—then a defensive posture that leads to identification with a social stratum as if it were a family. In other words, the ridiculous assertion that one would not want things any different than they are at present.

Sandra's new associates were innocent and naive in their picture of the world. They found it hard to imagine anyone living without many things they took for granted; and, in a way, they refused to acknowledge the lifestyle of anyone who did. Certainly they recognized the existence of the poor in their universe, but being "poor" and being "disadvantaged" were two different things in their book. No one, they felt, had a leg up on anyone else. With a lot of hard work, anybody could lift themselves up by their bootstraps and go as far as they wished. But a person couldn't be lazy and expect to be supported by others—no...hard work was the key. It's always ironic that those who work the least are always advocating hard work.

When Sean and Sandra entered the club dining room, Sandra knew immediately where their destination lay. Two young couples stood in a welcoming gesture the minute the newcomers arrived. And as they got closer to the table, big greeting smiles were added to the waiting dinner party.

"Sean," a large blond boy with the obligatory blue blazer and khakis called out, "where have you been keeping yourself!" He was one of those overweight boys who, being lucky enough to have access to money, still got the girls.

"What, are you crazy, Jason?" the other male, a rather skinny young man, laughed. "I think you can see where he's been."

Still standing, Sean made the introductions. Sandra couldn't get over how the five of them could be in the middle of the ultimate awkward moment and not appear the least bit ill at ease.

"Sandra, this is Amy," he said, nodding at a pretty redhead; "and this is Nicole," he said, smiling at a blond beauty who was obviously there with Jason.

"I'm so glad to meet you," Amy said. "We've all been wondering who the lucky girl would be who landed Sean."

"Yeah...Who'd have thought 'ol Sean would be the first to bite the dust."

"Oh, Jason, that's not funny," Nicole said. "Maybe it's about time you grew up a little yourself."

"Not me," said the antithesis of *cool*. "I've still got a lot of wildness to tame."

"Don't let him fool you," the other man said. "Jason's a dentist—not exactly the wild and crazy type."

"And I suppose running your father's men's clothing stores is outrageous."

"Grant has quite a future ahead of him in that business," Amy argued.

"Yeah…a two car garage and a mini van," Jason said.

"How about if we sit down," Sean interrupted. "I've been all over today, and my feet have about had it."

"The prime rib is very good here," Nicole said, sharing her already opened menu with Sandra.

"Well, that sounds good," Sandra said, at a loss for anything else.

"What do ya say we have a few before we order," Jason said, leaning back on his chair.

"I'm here to eat, not watch you get bleary-eyed," Nicole said sharply.

"That's right," Amy said. "We're starving."

"Women," Jason said in the tone of a man twice his age.

Most of the dinner conversation was aimed at Sandra, her being the new person in the group; so Sandra found herself answering questions and trying to expound on her answers so as to seem interesting.

"I don't think I've ever met a true artist," Amy said excitedly. "Oh, my mother goes to art classes with a bunch of middle-aged women who fancy themselves painters; but I've never talked with someone who has made a living from their artistic creations."

"Didn't I see an article about you in the entertainment section of the newspaper recently?" Grant asked.

"You read the entertainment section? What a dweeb!" Jason said.

"I read it because I like to try new things. I like to hear a new band or go to an interesting restaurant."

"Yes...the paper did an article on my work," Sandra answered, understanding that Jason was to be ignored.

"Well, if you were in the paper, you must really be good," Amy said. "I'd like to see some of your things."

"You have," Sean smiled teasingly.

"What are you talking about?"

"Your mother has one in the foyer."

"That's *yours*?" Amy asked excitedly. "My mother *loves* that painting. Sometimes she'll get up in the middle of a movie or something, and I'll find her out there just staring at the picture. She sees something there."

"Really? Which one?"

"The one with the basket of daisies," Sean said.

"My mother would just fall over if she knew I'd met you. Hey...I don't suppose you'd like to stop over some afternoon so that my mother could meet the artist who painted her favorite picture?"

"I'd be happy to," Sandra said, beginning to relax.

"What have you got on your plate for Tuesday?" Amy asked.

"I thought we were all going to the Shore on Tuesday," Jason complained.

"Oh, that's right," Amy conceded. "Why don't you join us, Sandra. Everybody will be there."

"Oh, I don't know..."

"Come on Sean," Grant said. "Take a day off from the old grind and go with us."

"I'm planning on buying a keg," Jason said.

"I'll see what I can do," Sean surrendered.

❦   ❦   ❦

Colin's new place was no mansion, but it was a far cry nicer than the last. First of all, it was much safer. The little house that he rented at the end of a block of connected homes wasn't exactly located in the best part of the city, but it was in a respectable enough neighborhood. People seemed a little more relaxed and less defensive. Sometimes Colin would sit out on his concrete door stoop to read the paper and find himself involved in conversations from porch to porch. The working people around him seemed very down to earth and friendly.

Of course, all is not a bed of roses wherever you live. Recently Colin had been struggling with phone people, trying to find a time when the wall phone in the kitchen could be installed. It seemed that the installer always came during those few times when Colin was out. And then there was that leak in his bedroom. He must have called his landlord's home a dozen times, only to get the dreaded answering machine. No call was returned.

Little inconsiderate things bothered Colin more than with most people. Like the time he had his garbage rejected by the trash men. The rules were that an individual was only allowed two cans of refuse. Having just moved in and finding the little place a mess, Colin had quite a bit to get rid of. Instead of putting the lids on the cans, he just piled them high with a few extra things, topping off one with boxes and placing a large bag of junk on the other. When he went out the next morning to retrieve his cans, a neat pile of three boxes with the heavy bag perched on top awaited him. It had taken these sanitary engineers more time and effort to separate and stack the extra items than if they would have loaded them directly in the truck. It must have been the principle of the thing.

Colin had settled into a regular habit of writing now that he was published. He would wake up at about 5:30 each morning and write for two hours before breakfast. After eating—usually at the greasy spoon down the street—he would sleep for another hour or two. Upon waking, he would write again—that semi-consciousness of the waking state seemed very conducive to his imagination. He wouldn't write again until late into the evening. All totaled, he put in about five or six hours a day.

He was happy about his writing again. *Smoke and Mirrors* had been reworked and sent out, so he didn't think about the fact that he had changed it so much. In fact, as time went on and the finished product hit the bookstores, Colin somehow convinced himself that all that he intended was still in the book.

Acceptance of the book was extremely important to Colin in the coming months, for he would be appearing at signings and on interview shows. To his surprise, Colin found these events thoroughly enjoyable. Of course, there's nothing better than greeting lines of people who think of you as a prophet, or letting daytime hosts treat you like the new Philip Roth.

The book took off like a rocket, and so did Colin's mood. He was feeling on top of the world when he ran into Sandra and a friend at the Starbucks in the new Barnes and Noble.

"Sandra!" Colin called from around the end of one of the rows of shelves.

"Oh, hi," Sandra said, a little reserved.

"I haven't seen you forever. What have you been doing with yourself?"

"Oh, same old thing," Sandra said a little distantly.

"Who's your friend?" Colin asked, not noticing that Sandra was uncomfortable.

"Oh, I'm sorry. Amy, this is Colin, an old friend of mine from college."

"An old friend—Hell, we've know each other for years and years! Used to date."

This last statement seemed to make Sandra even uneasier.

"So," she interrupted, "what have you been doing with yourself?"

"That," Colin said, pointing down the aisle of books.

"Colin," she said nervously, "...we don't know what you're referring to."

All of a sudden Colin realized that he was an embarrassment to Sandra—that she was trying to get their meeting over with as quickly as possible—before he made things worse.

"I was *referring*," Colin said with a touch of acidity, "to that display in the middle of the store."

"What—?" Sandra started.

"Oh, my God!" Amy all but screamed. And before Sandra could assure her that they would be getting away from this awful young man soon enough, Amy said, "Are you Colin Morley?"

"How did you know his—?"

"At you service," Colin said, bowing to Sandra's obviously impressed friend.

"You never mentioned that you used to date a famous author," Amy said.

"A famous—" Sandra stammered. "Colin, is that your book?"

"Why, yes," Colin said in mock intellectualism. "And if I may, I'd like to treat each of you ladies to an autographed copy."

"Oooh, that would be wonderful!" Amy said, literally jumping up and down.

"Yes, thank you, Colin," Sandra said, shocked but relieved.

After they left the store, walking to the car, Amy said, "You are so lucky!"

"Why?"

"You have such an interesting life…and such interesting friends."

"Yes, I guess I do," Sandra said dully.

❦   ❦   ❦

Jack could hardly wait to play the next night. They would be appearing at a stadium adjacent to a theme park in a western suburb of Pittsburgh. Jack stayed in his quarters in the back of the bus on this trip, choosing not to have his high brought down by cynical talk of showmanship. In fact, Jack had hardly talked to anyone from the time he left the stage the night before.

He waited till the very last moment before emerging from his trailer to take the stage. He felt now as if the audience was his only friend, and he would give all he could. By separating himself from the others, he would be sincere with his connection with his fans. Jack would use the energy from the audience to push himself to the limit.

But the concert had come to a halt. Just after a local warm-up band played their hearts out, the electrical hookup to the sound system went. Now the last thing a rock band wants to have happen is to lose power. And the worst thing that can happen at a concert packed to capacity with adolescents is to have a delay. Young, rowdy people—possibly drunk or stoned or worse—are not extremely patient, and there is always the threat of a riot.

While the electricians were working, Jack went down the side stage stairs and looked out the canvas-covered opening leading to the first rows of seats. Naturally people began milling around—there was too much adrenaline in this group to sit politely and wait for the show to proceed.

At his end of the first row—the expensive seats—Jack saw three girls of about 16 or 17. One was heavily made up with black ringed eyes, contrasting with bleach-blond straw-like hair. She was wearing hip-hugger jeans, which exposed a protruding belly that sported both a piercing ring and a tattoo that made here navel the center of a strange flower.

The girl next to her was bone skinny. Puffing madly on a cigarette, she paced back and forth in nervous disgust at having to wait. Jack watched as she started a new cigarette with the butt of the previous one, never stopping her manic walk.

Sitting on the metal chair with her head between her legs was the third friend. Every so often she would look up with a comatose stare. The concert hadn't even started, and she looked totally out of it.

"Those are your fans," Hale said from behind him.

"I hope they're all not like that," Jack forced a laugh.

"We've got some time. Let's circulate."

"You mean, go out there? They'll mob us or attack us or something."

"Here, put this hat on," Hale said, handing him his large brimmed headgear. They'll never guess."

"What about you?"

"Hell, nobody ever recognizes the backup band."

The two musicians circled around the back and made their way into the rear of the stadium. In the very back, young people gathered in groups on the grass, talking. Most stood in contemptuous stances, sneering or smiling evilly as they chugged beer from cans they had smuggled in or puffed cigarettes. Other than a small group huddled in a smoky circle by the brick wall, none of these kids seemed the least worried about using illegal substances in public.

"They seem kinda angry, don't they," Hale said.

"I guess it's the defensive guise of teenage years."

"I guess," Hale said. "Why don't we meet them?"

Before Jack could register a negative response, Hale had pulled him by the arm up to some tall hard looking young ladies.

"Hi," Hale said as they approached.

Neither girl looked up.

"My name's Hale, and this here's Jack."

"Yeah?" The prettier of the two said, "Well, fuck off Hale and Jack!"!

"Wow! Little scary," Jack said as they hurried up the aisle toward the front.

"I'll tell you what's scary," Hale laughed. "The guys that they'd be nice to—those are guys I wouldn't want to meet."

Just then Jack made an "oof" sound as he ran into a girl who had been dancing in the middle of the walkway.

"Oh, I'm so sorry," Jack said, trying to help her up.

The girl reacted as if Hale and Jack were not even there—as if she had not just hit the ground with a thud. She simply jumped up, shaking off Jack's offer of assistance, and began dancing again. First she danced in a dervish, round and round she went. Then she stopped suddenly and began prancing madly in place, her arms flailing at her sides. Before concerts and during intermissions, recordings are usually played to entertain or pacify an audience. This music, however, is pumped through the same sound system that had broken down. Thus, the dancer was making her own music—apparently from something deep in her own head.

"Shit!" Jack said. "What's she on?"

"She's just getting ready for the concert," Hale said.

By the time they made their way to the front, convincing security that they were with the band by pulling out stage passes, Jack was shaken. Nevertheless, he made his way up to the stage and prepared to give his best.

Once they were announced, the musicians quickly took their places, Jack going to the main microphone to salute the crowd. But where he normally would say hello to the town, Jack just stopped dead and looked into the audience. It was still daylight, so the stage lights had no effect on his view. What he saw was a cheering, waving, hooting rabble of strangers—the warm adoration he had perceived before turned into a hedonistic ritual of drugs and wild movement.

Hale, seeing Jack's apparent hesitance, recognized what had happened.

"It's an act, now, Jack," he said. "Do it for yourself...but give it everything."

And for those clear-headed enough to take in the true value of the show—and there were a great many—it would be an experience they would speak of for many months. To them, Jack had reached out. To them, the communication was complete.

Unlike the last time, however, Jack was exhausted rather than exhilarated when he left the stage. If he had had to do one more number, he didn't know how he would summon the strength or the motivation (but he would). When Hale met him at the stage entrance, Jack looked terrible.

"You gonna be okay?"

"Let's get drunk tonight," Jack said. "Let's get really hammered."

❦   ❦   ❦

Following the movie, Doc stopped at Barnaby's Place, a national chain pizza and sub restaurant. Barnaby's Place was arranged more like a hall than a restaurant. It consisted of four rows of wooden booths—two against each side wall and two in the center, a walkway between them formed by two half dividers. This walkway, accessible occasionally by a break in the divider, was the path the patron took to order and pick up food at a counter in the very back of the establishment. The eatery was kept dark, each table slightly illuminated by a faux tiffany lamp hanging over its center.

The place was jammed. Usually this would be the signal that would send Doc elsewhere, but not on this night. Doc actually waited for a table; and then, smiling all the way to the front to order, he purchased a pitcher of beer and a large pizza.

Once in a while, Doc would catch the eyes of another customer looking at him. He smiled at everyone and nodded, like he was a regular. Doc was even pleasant to the young boy behind the counter who took his order in a monotone of disinterest.

"What do you want on your pizza?" the boy barely found the energy to ask.

"What would you suggest?" Doc said brightly.

"What?" the employee said, the first hint of emotion in his automatonic behavior.

"What's your favorite?" Doc grinned.

"I...uh...whatever. I guess I like the double meat."

"And what does that consist of?"

"Sausage and pepperoni," the boy said with a hint of enthusiasm. "We really pile it on."

"Oh, yeah?"

"I usually have a piece on my break," the boy said, turning nearly human.

"Well that's good enough for me," Doc said.

Doc walked home with a full stomach and an unusual feeling of contentment. What was it about this evening that was so different? It couldn't have been the money that made so much difference. Maybe his selfish act had released something in him that the others had had all along.

He took the long way home. Returning to his hovel would surely put an end to this dreamlike experience. For the first time, Doc walked along Minneapolis Boulevard under the bright lights. He had always hated the neonic glow that the mile long stretch of businesses gave off. Doc had been living in the darkness. But tonight he looked up at each red and yellow and blue and green sign and read the words aloud, like a first grader who had just begun a phonics experience.

When he reached the end of the main strip, the businesses got seedier looking. Chain store after chain store now became reclaimed businesses with names one would never hear sung on commercial television. Just around the corner from Sal's Pre-owned Vehicles, Doc turned right on 25th Street. The lights became dimmer, and so did his mood.

On the corner of 25th and Garfield sat a single beacon of entrepreneurship in an otherwise business-dead district. A lone fast food establishment called Fabulous Taco sat, its dirty glass widows showing only one customer reading a newspaper in the far back corner. Doc's feet stopped dead as he approached the grubby eating place. This was an unconscious act, for Doc had no wish to halt. Finally he willed his feet to continue home.

As Doc walked, he heard a strange sound. It was like a dull moaning. His ears searched the air for a source, but nothing registered. Suddenly he realized that he himself was the origin of the pained tones. Suddenly he realized he was crying. Then he began sobbing, the tears becoming so thick he used the front tail of his shirt to wipe the blindness from his eyes.

And the crying jag would not stop. It did not stop all the way home. It did not cease when he reached his door. It did not come to an end when he crawled between his ancient blankets and lay in the fetal position, hoping for respite. Doc cried himself to sleep.

CHAPTER 35

Sandra began to spend more and more time with Amy. Though Amy was born with all the advantages and had little understanding of how cruel life could be, Sandra found her to be quite a nice person. Perhaps isolation from the stresses and hardships that most people go through created beautiful, happy people—and what's wrong with that.

Sean had not planned to go to the shore with Jason and Grant and the girls. He had only told Jason he'd consider it to shut him up. Sean found Jason to be a spoiled, boorish drunkard—but they had been companions through boyhood, so he continued to socialize with him.

"I understand how you feel about Jason," Sandra said as they ate their small lunches of shrimp cocktail, "but Amy has been so nice to me—we've gotten to be good friends—and she really wants to go."

"Because she doesn't want to be alone with Grant."

"What?"

"It's a long story. Anyway…if it means that much to you, I'll take the time off."

The "cottage" where they were to stay belonged to Jason's family—and was much, much more than a cottage. The five bedroom, three bathroom house was something that most Americans would find to far surpass anyone's Great American Dream. It was, indeed, a place on the shore—it was built overlooking the water. A long stone stairway led from the columned front porch of the "stately cabin" and concluded in the sand—a private beach—that led to the ocean. It was so exclusive it even had a name—"Graywood."

Graywood began with a large open foyer interrupted by a staircase leading to the guestrooms. Downstairs there was a complete gourmet kitchen off to the left of the marble entrance, and a sitting room off to the right. The entire back of the structure was a recreation area, complete with pool table, ping-pong, old-fashioned pinball machines, and the largest television Sandra had ever seen. Off the back was a patio with deck chairs and everything one would need for a barbeque. And then there was the new addition that was Jason's pride and joy—a hot tub.

"Well, let's get to serious drinking," Jason said, having obviously taken a long head start.

"I think we'll go upstairs and get settled first," Sean said.

"Suit yourself—but I can't guarantee how much will be left."

The room they would occupy upstairs was more a suite than a bedroom. A small fieldstone fireplace stood at the far end, flanked by two comfortable looking corduroy-covered chairs and an actual bearskin rug in front of the hearth. These were the kinds of trimmings that distinguished this building from a home in the suburbs. The large brass bed took up the remainder of the room, covered by a quilt just "down home" enough to have cost a small fortune to buy from some quaint shop in Dutch Country.

"It's wonderful," Sandra said to Sean, already unpacking things from his suitcase.

"It's been in Jason's family since the beginning of time," Sean said, unpacking a laptop computer.

"What's that?" Sandra asked, looking at the next item to emerge from Sean's bag.

"Never travel without a laptop and a cell phone," Sean smiled.

"But this is down time, Sean. Aren't you planning to relax?"

"Relax? Only pampered rich kids like Jason can really have the luxury to relax. I have a business to run. Jason is old money—we're new money."

"Are you planning to sit cooped up in this room and do business all day?"

"Of course not, honey," Sean said, taking Sandra in his arms. "I'll just do a little work here and there on a deck chair while you and the girls have a good time."

Just then Jason bellowed from downstairs, "Pussyman has arrived!"

"What's he talking about?"

"Oh, that's what Jason calls Grant—and not just behind his back."

"But why?"

"Grant is a bit anal. Everything in its place—if you know what I mean. He can get to be a little too much after a while."

Sandra's forehead furrowed. "But Amy is so carefree and full of life."

"Exactly...and that's the problem. Grant is constantly correcting and berating the poor girl. We're not sure why she takes it, but she must love him or something."

"Wow! Grant and Jason are exact opposites!"

"That's another problem. There's a constant battle going on between them. Luckily, Jason has enough liquor around for the rest of us."

"Isn't Nicole coming down?"

"Oh, she's here somewhere. She just kind of does her own thing—apart from Jason. He disgusts her."

"Then why—?"

"Jason has everything. Nicole values that. A rich boy always has some beauty hanging on his arm. Fortunately for Nicole, he's always too smashed to notice how much she hates him."

"Does Nicole come from a poor family?"

Sean laughed. "Far from it! It's just that there are degrees of rich. Nicole is reaching a little higher."

Sandra stood quietly, noticeably disconcerted.

"Oh…they're not that bad," Sean said. "Everybody's got their little 'things,' you know. I'm sure your friends have their idiosyncrasies too."

"Oh yes," she said distractedly.

"Come on. Let's join the others. Don't worry—you'll have fun."

Part of the fun Jason had planned for them was sitting in the large outside Jacuzzi sipping drinks. Sandra felt uncomfortable enough having to sit beside the plump rich boy, but the fact that she was his focus of attention was unnerving. When he would speak to her, he would touch—nothing considered inappropriate, exactly, but there was lots of touching. Then he would lean in close to her ear to tell her something—just inane chatter—after which he would laugh uncontrollably as if they had just shared a naughty secret.

Sandra looked over at Sean occasionally to note his reaction to all this, but her fiancé seemed occupied in conversation with the others. Apparently the consensus was that Jason was harmless and that indulging him prevented him from becoming even more obnoxious.

Then Jason's hands became busier. This activity took place below the water, however, so no one was the wiser. Soon Jason's right hand was on the inner thigh of Sandra's left leg—at which point she elbowed the young man sharply in the ribs. Though this made Jason remove the wandering hand, it also threw him into convulsions of drunken laughter.

When Sandra looked to Sean at this point, he was busily talking on his cell phone—apparently about business, based on his serious expression.

🍁　　　🍁　　　🍁

Jack spent most of his night vomiting over the bus's stainless steel toilet. The motion of his motorized home and the liquor he had put away after the concert were a horrible combination, and he was paying dearly.

When they got to the hotel, Jack wobbled off the bus last, only to be met by Chuck.

"You alright, kid?"

"Yeah…yeah, I'm alright."

"You've got to take it easy, or you'll be shot before we're half way through with this tour."

"Don't worry, Chuck. I'm not doing that again for a long time."

"Then how about breakfast?"

Jack looked at him with wide panicked eyes before puking on Chuck's Gucci loafers.

🍁　　　🍁　　　🍁

Colin's advance from Double House had been a long time coming; but when he arrived home from a promotional trip to Cincinnati, a check for a hefty amount greeted him in the mail box. Now Colin was in no great hurry to change his lifestyle, but there were a few things he had done without for quite some time. His biggest need was clothing. While the shabby threads that he purchased from second hand stores emphasized the image of a writer, he was anxious to get some new things.

Some people like to shop. And it's not only women. Many men like to take their time and select just the right thing at just the right price. Colin was not one of these individuals. The thought of going out to a mall and walking from store to store both wearied and frightened him. Besides, Colin always had an idea of what he was looking for. Why, he wondered, did he have to spend so much energy and fray so many nerve endings searching for it?

Though Colin had enough in his bank account now to purchase a car in cash, he waited at his usual bus stop for the Number 1. The Number 1 was the best route in the city. It hit all the most essential places. It also stopped at Lancaster Mall. This would be his destination for clothes shopping.

Entering the main entrance of a shopping center must be an exciting experience for most people. It's kind of like entering a different world, with the big contemporary fountain in the center, pointing through three floors to its highest point. Escalators going up and down, people standing instead of walking from level to level. Music piped through without pause so that no one has to think in silence. People eating and drinking, eating and drinking, eating and drinking. And movement—constant movement. Everyone has a direction. People were streaming from one end to the other and back again. Upstairs. Downstairs. Kiosks. Food court. Bank machines. Fashion show. Jewelry. Designer coffee.

The minute Colin entered, he found he had to sit down on one of those slatted wooden benches surrounded with mammoth planters and unappreciated modern sculpture. Colin looked for an empty area—away from mothers and their babies and lounging teenagers. He felt safe…for a minute.

Then an old man sat next to him. There were empty seats all around the area, but the man sat right up against Colin. Colin, not wanting to seem rude, secretly scooted a bit to his left. The man, sensing more room, spread out more, invading Colin's space. Thinking it wrong to jump up and sit somewhere else, Colin tried to pretend he was not bothered.

"Waitin' for the old woman," the man said.

"Huh?" Colin asked, not expecting a conversation.

"The wife. She's in there looking for something to wear to our granddaughter's christening. She wants to look nice."

"Uh huh," Colin said, staring straight ahead.

"Ain't gonna help. She ain't gonna look good no matter what she puts on. Why the hell waste good money!"

"I...uh...don't know," Colin said.

"You married?" the old man snapped.

"No. Not yet."

"Do yourself a favor and don't. It all seems great in the beginning—you know, sex with this young girl anytime you want it. Hell, later on you pray she don't think about it no more."

Colin coughed nervously and picked up a newspaper someone had left under his seat.

"What you do?" the old man demanded.

"Pardon?"

"How do you make a living?"

"Oh. I'm a writer," Colin said proudly.

"So you haven't got a job."

"No, I'm a writer. I make a living writing."

"Shit!" the man snorted. "That ain't no way for a man to make a living."

"Why not?" Colin defended. "I make good money."

"A man should work with his back and his hands. All the brainy stuff ain't real work."

"It may not seem like real work to you, you nasty old geezer," Colin said, giving up politeness, "but I'll make a hell of a lot more money than you'll ever see."

"Shit," the old man said. "Even I'm smart enough to know that writers don't make no big money...unless you're Tom Clancy or somethin'."

"Or Colin Morley?"

"Who?"

"Over there," Colin pointed to a display in Brentano's window. That's mine."

"No it ain't," the man said.

"Here," Colin said, pulling out his wallet and dropping a twenty in the old man's lap. "I want you to go over there and buy one of those books. Then I want you to look on the back cover for my picture. After you're convinced that I am indeed the author, I want you to then take the book and shove it forcefully up your withered old ass."

As Colin stalked away, he could hear the old man say, "Shit!"

CHAPTER 36

❦

Doc sank into a deep depression. Now, Doc was no stranger to melancholy, but this was the worst that he could remember. His eyes would open at about 5 a.m. each morning, and he would pull the blankets up over his head to block out what little light had entered into the dismal apartment. Then he would lie there—frightened of his own thoughts—until a sick semi-sleep carried him for a few more hours. The cycle repeated itself over and over until nightfall. Somehow safer in the cover of darkness, Doc would get hours of sleep he did not need nor did he deserve.

One would think it was the dead man that haunted Doc's conscious state. It was not. Doc had an easier time putting that episode behind him than most would. Doc's problem was his flirtation with the flow of the world. He had forgotten for awhile who he was and what he believed. Doc had let himself enter the realm of *the others*, and he was disgusted with himself for it. The sham existence that Doc had always rejected was what most saw as life's purpose. Doc renounced this as a lifestyle, hoping that his refusal of inclusion meant that he would lead a somehow higher, if not happier, life.

Often those among us who do not participate in the mainstream of things do not do so because of some sense that they do not deserve to be happy. Doc's case was more like a holy hermit. He believed somehow that turning his back on the trivial, on unearned contentment, on shallow happiness put him closer to what he imagined to be a greater truth. Perhaps that greater truth could be called God—though he would be the last to admit to it.

His pain at present was derived from the fact that his small taste of the absurd and frivolous—his sampling of *the others'* value system—left him thirsty for more. The idea that there was little to life besides the silly entertainments people made for themselves suggested that it was, in fact, he who was the fool. He was the fool because if there was nothing more out there than what most people called lives, then he was wasting his time with his heavy thoughts and his deep conviction.

Now, even a man with Doc's penchant for the truth will refute evidence if it goes so much against strong beliefs of the past. So instead of giving in to the lightness of living, Doc withdrew further as one draws away from the temptation of Satan. Giving in to the inane frivolity that most humans use as an excuse for rising in the morning was more than Doc could allow himself to accept. He had to, therefore, find some way of warding off its inducement. Thus, the depression.

The worst thing for mental illness, of course, is isolation. Joining one's kind is part of the definition of good mental health. Sociability, in fact, is one of the criteria for evaluation of an individual's ability to cope. Assimilation is the objective. Otherwise, one is considered deviant, like Winston in *1984*. The mainstream doesn't have to make sense for it to be considered sanity. The whole idea of rationality is a democratic one. The man who is a minority of one is deemed mad.

Therefore, one sinks deeper and deeper into his madness as one becomes more and more alone. Others are our check of our very being. Without their witness, all may be a dream. In lunacy, all *is* a dream.

At first, Doc would have Colin stop by—ironically for advice. Lately Colin was wrapped in a world of his own making and was doing just fine alone. The bartender job was another way of reaching out to others, but Doc could no longer force himself to leave his place. Other than that, Doc had nothing. All he could hope for was that everybody but him was useless breath and that possibly he was the only one that could see things for what they really were, and that could hardly be the case…could it?

Eventually Doc was unable to sleep. Even the floating phantasmagoric images that served as a small departure from reality could not be summoned. He found that he was trapped with his demons and that he could not run—he had nowhere or no one to run to. For survival—and Doc often wondered at how much he seemed to value it—Doc needed to do something to bring artificial respite from his torture. Cold turkey is only good for ridding oneself of something chemical, not ridding oneself of oneself.

When he could stand it no more, Doc made his way to the doorless cabinet over his single water source and located half a bottle of cheap vodka in the back corner. This was not enough. But, like others with Doc's chemical makeup, he had a backup plan: a cache of Valium he had been prescribed right after his wife's death. At the time he had felt guilty about numbing his pain. Now, he had no choice. So, down went a small handful of the pills—Doc was always aware of a body's tolerance—followed by a good portion of the drink. Soon he felt much better.

CHAPTER 37

❀

The day of Sandra's wedding quickly approached. For some reason this panicked her a bit. Not because of all the things she had to accomplish beforehand—she wasn't exactly sure why she had so much angst. But when she caught herself frowning about the situation, she would shake her pretty head and smile—as if a silly negative thought had crept into her wonderful life.

Though most of the invitations had been sent out, there were three she had held back. Of course she intended to invite her friends, but something prevented her from mailing the three small envelopes that sat on her dressing table. When she would look at them, she would feel extremely guilty. In was not subconscious thought that stood in her way. She knew that these three men that had meant so much in her life were from a time that she did not care to acknowledge anymore. But they also represented her conscience. She already felt their disapproving gazes as they saw her with her perfect groom. They would say nothing, but their eyes would condemn her.

And there was something more. She was becoming a bit of a snob. The three would not fit in with the other guests at the affair. Successful or not, they were cynical and crude men who would surely offend someone.

But worst of all—Colin, Jack and Doc represented who Sandra had been. Sean's relatives—especially his mother—would see that Sandra was not good enough for this young man. They would determine that she had no right to consider entrance into the elite part of society.

Besides, how would they look? Colin, of course, would wear some of his Salvation Army recycled clothes—complete with stained jacket and work shoes. Jack would feel he had to look the rock star in some strange, gaudy costume. And Doc—well, she could not imagine what the arty and eccentric street person would have on for the occasion.

And then she would be thoroughly and completely ashamed of herself. She should not be embarrassed of who she was or whom she valued as friends. With this resolve, she would snatch up the invitations and head for the door, only to return them—promising herself that she would mail them later.

❦　　　❦　　　❦

After awhile, Colin's wardrobe began to become quite extensive. Now the baggy second hand pants and oversized shirts were replaced with expensive sports jackets and slacks. Armani shoes took the place of his friendly old work shoes. He still would not wear a tie—this was not the uniform of an author—but his shirts were made of fine material, costing him much more than he would ordinarily pay for a whole outfit.

Naturally, he rationalized his new appearance by the demands placed on him by the promotion of his book. Steve had always suggested a nicer look for interviews and book signings—and didn't Steve know best when it came to promotion? These days a writer had to give in a little to get his work read—but it was worth it if he could reach his audience.

Colin's new attire came in handy because he now found himself included on many party lists. People of means loved to have writers and artists at their functions—possibly as a demonstration of their interest in culture. Colin, becoming more and more the newest celebrity in the literary world, began spending nights and weekends at some of the most expensive homes in the city. Here he would run into other artists, musicians, actors, and even some sports figures who had also been tapped.

At first Colin felt awkward at these affairs. He felt inferior among these people who had been selected by God to be at the top of society. Of course, he would never acknowledge his feelings of inadequacy—but down deep he knew that he was in over his head.

Then he began to secretly aspire to this level for which he held so much disdain in his earlier days. After all, his literary achievement had entitled him to rub elbows with the privileged and influential, hadn't it? Maybe he was destined to be with the cream of the crop all along. Maybe his misplacement was in his previous life.

❈   ❈   ❈

At the beginning of the tour, Jack had diligently written to Michelle. It would have been easy to simply call her, but somehow he knew hearing her voice would make him feel embarrassed. This, of course, was not Michelle's doing. It was just that she was so real and together—and he was creating an identity daily. How she could tolerate his lack of self-determination, he did not know.

Eventually he stopped even the writing. He felt horrible about it. Michelle was the one individual on the face of the earth who knew who Jack was and accepted him—and she made him feel ashamed and frightened because of it. And—infuriating to Jack—she would understand. She always understood.

Jack was now getting a treatment from others that he had never expected. Even Chuck seemed to be showing him more respect. When Jack walked into a hotel room, it was "What can I do for you, Mr. Benson ?" and "Has everything been satisfactory for you, Mr.

Benson?" Disc Jockeys, who had a natural arrogance when behind the microphone, were suddenly intimidated by him during the promotional interviews. And when he walked into a restaurant, talk would stop—replaced by whispers of awe.

At first Jack felt strange with the new treatment. Then he secretly felt a thrill at the adoration from others. Finally, he began to expect it. He would no longer acknowledge crowds who had waited hours to see him with anything but a bothered wave. He was flip and insolent with the media. He even became impatient and demanding with Chuck.

As far as his band mates went, he no longer used the pronoun "we" or "us" when referring to performance at a show. In fact, he ceased talking about on-stage activity at all with the other musicians. It suddenly dawned on Jack that he was the star, and that these men behind him were simply a replaceable backup band. They served at his will. And if a mistake was made on stage, he was quick to assign blame to one of them—even if it was his own blunder.

Jack no longer felt silly in his "rock star" clothes. Now he was wearing them off stage too. Gone were jeans and sweatshirts—replaced with a peacock wardrobe of gaudy pretentious adornment. And rarely would he wear the same thing twice. He even began wearing unusual headgear—large velvet hats or strange variations of western toppers in bizarre colors and materials.

And those around him understood their new status. Tones of deference from the band members were in every exchange—even from Hale. Chuck began making appointments rather than barging in. Even the stagehands and drivers would cease conversation and "hop to" when Jack entered a scene. Jack began to realize his own greatness.

CHAPTER 38

❀

Eventually, Doc came out of his depression. He always did. And in a strange way, he hated himself for his emergence from the pit. It meant that he clung cowardly to this ridiculous life—that he was too afraid of the alternative. Doc disgusted himself.

But he went on—as many of us do. The alcoholic or drug addict who can hardly tolerate the feeling of existence—continues. The abused wife whose days have become worsening hells—goes on. And even the mentally ill who are not even able to understand "normalcy" with even its most abject face—linger. Cowards! But aren't we all? Eventually we begin to understand the meaninglessness of it all, but that does not stop us. We cling to little pleasures—a cigarette, music, ice cream—and we all *consider the alternative*.

Because he stopped going to work, Doc lost his job as a bartender. Now he swept out the little grocery and package liquor shop on the corner at night. The pay was much lower, but he was paid in cash. Unfortunately, the new job gave him more solitary hours; but the physical action involved helped him through. Most of the time he would listen to late night talk shows on the little radio behind the counter; people would phone in with horrendous problems—but they would always sound as if their woes were temporary and could be eventually solved. Doc was forming new habits and continuing to fill his days.

There were others living a similar life. A number of men lived only one step from the street. These were usually not men of intellect, but Doc began to find some interesting personalities. He couldn't help but feel superior to these poor wrecks—and he felt terrible about his feelings—but he used the creatures as safe companions who would expect nothing from him and would not know how to hurt him. These were men so cut off from the rest of the social order that they could not employ the tricks and deceit. Naturally they had been exposed to the treachery required for comfortable survival—but they had grown weary of it. In fact, they were tired of life altogether and were hanging on by a thread—but they were too ignorant, Doc thought, to feel cowardly because they did not let go.

Doc's relationship with the dregs he found as company reminded him of George and Lenny from Steinbeck's *Of Mice and Men*. At first one thinks of how lucky large, retarded Lenny Small is to have someone like George for guidance and protection in the cruel world. Later, one realizes that it is George who is the lucky one; for in this oversized simpleton, he has found the best of persons. He has found true friendship and loyalty, as one finds in a dog—but in a human.

Mack, one of Doc's new acquaintances, picked up garbage and washed windows at the gas station. He also stood guard at night at the scrap yard. Mack came by his situation naturally. No one in his family had ever stayed in school past the mandatory age. He was raised in a tin box that had once been called a mobile home around which were the odds and ends collected by his parents. Sometimes they would sell the junk, and sometimes it would remain as yard decoration.

This idiosyncratic behavior was a way of life for him, and he did not question it. He would have it no other way. It was similar to the way a person from a poor family craves the meager concoctions that his mother had called meals, even when his life has risen above his beginnings.

So Mack could not change his own perspective of the world any more than an educated man like Doc could adopt Mack's uncomplicated attitude. But Doc marveled at the sense Mack made. Not that everything Mack said seemed perfectly rational. But talking to him felt like watching a deer stand in the forest or birds making a nest.

In a way, Doc envied Mack's ignorance. He admired it in the same way he admired those that were succeeding in this world by not questioning it. Neither the bottom nor the top had a taste for contemplation. Doc, on the other hand, could not turn it off—and he pitied himself because of his awareness.

"What's up, Doc!" Mack called out to him from the front concrete steps of his rooming house.

"That's funny, Mack," Doc said.

"What's up, Doc!" Mack repeated, doubling over with laughter at the joke he had made.

"Have you eaten tonight?" Doc asked as Mack finished up his cackling.

"Wuh?" Mack said through teary eyes.

"I said, have you eaten tonight?"

"Well, I don't know as I have yet," he answered, taking out a well-used railroad handkerchief to blow out the nose rattle caused by the hilarity.

"Why don't we get a couple of hot dogs?" Doc suggested.

"Can't stomach 'em," Mack waved his hands. "You know what's in them things? They ain't good for you! Let's get us some of those big hamburgers with all the bacon piled on instead."

Now it was Doc's turn to laugh. Mack, not caring what the joke really was, joined along.

"What's up, Doc?" he said, and they both laughed until they hurt.

"Okay, Okay...we'll get bacon burgers."

"What's up with that hot dog thing of yours, anyway?" Mack wondered.

"Oh...I don't know...I just like to have a couple of hot dogs smothered in onions and catsup...with a friend...once in awhile."

"Hmmm," Mack mused. "Well, if it's for friendship, why the fuck not. Hell, it won't kill me."

"There's a stand at the end of the block. Pretty good dogs. Only...I've had better."

"Never could tell the difference. A hot dog's a hot dog."

"Yeah," Doc sighed, "I guess you're right."

And that was as deep as their conversations got. They never discussed existence; they didn't talk about God. And new thoughts were never introduced. The lack of stimulation helped Doc to sleep better at night.

Except Doc knew that this vacation from himself was temporary. He could play the game for awhile—even begin to believe it—but it would not last. He didn't belong with people like Mack, just like he didn't belong with those who functioned well in society. Eventually Doc would need books and academic discussion. Soon he would be compelled to throw himself into his art. Was it his superiority, or was it simply self-destruction that would lead him back?

CHAPTER 39

❦

Sandra had planned the perfect wedding. Everything was right out of the pile of bride's magazines she had collected. And everything was just as expensive. But Sandra's art had become more and more valuable as she ironically began to pay less and less attention to it. Shops were virtually begging for more pieces, but Sandra didn't heed the call. She was wrapped up in the pomp of the grand show she was about to put on, and that was plenty for any young girl's head.

Strangely enough, Sandra's biggest problem was finding a maid of honor. She found volunteers-a-plenty for bride's maids, but the special role did not have a player. She wondered that she had so few close girl friends in her youth. Of course, she had many superficial acquaintances in high school and college, but her interest in art seemed to separate her from the others. While they had tried out for the cheerleading squad or gone on shopping sprees or mooned over football players, Sandra had occupied herself with painting. Oh, she had never been all that consumed by her talent, but she was just serious enough to make her different.

Actually, now that she thought of it, Colin was the first close friend she had ever had. They had had a relationship, but she guessed it was only because they didn't know how to handle a male/female friendship without it being accompanied by a sexual pairing.

That's why they had continued to be around each other even when there did not appear to be anything romantic going on. Though their association seemed strained, even volatile at times, it had lasted a long time.

Sandra supposed she could have asked her old college roommate to be her bridesmaid, but that would have seemed odd after all these years. Besides, this marriage was about Sandra's future, not her past. So she decided to ask her new friend Amy.

"Oh, I am so honored!" Amy said, tears forming in her eyes. "Of all the wonderful friends you must have, I can't believe you want me."

"You're my new friend," Sandra said. "Besides, in the short time we've known each other, I feel we have become very close."

"Oh, yes," Amy said, overcome with her joy. "I consider you to be one of the dearest people in my life."

"Why?" Sandra found herself asking before she could stop her inappropriate response.

"Because of all the people I know, you are the most *real*," Amy said. "Most people are shallow…not sincere. You…well…it must be the soul of an artist or something…but you are so natural and unaffected…and so deep."

"I don't really think—"

"Oh, no…it's true. Most people lead shallow lives…kind of artificial, you know? And I don't mean that in the way most people would. I don't think the majority of people allow themselves to recognize the triviality of their lives. I mean, they pretty much accept what comes along as their main focus. They don't do it on purpose, though. It's just that it's easier to go with the flow. You know what I mean?"

"Uh…yeah…I think I do," Sandra said hoarsely.

"I get caught up in the everyday stuff too," Amy said. "But I don't want to be that way. I want to think for myself. I want to be an individual. You've helped me with that, Sandra."

"What do you say we look at some bridesmaid's dresses in my magazines?"

"That sounds like fun."

❖   ❖   ❖

Colin found himself a regular at the parties given by Mr. and Mrs. James Matson. Matson was one of the wealthiest men in the city. But he had no real business to speak of. Oh, he followed investments and funded real estate projects, but these activities were only hobbies. Matson really saw himself a philanthropist and patron of the arts. He was of the old money who believed in the idea of noblesse oblige—the idea that the fortunate at the top should give back to the people. Some of his ilk felt that politics was the way they could help. Matson, on the other hand, had a penchant for constructing buildings like community centers or libraries or museums for the masses—and he never balked when it was suggested that his name be attached.

Matson's wife, Charlene, was a beautiful Southern bell, ten years younger than her husband. She was a young 35 and full of life. Her husband, while socially active, lacked her youthful vitality. As the years went by, she began to see him as more of a father figure than an equal. She still loved to please him—and he was proud to have her on his arm. But Charlene had passions that were not satisfied.

Charlene would never think of leaving her husband—or her lifestyle. She did, however, like to satisfy her desires by dalliances with younger men. Now, of course a woman like Charlene would not often find herself in the company of the kind of men she was attracted to. Like many younger women, Charlene wanted her men to have a sense of danger about them. And she knew where to find them.

Charlene, as the perfect aristocratic Southern woman, was well educated in the fine arts. She knew her music and her paintings and her quality literature. She was brought up that way. So when she would suggest that a young artist or musician or writer might be an interesting dinner guest, her husband never suspected that she had more than culture on her mind.

The artistic temperament, Charlene discovered, held some of the same ideas about sexual liaisons—that they were to be enjoyed for the moment, but were not to have any permanence. Therefore, Charlene was able to work her way through a number of the most creative young men in the country without the worry of it being discovered by her husband. After all, a patron as rich as James Matson would not be as generous to an artist who was sleeping with his wife.

Charlene found Colin at one of his book signings. She was not there because she had heard of the event. Actually, she stopped by for a Columbian coffee and a croissant. Rarely did Charlene associate with the rabble that inhabited the common retail establishments, but Reboard's Books attracted a crowd that she considered a step up. After all, a person required some degree of intelligence to appreciate reading. It seemed like a select few nowadays who could even claim to have read an entire book.

While enjoying her snack, Charlene looked over the designer magazine that she was pretending to read to see a crowd gathering in an area of the store just in front of where she sat. Because Colin's autograph table had its back to the coffee shop, Charlene had an unobstructed view of the back of Colin's head. She watched his movements for a while and became intrigued by his body language. When he turned around and revealed a cleaned up bohemian type, she was hooked. She made up her mind then and there that she would pursue the new author.

"I've heard many good things about your work," she lied as Colin packed up his things at the end of the session.

"That's nice to hear," Colin said, inured to praise at this point in the day.

"May I still get you to autograph a copy?" she said, batting her big eyes.

"Sure...yeah. What's the name?" he said, pulling a pen from his shirt pocket.

She looked him straight in the eyes for what seemed like the longest time. "Charlene."

"Charlene," Colin said, a bit unsettled by her behavior. "Okay, Charlene. Hope you enjoy it."

"Oh...don't sign it now."

"But I thought you wanted—"

"It wouldn't mean as much if you signed it now. I mean...you don't really know me."

"That's true, but—"

"I have an idea. My husband and I are giving a big dinner party. Everyone will be there. People you'd like to meet. Why don't you come? You can sign it after the party. You'll know me better by then."

"I don't know—"

"Oh please," Charlene purred. "Here's my husband's card with our address. The house is easy to find. It's right at the top of Mulberry Hill."

"Mulberry Hill?" Colin was impressed. "That's the classiest area in town."

"We find it pleasant," Charlene said. "Then you'll be there?"

"Well...yeah. Yeah, I'll be there," Colin gained enthusiasm.

"Oh, wonderful," Charlene said. "I'll make sure we spend lots of time together."

And she did, indeed. As Colin politely said his goodbyes to his hosts at the end of the evening, Charlene placed a piece of paper in his hand. When Colin opened it as he made his way down the front steps of the mansion, he saw that it contained the name of a hotel in the suburbs and a room number.

Usually Colin was thick about whether he was being flirted with, but this was an undisguised proposition. The question was, Would he meet her there? Charlene was definitely a beautiful specimen—and there was something about her that shouted sexuality. Though he was luckier with the fairer sex lately than he had ever been before, it had been awhile since Colin had been with a woman—especially a woman of this caliber. He decided he would go for it.

Colin, like the others before him, was not disappointed by the wily Charlene. She was every bit of what she promised—and more. When they were finished, they lay quietly together for about a half-hour before Charlene got up and began dressing.
"Where are you going?" Colin asked.
"Why…home, of course."
"But—"
"Don't worry, my darling," she smiled, "this is not the end for us."
When Colin started to speak, Charlene put her finger to her lips.
"The room is paid for," she whispered as she backed out the door.

❦   ❦   ❦

Celebrity and ego are strange things. The best of us are taken in by their destructiveness. Those well-known televangelists might have been quiet, pious, and devout before their television shows became so big. And politicians were probably very idealistic before realizing their influence. Movie and television stars? Well, something happens to them when they make the transition from bus boy, trying to break into show business, to successful movie or television show personality. People forget who they were.
Jack, like the rock stars that had proceeded him, was also taken in by the worship of his fans and the obsequiousness of those who made their livings on his coat tails. All of a sudden no one is rude, nothing is difficult, people are awaiting your every wish. One begins

to think that he must deserve such treatment—if he didn't, the guilt would be overwhelming, and humans aren't built that way. Finally, he not only gives in to the fact that he must surely have something great about him, but he begins to identify it. Slowly he gives great credit to even the least of his accomplishments until he believes his genius to be almost divinely ordained.

Now, Jack was a good person—some might have even called him "down to earth." But struggling against the role that others feel you should be playing becomes stressful after awhile, and you must either stop the hypocrisy or become the character. It's a survival thing. Acceptance is easier than fighting it—especially when the result is gratifying.

So Jack began with groupies. Having his pick of the harem awaiting him backstage every night was a welcomed perk which his mind turned into a given. At first it had been hard to simply take advantage of an emotionally defenseless young girl. He felt that he must get to know her—maybe even take her some place. Then later he went directly to his room with his acquisition—or acquisitions—and rudely showed them to the door when his lust was satisfied.

And he became extremely demanding. His hotel room had to be superior to everyone else's. His dinners were purchased at the finest restaurants and brought to his room. He began being picky about with whom he would do interviews and which photographers from magazines he preferred to work with.

Jack felt he deserved it all.

CHAPTER 40

❀

It had been a long time since Doc had bought a newspaper. With his recent campaign of ignorance, the news of the day would have only interfered and brought him back to reality. But now—well, Doc was ready to return to thinking. The experiment had failed, and he was back.

The newspaper headlines were quite disturbing—odd that he had heard nothing. It seemed that terrorists had overtaken our U.S. embassy building in Kubalistan. The ambassador and other staff were able to get out to safety, but the crime could not be ignored. American fighter jets were sent immediately to the terrorist strongholds, and a lesson was taught—or so we hoped.

Arab terrorists were a mystery to Doc. Here were men with little in life as far as material things, who were willing to die for a religious or political cause. What's worse, they were able to somehow rationalize any casualties involving innocent people. In fact, they considered these innocents the enemies. What drove these fanatics? And why was their thinking so convoluted?

Actually, Arab terrorists were not much different than the rebel forces in Northern Ireland. For decades young Irish boys have killed and bombed and destroyed in the name of idealism. Never was there guilt if a child was involved. Never were they disturbed that their actions had kept an entire country from the progress that it could have made.

The most disturbing thing about both groups was that the idealism in the individual foot soldier did not run deep. Sure, there must have been leaders who could go on and on about the purpose of their crusade; but most of the men involved had little idea why they were committing the violent acts. They were driven by a superficial hatred that, when explored, revealed nothing but unfounded prejudice (a redundancy if there ever was one).

Doc took the paper and sat down on the stoop of Hank's Shoe Repair to examine the details. Then he folded the paper as if he were about to deliver it and just sat there tapping its end on the sidewalk as if he were swatting ants. Deep in thought again, Doc tried to understand.

But wasn't it obvious? People do not question their motivation. They just go with the flow. But everyone needs a direction to flow—so they *follow*. It might be a lifestyle that they emulate—they might be a yuppie or a biker or a redneck or an intellectual. Each lifestyle was complete with proper clothing, vehicles, obligatory music, political leanings, even thought processes. Once one joined a movement, life was easier. Instructions were provided. One got up in the morning knowing what to wear and how to act. It was uncomplicated. It offered a kind of twisted security.

And maybe a terrorist group or a revolutionary movement or the Neo-Nazis organization wasn't much different from the Lions Club or the Daughters of the American Revolution or the Moose Lodge in the sense that it provided identity and direction. Of course, a group that exists on hate and destruction is morally different from a group that is formed to help the community—but each performs the same function for the individual.

Religion alone did it for some people. And with religion, the guidebook was usually written down. You knew exactly what was expected of you. And with religion, there was no requirement for thinking—everything was faith-based. So if one destroyed lives in the name of Allah, there was no guilt. If a devout Christian murdered an abortion doctor, there was no remorse. Only a higher power could judge such acts.

It was interesting to Doc how society distinguished insane acts of violence and carnage from those that were considered organizationally driven. For example, a serial killer who is given instructions from his dog, or a man who kills because of some distorted idea of justice which is his and his alone—these individuals are considered *monsters*. But if people slaughter in the name of some organization, they are *zealots*. It pretty much boils down to how *many* people share one's crazy notions. If a group has a shared twisted idea, it's a cause. If one man has a warped agenda, it is insanity. The insanity of one.

It was strange, Doc thought, that in a country that ostensibly valued individuality, the group had such importance. But it was this group—good or bad—who instructed people on the way to react to their world. Very few people knew how to deal with things on their own. They needed to look to others—authorities or support groups or whatever—to tell them how to feel, how to respond, what to do! It's not really the fault of these people. They truly don't know what to think or do on their own.

From time immemorial, whenever there was fear or calamity or disaster, the crowds would gather at the door of the king or chief, ready to be given directive on how to respond to the new hand being dealt. And, of course, a clever leader could always exploit his own status and power by using their panic for his own ends.

Oh, how pathetic the human condition when we plead, "Tell us what to do!" And often more pathetic is the answer that the charlatan in charge cooks up. Whether he asks them to chant or present a sacrifice to the gods or wear a symbolic emblem on their breasts, they do not question; they are simply glad for the answers.

Doc's brain took a break, and he opened his newspaper again to the classified section. Here he began looking through jobs. It was time that he moved on.

CHAPTER 41

❀

An engagement dinner is an awkward affair. Here the families and friends of both the bride and groom get together for sometimes the first time. Therefore, in addition to the business at hand, the strangers have to go through a sniffing activity when they take stock of the new people that will soon become a part of their lives.

Sandra's parents were obviously intimidated by Sean's family, but they were excited to be in their presence. It was as if they had been allowed backstage to mingle with celebrities—they could hardly contain themselves. And instead of going out of her way to make them feel comfortable, Sean's mother seemed to become haughtier as she sensed her ability to create apprehension.

"Oh, my," Sandra's mother whispered to her as they watched Sean's mother circulating among her relatives, "that dress must have cost a fortune. I can just imagine what she'll be wearing to the wedding."

"Oh, she'll have something special," Sandra said, glad for the sarcastic release she could have while talking to an ally.

"We're around money now," Sandra's father said, impressed as he scanned the hall. "Sandy, you've landed the big one."

"I didn't land—"

"What are you doing way back here?" Sean interrupted from behind.

"Oh just—" Sandra started.

"We're admiring your family," her mother said. "It must have been so wonderful for you growing up with such advantages."

"Well, there's more to life than power and money," Sean said.

"Yeah...Easy for somebody who has always had it to say," Sandra's father said, slapping Sean on the back.

"Yes...well...Sandra, my Aunt Eileen would like to talk to you."

"Right now I'm with my parents," she said, a bit defensively.

"Oh, go on, Sandra," her mother said. "We're just fine."

"Yeah. We're happy to just stand back here and watch the rich people," her father said.

Sean's Aunt Eileen seemed the stereotypical dowager, complete with jewels and the hefty bank account from her late husband.

"My sister tells me that you like to paint," Aunt Eileen began as soon as Sean left them.

"That's what I do," Sandra said. "I'm an artist."

"Oh...I had no idea. The way Claudia talked it was just a pastime. I'm very interested in art myself, you know. Before I was married I was quite the watercolorist. Very abstract stuff. I worked in oil, but water color seemed to lend itself to the ethereal subject."

"That's true," Sandra said, suddenly warming to her.

"I only wished I had kept up with my painting after I was married."

"Why didn't you?"

"Oh, my dear, my duties as a wife did not include silly endeavors like that. My husband expected me to play the role of wealthy business wife. There was no room for the creative personality. I had expectations to fulfill. My time was very limited."

"Then you just stopped?"

"Funny...On the night before my wedding—when most girls would be excited about the ceremony and the life they would be beginning—I painted. I painted until three or four in the morning—until I was exhausted. And that was the last time."

"How could you just give it up?" Sandra said, reddening.

"Oh, I gave up more than painting, my dear," Eileen shook her head. "I gave up a lifestyle. I gave up friends. In those days, they called us the 'beat' generation. The people I associated with were mostly writers or musicians or other artists. Of course, these were hardly the people that my husband would have wanted me to associate with—so I walked away. Just like that."

"But how did you even meet a man so different from you?"

"Oh, Clifford was the American dream. He was what was drummed into every little girl's head from the time she was playing with dolls. Clean cut, rich, successful, confident. When he became interested, I was swept off my feet. Apparently I was not as proud of the life that I was living as I thought I was. This seemed like my big opportunity. It seemed like what I ought to do. After all, living the 'beat' life was childish and immature in a way. I mean, one could not be a beatnik forever. Eventually I would have to grow up. Clifford represented the world of grown-ups and responsibility. The wealth aspect was exciting too. All of a sudden, I began living in a different world of luxury. It can all turn a girl's head."

"But you were happy, weren't you?"

"Happy? I thought I was. I mean, Clifford gave me everything a young girl could want. But as time went on and the excitement wore off, there was a need for a companion in addition to a sugar daddy, you know what I mean? Well, Clifford escaped more and more into the business. I, in my loneliness, began to resent him for what I had lost."

"Wow. That's so sad."

"I'm sorry, Sandra. Believe me, I don't normally tell my life's story to people I just meet—or anybody else. It's just that…well…I find you comfortable to be with…and maybe we share something."

"Do you paint now?" Sandra asked hopefully.

"Oh, my no. Now I travel the world spending my dead husband's money. I've seen all the masterpieces, though. I get a certain satisfaction using his wealth to make trips to Europe just to see a painting or a sculpture."

Before Sandra could react, Claudia Brady approached from just behind Eileen.

"I see that you two are getting along fine," she said, almost disdainfully.

"Why, yes we are, Claudia. It seems that we are very much alike."

"I can't imagine the family having two like you in it," Sean's mother said with light contempt.

"Oh, there are lots of independent, interesting people in the world, Claudia. Who knows, this one here might add some pizzazz to an otherwise stuffy gene pool."

Mrs. Brady just slightly shuddered and went on to other guests.

"Oh, you're in for a battle," Eileen smiled. "Poor Sean is going to feel like a pull toy."

"A what?"

"Ever hear of Chinese handcuffs?"

"Sure," Sandra said, "those things that go on your finger."

"Yes, that's it. Each person puts his finger in one side and pulls. And the more the opposing forces pull, the harder it is to escape."

"What does that—?"

"Oh, you'll have to excuse me, Sandra," Eileen said, looking across the room, "I haven't spoken to old Cousin Norton in years." And she hurried away.

Going to the mailbox each afternoon is such an important event in everyone's day. Of course, rarely is there anything waiting there of any interest. "Advertising and bills!" is the response from just about every inquiry about what one has found in the mail. Yet that doesn't diminish the excitement before the next postal visit. We're always intrigued by the unknown.

There's a game that some people play at parties with brightly wrapped gifts. The host wraps objects in various shaped boxes and containers, complete with ribbon and bows. Each guest can select the gift of his choice. Then the players try to obtain the gift that they *really* want. Of course, everyone else's gift looks better. And the shapes drive the participants crazy guessing. In the end, when the gifts are unwrapped, the objects turn out to be dull and ordinary, like a tube of toothpaste or a round box of Quaker Oats. But the excitement comes in the anticipation of the unidentified.

Colin approached his mailbox every evening like a Christmas gift wrapped in shiny red paper. There would be nothing extraordinary behind the little arched door; there never was. *But maybe this time.*

As Colin shuffled disgustedly through the pre-approved charge card come-ons and the book and record club ads, he came upon a little card-shaped envelope of pale yellow. Across the back was his name and address, written in a familiar hand. In his excitement, Colin tore the envelope off the card.

As he opened the cover, his heart sank. It was a wedding invitation. From Sandra. Though he recognized that his reaction was one of disappointment, Colin refused to be honest with himself about the source of his distress. He reasoned that it was always tough to lose a good friend—that it was too bad they had grown apart. He told himself that they were all growing up and that there was a certain sorrow attached to that. Colin guessed that those innocent evenings they had all spent together were the cause of a kind of bittersweet feeling that he now had. But he stopped searching for the truth at that point.

He wasn't sure why, but he felt he had to sit down for a moment. His legs felt like Jell-O as he dropped onto the curb by the mailbox. The other letters fell from his hands into the street while he stared at the announcement of Sandra's nuptials as if she were a stranger. And though he did not intellectualize his emotions, he could not tear his eyes from her name. It was a full ten minutes before he awoke from his reverie.

❦   ❦   ❦

Jack got a sick feeling as the tour bus rolled into his hometown. He was home, but he was someone else now. Home represented a visit to that man he left behind. Jack wanted no challenge to his new image. On the road, he could try out any personality he wanted. Here they would see a change.

And then there was Michelle. He knew he would have to see her. How could he explain how things had changed for him? She would smile as if nothing was really any different. But it *was* different—and he didn't care to have her judge his new behavior. Of course, Michelle would never say anything, but he would know.

Jack had retained his little apartment when he went on the road—another reminder of the old Jack. How could he return to it now? He owed it to himself to get new digs. Hell, he owed it to his fans. Imagine what people would think if they learned that he still lived like a pauper. So Jack checked into the VIP suite of the Hyatt downtown.

On his way to his new residence, Jack was forced to go by his old place for personal things and mail. It was horrible. His little efficiency was an embarrassment now, with his hide-a-bed couch and his little two burner stove. CD's were stacked all over the place, and his old acoustic guitar sat propped up against the corner. What a pitiful existence, he thought. Then he saw the picture of Michelle on the little 13-inch television. Quickly, he grabbed a few things and rushed out the door and down the creaky wooden stairs.

Jack threw the things into the back of the car he had borrowed from Chuck. Then he tentatively approached the mailbox. Whatever it contained would be further proof that he had been a loser.

It was odd that Jack thought of things as "his old life." He had only been gone for six months. How much could he have changed? Yet, the new Jack seemed years away from what he had been before the tour. Things were quite different now.

As he slowly looked through his letters, he felt as if he were handling someone else's mail. Then he came upon the pale yellow envelope. Jack froze as he stared at what was obviously a card. Michelle? Most likely. And it would be something meaningful to what their relationship had been—and she would write something heartfelt before signing.

But it was not from Michelle. Still, a wedding invitation from Sandra was a blast from a time he chose to put behind him. Maybe, he thought, Sandra had changed too. Surely she had. They were all growing. It was ridiculous of him to think that he was the only one to reach beyond their little circle. From what he had heard, even Colin's life had taken big leaps. It could be that the friends would not be the threat that he feared.

Jack held the little invitation to his mouth in thought. Yes, he decided. He would go. And he would go as the new Jack, complete with his rock star attire and attitude. He could see it now. His entrance would get as much attention as the bride. The press might even hear of it and send photographers. Naturally Sandra would be pleased that he could lend his celebrity to the occasion.

When the phone rang in his hotel room, Jack knew it was Michelle. He picked it up slowly and spoke in an unsure rasp.

"Hello?"

"Jack? You're back!" she said enthusiastically.

"Oh…hi, Michelle. I was just going to call you."

"Sure you were, Jack. Don't worry; it's okay. It probably takes a while to unwind from the road."

"Yeah…that's it."

"Jack, why didn't you call?"

"Things are just so different on the road," Jack said nervously. "Everything is so hectic."

"I understand."

"I knew that you would," Jack said, trying to hide the negativity.

"Listen, Jack, I guess your being gone was just too hard on me. I mean, I never heard from you at all."

"I'm sorry, Michelle," Jack said with a hint of irritation. "I just got so busy."

"I've met someone, Jack."

"Wha—?"

"Our relationship just could not work the way things were. I've been so terribly lonely."

"But—"

"I found someone who's able to be satisfied with just simple things, like me. You, well, you've got your career. It's where all your energy goes. Gary, well, I'm his main focus. I know it sounds corny, but I like that kind of treatment."

"But what about us?" Jack asked the woman who suddenly seemed more important in his life.

"There is no 'us,' Jack. There's you and your music, and there's me waiting for you. Anyway, I'd like to stay friends. Maybe you could even meet Gary sometime."

"Yeah, sure," Jack said toughly. "You're right. It wouldn't have worked. I'm glad you saw that."

"Bye, Jack," Michelle said, and she hung up.

Jack wasn't sure why, but he was hit hard by his own thick wave of loneliness. Why would the loss of a woman who made him feel so uncomfortable make him seem so suddenly empty? The fact was, he was trying to figure out a way of leaving her. Would he have done it?

Jack's thinking had changed so much that he no longer let a real thought in. It was far too dangerous at this point to examine his true feelings. He was now who he felt he should be, and that was enough. Was there really any more to anyone? Doesn't each person adopt a persona based on characteristics that they have found attractive along the way? There really isn't anything truly original, is there?

But Michelle had reminded him of something he could not be rid of. She had always been in touch with his childish worries, fears, and insecurities. How could he ever be truly "cool" with someone so aware of his inner inadequacies? Still, losing her was like losing a part of himself—a big part. Now he would play a role, denying that part of himself that was pathetically human—that part of himself that was as close to real as a person gets.

Jack reached for the phone. "Chuck," he said when he had reached the man responsible for his new life, "I want women. Get me some women."

CHAPTER 42

❊

Doc had fallen asleep while reading an old volume of the philosophy of Niche. Doc often consulted Niche's works when he felt particularly weak and vulnerable. And it wasn't just the famous quote about the things that don't destroy us making us stronger. There was much, much more to the man.

Hitler had read Niche. In fact, it's been said that Hitler's motivation for much of what he did came from the philosopher. Actually, Hitler had misread Niche's writings. People do that. They latch on to a poet or a quote or a Bible verse and use it as a life guide—and they've interpreted the whole thing wrong. Much like Ronald Reagan who thought the Boss's *Born in the USA* was a patriotic song.

Doc guessed that we pick our influences based on the truths that we have already formulated. If we see a line or hear a song that reinforces our own philosophy, we use it as evidence of that viewpoint's credibility.

When Doc was in college, he had collected quotes. And, of course, he had done the same thing as everyone else—only being attracted to the beliefs that reflected his own. But the more he had collected, the surer he was that he had had a grasp on the universe. Now he wondered if anyone ever understood the world.

One quote that he especially liked when he was young and innocent seemed to be popular with a great many people recently. It was when Frost said, "Two roads diverged in a wood, and I—I took the one less traveled by, And that has made all the difference." Now you found the line on calendars and greeting cards. Everybody liked it. Hell, it was *acceptable*. Enough said.

Crane had written a similar, but more accurate poem on the subject. In Crane's poem, the author elects to take the less traveled road, only to find that it was overgrown with weeds. The author laughs at the lack of courage and individuality of others until he observes that each weed is a sharp knife. He then decides to take another road.

Didn't everyone see that that "less traveled road" thing that the masses had made into cliché was simply bullshit—at least as far as they were concerned? The "road" is a tough, painful one. Doc knew, because he had forced himself to travel it. What kind of an idiot, Doc thought, would take a little traveled bumpy road when one could glide along happily on the main highway?

Doc groggily took a sip of his coffee cup full of vodka when he heard the hinges of his mail receptacle squeak rustily at the front of his building. Odd that he could always hear that little sound through all the street noise. Apparently he did not know the importance that he placed on communication from the outside world. But he received very little in the way of mail. Usually the postman did not even stop. But when he did, the imagination promised more than the prize he would find.

This time was different, however. A warm feeling overtook Doc as he read the wedding invitation. Doc had always had a soft spot for Sandra. She always seemed so open—and so confused. But Doc would find himself smiling when he heard her talk, just like he was doing now. He could not imagine anyone ever wanting him to attend any ceremony or social gathering. Doc was overcome with emotion that Sandra had even thought of him.

But this presented a dilemma. Of course, he would not attend. He hadn't been to a public event for decades. Not only would he not know how to act, he would surely make those around him uncomfortable. How could he do this to such a sweet girl like Sandra? And then, how could he disappoint her by ignoring her request? Should he get hold of himself—clean up his act for one evening for the sake of the girl? He would have to give this some deep thought, but he was pretty sure he knew the right thing to do.

Doc had spent a great deal of his life building a protection around himself. Oh, he had done it by telling himself that his idiosyncratic, antisocial, misanthropic life was courageous. Now he wondered if being an iconoclast simply meant a fear of rejection. Sandra had really thrown a wrench into the works. He could no longer read or create or even think straight. All he could do was suffer with the anxiety that the invitation presented.

How weird it was to be incapable of associating with your own species. Man was a social being—that was plain. Doc's antisocial behavior was indeed aberrant rather than simply individualistic or unique. His existence was undeniably freakish. But like with any physical or chemical deviation from the norm, he could not change himself.

Rather than have his first return to human contact be at Sandra's wedding—where he would surely have an anxiety attack—Doc made the decision to connect slowly. He decided to contact the person he had had the closest attachment to in the last year—and that was Colin. It took every bit of courage he could muster to dial the payphone at the gas station kiosk. Twice he had hit the receiver, hanging from it in cowardly pain before trying again. He was sweating profusely and shaking uncontrollably when he finally succeeded in dialing the number. The phone rang twice and then there was a connection.

"The number you have called," the recording stated, "has been recently disconnected. Please check your directory for your party's new number."

After all that, he could not even complete the call. A feeling of relief and defeat came over him. There was no one else. Though he knew he was alone, he now felt incredibly isolated. He was no nonconformist; he was a misfit.

When Doc returned to his place, he sat in his miserable chair wrapped in a blanket he took from the bed. He wrapped himself tight, struggling to feel secure—lifting his legs up onto the chair in the fetal position. He was a scared animal crawling into as small a space as possible for protection.

CHAPTER 43

❀

"You love me for who I am, don't you Sean?" Sandra asked as they drove to the travel agent.

"Who else would I love you for?"

"That's not funny."

"Okay," Sean said, realizing that Sandra had some issue to the discuss, "I'm sorry. Of course I love you for who you are."

"I mean, you accept my personality and my career and everything that goes with me—the good, the bad—"

"And the ugly? Sorry, I couldn't resist. Why would I marry someone I didn't accept?"

"I was talking to your Aunt Eileen at the engagement—"

"Oh, so that's it!"

"What's it?"

"Aunt Eileen has been telling her story of oppression of years and years!"

"So, she's not telling the truth?"

"Oh," Sean smiled, "I suppose she's telling the truth—as she sees it."

"What's that supposed to mean?"

"Sometimes we blame others for our own lack of courage and initiative. According to my mother—and that's another whole set of truths, I admit—Aunt Eileen wanted to be a hippy or beatnik or bohemian or whatever they called them then. Only, she came from a privileged family—so she would never have to starve or suffer for her art. Anyway, she most certainly had talent—but there's a big difference between having talent and being a great artist. In other words, Aunt Eileen was a 'wanna-be.'"

"A 'wanna-be'?"

"Yeah," Sean continued. "She would have flopped if she had tried to make any career of her art, so she stopped. Fortunately for her, she had Uncle Clifford to blame."

"But how do you know she wasn't any good?" Sandra argued. "You said yourself that your mother has her own set of truths."

"Because I've seen Aunt Eileen's work. My mother has a few paintings stored in the attic. She's very fond of them, for some reason. Many times when I was a kid I'd find her up there sitting on a trunk just staring at one after another."

"Wait…Now you're confusing me. First of all, how do you know how good her paintings are?"

"Well, I didn't really know when I was younger—but I think I've gained a little taste over the years."

"Hmmm…"

"And as far as my mother goes, I think she's always admired my Aunt for being a free spirit. My mother always did what she was expected to do in life—get married to a successful man, make his home beautiful, raise his children, support him in any way possible in return for security. She never took a chance in her life."

"So she doesn't really hate Eileen. She's just jealous."

"No," Sean frowned, "I don't think it's as petty as that. She's just uncomfortable when Aunt Eileen is around because Aunt Eileen represents my mother's other side—a side she no longer chooses to acknowledge. You see, going with the flow is my mother's philosophy—you know, doing what's expected, fitting in with her station in life. For some people, though, going along with everything is tough.

It's going against the grain. My mother knows that being different is not easy or productive, so she works at shutting out any natural tendency for rebellion. And just when she feels she has successfully squeezed that uniqueness from her soul, my Aunt Eileen comes around and reminds her again of who she really is."

"That's very sad."

"Only sad if you let it be. My mother works very hard at keeping emotions like that out. You see, she sometimes—all right, more than sometimes—is a little tough to take. She comes off as angry and scornful. Actually, her struggle is with herself. So she plays the part of the supercilious high society wife."

"But it's not natural to her."

"Well, we all play roles. Let's just say that hers requires a lot more work."

"So she really doesn't hate me," Sandra deduced.

"Of course not," Sean said, "but you're more of a challenge to her."

"A challenge?"

"You're like Aunt Eileen—with your art and everything. That's why she has to diminish the importance of your painting all the time. It would kill her to think that you could really pull that off and get the security of a successful husband at the same time."

"My God!" Sandra exclaimed.

"Yeah…what some people live with."

※　　※　　※

When Colin awoke that Thursday morning, he was not alone. As soon as his mind began to focus, he looked over at the digital alarm clock. It was 8:14 a.m. Charlene, it seemed, had overslept.

At first Colin panicked. Damn, he thought, now she's going to be found out. Then a smile spread across his face. Charlene would have to face the music like anyone else. Her little game of "boy toys" was up.

Colin hadn't realized until this moment how much he resented his role in this playtime of hers. But he felt empty and lonely in the mornings when she would leave. Never was there any more than the sex. No phone calls, no secret notes—nothing. This must be how a lot of women felt, he thought. Used.

Sensing that Colin was awake, Charlene began to stir. Then she turned over toward Colin, opened her eyes, and grinned.

Colin looked down at her. "You know you're in deep shit now."

"I am?" she said almost condescendingly. "And why is that?"

Confused, Colin just looked at her.

"Colin," she said in pedantic tone, "I know what I'm doing. I *always* know what I'm doing."

Now Colin just stared.

"James is out of town," she laughed.

"Oh."

"Colin," she said, "I do believe you're disappointed. I think you wanted me to get caught."

"I think you're right," Colin said.

"Colin, haven't things been fun? Haven't I pleased you?"

"No doubt about it," Colin said.

"Then what? What is it?"

"I don't know, exactly," Colin said. "It's just that…well, do you realize that this is the first time we've ever talked?"

"We talk."

"We talk *dirty*. I mean, we don't talk like people."

"I can't believe my ears," Charlene said. "I thought it was all sex with men. I thought it was women who wanted the relationship."

"Don't get me wrong," Colin said. "I love the sex! And for a long time that's all I wanted."

"But things are different now?"

"I'm lonely. I'm missing something in my life."

"Like what?"

"Like marriage."

"Marriage? Oh, Colin, you have no idea what you're talking about. Marriage is nothing like it's supposed to be. It's unnatural for a couple to be monogamously committed."

"You're talking about sex again."

"What more do you think you get from marriage?"

"You're married."

"I have money and security. He has a pretty wife and hostess. That's all."

"And you don't think there's any more than that?"

"What's all this talk amount marriage anyway?" Charlene interrupted.

"Oh, nothing…it's just that a close friend of mine is having her wedding soon."

"*Her* wedding? Is this someone you care about?"

"I just told you that she's a close friend."

"Listen, Colin," Charlene put her hand on his, "there are no close friendships between men and women. One party or the other is always secretly thinking of more."

"No…you wouldn't understand…We've been friends forever," Colin protested."

"Oh? So you've never entertained the idea of a relationship?"

"Well…we dated for awhile…but now we're just good friends."

"I know you think I'm a cold woman who can't possibly have any emotion east of lust—but I'm a human being too. I know about men and women and love—believe it or not. People don't turn off one kind of relationship and begin another. Couples who have been romantically involved can never forget what they had—no matter what the circumstances. I think you're still in love with this girl."

"What!" Colin reacted a bit too strongly. "That's stupid!"

"Stupid? No, I don't think it's *stupid* or ridiculous. I think her upcoming union is throwing you."

"Well…maybe it is…but that's because I'm not sure if this guy's right for her."

"You've met him?"

"Well...no."

"Then how could you possibly—"

"Sandra is a special kind of person," Colin explained. "She's an artist."

"And?"

"Well...it just wouldn't be right if the man she married did not appreciate her talent and temperament."

"Ah," Charlene said knowingly.

"What?" Colin asked.

"Nothing. Nothing at all," Charlene said, starting to get up to get dressed.

"Where are you going?" Colin asked. "I thought you said James was out of town."

"He is. I planned on having the whole morning with you, Colin."

"Then what's the problem?"

"I just don't think your heart is into it."

❦   ❦   ❦

Jack also awoke in a hotel room with a beautiful woman next to him in bed. Only Jack's companion was considerably younger than Colin's. The girl couldn't have been more than 18 or 19 years old—but that's what constituted Jack's taste lately. After all, this was most likely the average age of his fan base.

The perfect specimen lay next to him, uncovered and completely naked. Jack, now sitting up, just looked at her smooth, flawless body. Lately he had been with many young flawless bodies. Never in his wildest dreams had he ever thought that women of this caliber would be so available to him. It was like having *Playboy* magazine and a porno movie come to life every night.

"Hi," the girl said sleepily in a high school voice.

"Hi, Heather," Jack said.

"Hillary."

"Oh, I'm sorry!" Jack said.
"That's okay...I don't mind. What's on for breakfast?"
Jack began to panic. Breakfast? How was this part of the bargain?
"Uh...well...we could go down to the hotel restaurant."
"That sounds awesome!" she said, jumping up to find her things.

Breakfast was more awkward than Jack could have imagined. He could not think of a thing to talk about. Heather, or Hillary or whatever her name was, however, took up the slack.

"These waffles are so good. I think it's the strawberries. I love strawberries. I don't like strawberry flavoring though. I don't even see how they can call it strawberry; it doesn't taste like strawberries...When I was a senior, the cheerleaders would sometimes skip first period and go out for breakfast. We never got in trouble, though. All the teachers liked us. All except Mr. Leonard—the tight-ass. It's always math teachers that can't lighten up, you know? I graduated from Roosevelt High. Where did you go?"

"Uh...Hessville...I went to Hessville."

"Hessville? Did you know Jamie Hanson? She's my cousin. Class of '97."

"No...I left long before then."

"I hated school. Oh, I don't mean the social part. I just don't see why we had to learn some of that stuff. I mean, you don't use Shakespeare or algebra in real life. And what was up with Phys. Ed. I mean, I liked it and all...but what did that have to do with the real world?"

"I...I never thought—"

"So, what are we doing after breakfast?"

"Oh...I...there are things I've got—"

"You think you can drop me on the way? I was supposed to meet Mindy at the mall. I told her I might be a little late because...well, you know. Banana Republic is having a big sale. Usually everything's overpriced...but I love their clothes."

"Sure...sure," Jack said. "I'll drop you."

CHAPTER 44

❀

The worst thing about going for a new job is the interview. Naturally, there are different kinds of jobs, so there are different kinds of interviews. Professional jobs have the most pretentious kinds. Possibly this is because a single skill is not what the employer is looking for. In fact, in many cases, the employer has no idea what to measure in the interview process. Thus, many people are hired for high paid positions based on presentation and personality. An individual could possibly land a job because he or she is bubbly or because he or she asks interesting questions. Sometimes it boils down to the brand name of the person's clothes.

Doc had worked with a man at the university who had stepped in to take over a class when the previous professor had suddenly left town with a pretty co-ed. Being mid-semester and the fact that the previous instructor had been extremely popular with his students—perhaps too popular—the task of substitution was a tough one. The stand-in, however, through hard work, had been extremely successful. He continued the flow of the class—and also became admired among both students and colleagues.

At the end of the year, this successful replacement interviewed for the job, along with three or four other candidates from around the country. He didn't get it. When he asked why, he was told that the interview was not good—that he didn't show enough spark—that he was too laid back. The man they hired was dismissed at the end of the next semester.

Doc was hardly going for a professor's job at a university right now. The interview he had set up wasn't even close to professional. But it was far different from that of bar tender or clean-up man. Doc was applying for the post of night manager at United Package Delivery. This was a big step for the man who kept all personal contact in the past at its simplest level—aside from his meetings at Fabulous Taco, of course. It was a necessary step, though, if he wanted a little mental challenge to his days. Also, since he had received Sandra's wedding invitation, he had felt silly and guilty about some of his life decisions. He felt he needed something else to grow.

Doc entered the office of human resources dressed in a suit that he had packed away years ago when he had gone into emotional hiding. It was a gray three-piece—though he dropped the vest—which may have been a bit out of style—but the suit was in good shape. Under this he wore a white shirt, fresh from the cleaners—15 years ago. His blue and gray striped tie was conservative enough to have fit in with any time period.

"I'm here for an interview," Doc meekly told the receptionist, who had not even acknowledged him from the time he had come through the door.

"Have a seat," she said without looking up from her typing.

That was another problem with going for a job. You were supposed to be polite—a hat in hand approach—and everyone you had to deal with had license to be rude to you. It was as if they were rubbing it in that they already had jobs and were somehow superior.

Doc's interview was at 9:45 a.m. When the clock hit the 10:30 mark, Doc walked back up to the receptionist's desk.

"Yes?" she asked with nasal impatience.

"My appointment was for 45 minutes ago," Doc said as respectfully as he could. "Is there a problem?"

Immediately the secretary stopped her typing, hands dropping in her lap, not moving from her position. Then she swiveled around in her chair to meet Doc's eyes. She had ratty reddish-brown hair with a bad dye job. Her blue eyes were circled in such dark liner that she reminded Doc of an early Egyptian. Now her hardened, make-up caked face looked angry.

"Mr. Anthony is a very busy man," she said curtly. "He does more than interviews, you know."

"No, I wasn't aware of what his duties were," Doc began to lose his intimidation. "I only know that I have an appointment with him."

The secretary, noting that she might not be as daunting to the man before her as she originally thought, turned her aggression to passive.

"I'll let you know when he's ready," she said flatly, turning her chair back to her work.

After another 15 minutes, Doc approached the desk again. This time she did not address the man in front of her, but simply picked up the phone and spoke.

"Mr. Anthony, your appointment is here. Yes sir." Then turning to Doc and smiling, she said, "Go right in."

The office was a cluttered, smoke-filled room. Anthony was on the phone as Doc came through the door—a cigarette dangling from his mouth as he talked—but he motioned for Doc to sit in the chair facing the large desk. Finally, after what seemed to be about ten minutes, Anthony hung up the phone and faced Doc."

"So, he began, you want the manager's job?"

"My name is Jacob Crenshaw," Doc said, obviously pointing out the rudeness of the situation, "and I'd like to know more about the position."

"You're obviously an educated man," Anthony said, not to be threatened. "What brings you to a job like this? Alcohol? Been in trouble with the law?"

Doc's cold looks even penetrated the callous and cynical Anthony. "Insanity," he said forcefully.

Anthony looked suddenly apprehensive. "Wha...oh...you have been in a hospital?" he stammered.

"No," Doc said calmly. "I haven't."

"What—?"

"I'm crazy, loony, cracked, psychotic. But I haven't been diagnosed. Do you know *why* I am insane?" Doc spoke with the tone of a Charles Manson.

Anthony, visibly shaken, only shook his head.

"Because I can't understand you or the rest of the fucking people in the world. You make no sense to me. You all seem like a bunch of assholes. But you aren't, of course. I'm the weird one. Do you know why I know that?"

Again Anthony only shook his head, pushing his chair back slightly.

"Because if everyone acts one way—no matter how rude or bizarre or evil or selfish or even banal—then the person who chooses *not* to is the nut."

"Uh huh," Anthony choked.

"So," Doc said standing up, "I want to thank you, Mr. Anthony, for reminding me why I have rejected the 'sane' world."

As Doc passed the receptionist he paused. "And fuck you, you skinny piece of shit!"

CHAPTER 45

❀

The weather on the day of Sandra's wedding was perfect—of course. Now, the ideal month for a wedding is supposed to be June, but Sandra chose the second week in September because of the weather. This provided the feel of summer while minimizing the threat of one of those sticky hot days. And her planning paid off, because she awoke to a beautifully sunny day with clear skies and a projected midday temperature of around 74 degrees.

If only Sandra's disposition could have been as sunny as the weather. The moment her eyes opened to greet a fresh day, Sandra could feel that she was in a funk. Sometimes people awoke that way, she reasoned. Maybe it was an unremembered dream that caused the feeling. Or maybe it was chemical. Sometimes a person was just not right because the chemicals in the system did not have the correct balance. Regardless of the reason, Sandra—usually a morning person—was not in a particularly good mood.

"Good morning, sunshine," her mother greeted her as Sandra walked into the kitchen. Her mother had used that expression since she was a little girl. Most of the time it had made her smile, but today it caused her to wince inside.

"Morning," she grumbled.

"I thought you'd be up at dawn—like on Christmas day when you were a kid."

"Why, mom?"

"Why? From excitement. This has to be the biggest day of your life. If I were you, I'd be feeling so excited I'd be about to burst. In fact, I'm close to feeling that right now."

"Where's dad?"

"Oh, he's out getting some last minute things taken care of. You should have heard him this morning—I'm surprised you didn't. He was whistling! I haven't heard your dad whistle in the morning since he was a young man. I used to lay in bed on Saturday mornings and listen as he did his little chores. He just loved to putz around on the weekend. Told me once that sleeping was a waste of life. That we'd all have plenty of time to just lie there and do nothing someday."

"Yeah, he always did get up early on Saturdays. The one day of the week he could sleep late, and he's up at 5:30 or 6:00."

"I made your favorite," Mrs. Louder said rushing around the kitchen.

"Pancakes?"

"Mickey Mouse pancakes. You remember how I used to put little ears on each…"

At this point her mother became silent, causing Sandra to turn around in her chair.

"Mom, are you crying?"

"It's…just…that my little girl…won't be my little girl anymore."

Sandra stood and walked over to her mother who was facing the sink, both hands supporting herself as if she would faint.

"Mom…you're not going to lose me. I haven't been a kid for years, but I'm still around. I'll always be around."

"No," her mother sniffled, now mopping her wet face with a paper towel, "a married woman changes. She belongs to her husband then. She takes on a new life—her husband's life."

"I hate to tell you this, mom, but I won't *belong* to anybody. I intend on being Sandra Louder—husband or no."

"Oh, don't talk like that. Especially today. The whole idea of marriage is for a man and woman to become one."

"Whose idea?"

"Well...the Bible says something about that."

"Maybe there are different ideas about marriage today," Sandra said defiantly.

"Why are you talking that way?" her mother asked, a look of mild shock on her face.

"What way?"

"Your attitude. Your tone of voice. You've never spoken this way about your relationship with Sean."

"I don't know. I guess I've been thinking a lot about this whole thing."

A look of pure horror took over Mrs. Louder's face. "You don't have second thoughts, do you?"

"No. Don't worry. Maybe I'm just a little nervous," Sandra assured her mother—and herself.

"Well," her mother's face changed suddenly to a warm, knowing smile, "that's to be expected. Now you just eat a good breakfast. You're going to need all your strength for the day ahead."

🍁 🍁 🍁

Colin was a bundle of nerves. He had never been a calm person. It was because his mind raced—never stopping for a split second. Always one thought after another—boom, boom, boom—like changing channels quickly on a television set with the volume up.

Once he had asked a date what she was thinking about. She replied, "Nothing." "Oh, you couldn't be thinking of nothing," he had laughed. "No, really. I wasn't thinking of anything." This had been a revelation to Colin. He had just assumed that everyone had runaway thoughts. Maybe not as intense as his, but constant. The idea that someone could have a truly blank mind was beyond his comprehension.

Occasionally he had a sleepless night. This was usually due to a little something extra occupying his thoughts so that his mind was working overtime. Sometimes he could put his finger on the problem, and sometimes he couldn't.

When Colin was feeling a great deal of anxiety about something of importance, his mind triggered a mechanism for coping with it. Unfortunately, the mechanism brought little respite from worry. What it did was fill his head with a plethora of little irritations that had been usually suppressed. When under pressure, the little things plagued him.

For example, suddenly he would fret about the perfection of things. A crack in the plaster or a scrape on his shoes. Whether his hair was thinning, or if a mole was getting larger. He would become full of self doubt and take everything anyone said as an affront. In short, he would become a mess. But the little things would take his mind away from the item that was so extremely troubling.

The problem with even the slightest neurosis is that the neurotic can never identify it in himself—even when it is transparently "in-your-face" obvious. Here he was, on the day of Sandra's wedding—and he was coming apart at the seams. Nothing went right from the moment he got out of bed. Everything irritated him. The television newscaster's voice, the consistency of his microwave oatmeal, the way the sun shone right into his face as he was trying to read the paper—which, incidentally, was chock full of grammatical errors on this particular morning.

Because Colin had recently taken an interest in his clothes—and because he wanted to make a good impression at Sandra's wedding—he decided to lay out the suit, shirt and tie that he would wear. Colin had a number of expensive suits now and a variety of silk ties, so deciding what to put on should have been no problem. He had decided to wear a white shirt to the wedding because of the formality of the event. Unfortunately, the collar of the one clean white shirt he had was stained and had not been cleaned properly by his laundry. Of course, that changed everything. If he wore a blue shirt, he would have to change suits. The suit he had in mind, though, had a loose button on the jacket. The button would have probably been just fine for one more wearing, but Colin began to obsess about it until he magnified the problem to the point that he could no longer even look at the jacket. Colin started attacking his closet for something else. Nothing seemed to be right. Here was a man, clothed by the Salvation Army for years, and he could not find the attire to suit him.

Colin literally shook when he finally forced himself to sit on the couch and stop his maniacal search. What was wrong with him? Maybe it was the prospect of seeing his old friend after so long. Maybe it was the fact that he would see others he hadn't seen since his life had changed. He wondered if Jack would be there. Of course, he would. Sandra wouldn't have invited Colin without inviting Jack. And what about Doc? Surely she would invite Doc. Maybe not.

At length Colin got himself together. He decided to wear what he had originally put out. A relative calm began to take over. It was the calm before the storm, however, because getting ready involved tying his necktie.

Neckties are really no problem, as long as one is not nervous or in a hurry or irritated or angry. Unfortunately, it is sometimes necessary to hastily tie one of these ridiculous bands of color under the wrong conditions. The difficulty is all in the length. If one is after the perfect length, one has to have a feel for just the right place to make the knot. The difference as to whether a knot is correctly positioned is very slight at the top of the tie where the tying takes place and can cause a great difference at the bottom of the tie, near the belt. Just a fraction of an inch can make the tie ridiculously too short or way too long. And when the individual finds that he has judged wrongly, he must adjust carefully and to a very small degree, or the opposite extreme will be the result.

Colin, who had tied a necktie many times in his life, never seemed to have a big problem—until today. His first attempt left the point of the striped piece of cloth about three inches above his belt buckle, making him look like a member of a Wisconsin polka band. His next try was a little better, but on this day things had to be perfect—so he tried again. Because he could not leave well enough alone, Colin found his new length to be halfway down the zipper of his pants. How could such a small adjustment do so much? After three more tries at exactitude, Colin ripped the tie from his collar and threw it across the room—where it landed on a cold piece of Domino's mushroom and pepperoni pizza, left over from the night before.

Immediately understanding his mistake, Colin ran across the room to rescue the tie, which was now the only tie he could ever consider for the occasion. Luckily it looked just fine. Apparently the grease had congealed just enough in the cool air to make the pizza harmless. To be sure, though, Colin reached for his reading glasses on the nearby desk and clicked the lamp on. Now, upon perusing the whole tie, Colin found a dark spot about the size of the head of a small finishing nail. This set him off in a new tirade, which ended with him pulling every tie he had ever owned out of the closet until they formed a pile on the floor. This he stomped on the collection, jumping up and down, up and down, cursing the ties as he pummeled them into the carpet.

The best thing about a tantrum is that it releases the body's natural drugs; so that when it's over, a calm prevails, and one is finally able to think rationally. When Colin composed himself, he made the decision to wear everything that he had originally decided—spots, ring-around-the-collar, and all. And he decided to walk to the church because he thought the exercise and the fresh air would further relax him.

❦   ❦   ❦

Listen, Chuck, I need a fuckin' date!" Jack screamed into the mouthpiece of the phone.

"So get one," Chuck said. "You've got girls throwing themselves at you. How hard can it be?"

"You don't understand! I can't bring some bimbo! I've got to make an impression at this reception!"

"So take that girl from the other night. She was a looker! Just tell her to keep her damn mouth shut," Chuck said.

"What happened to you, Chuck? I thought you were the savvy showbiz guy. This wedding is a public event. When they find out I'm attending, there will be photographers everywhere."

"It sure didn't take you long, kid," Chuck said, laughing sardonically.

"What the hell's that supposed to mean?"

"It takes most of 'em a couple of years before the head begins to grow. Son, your ego was just waitin' to be released!"

"Maybe it's just that I picked up an understanding of the business faster than most. Maybe I understand it better than *you*. Maybe I don't need you anymore."

"Oh, you need me alright, kid. But there's nothing I can do to convince you of that—you're gonna have to find out for yourself," Chuck said coolly.

"Yeah? What is it that I have to learn?" Jack sneered.

"Just that you're a flash in the pan. Who do you think you are—Elvis? How many young, talented musicians do you think come and go in the music world? If you're lucky, you'll make it a few years."

"That's where you're wrong, old buddy," Jack spat. "I intend to do whatever it takes to be around a long, long time. Oh, don't you worry, Chuck—I'll make it. But it will be without you. You're fired!"

"I'm what?" Chuck laughed. "That's where *you're* wrong, old buddy. We've got a contract. If you want me out of your life, you're gonna have to pay big. Besides, I've outlived a million punks like you in this business. They come and they go, but Chuck Henderson sticks around. Hell…you've got it *all* wrong, you little shit. I don't work for you; you work for me!" And Chuck laughed until Jack hung up the phone.

CHAPTER 46

Sandra's father drove like an old man. When the sign read 30 mph, that's what he did, and not a bit faster. In fact, he would actually drive slower than the allowed limit, just to make sure he didn't go over.

"Dad, we're never going to get there on time," Sandra complained from the back seat.

"Oh, don't you worry, honey," her mother said, "we'll get you there in plenty of time."

"Hell, they can't start without you," her father laughed. "Besides, it's better to get there at all than to risk an accident.

Just then her father slowed to a crawl.

"What's the problem now?" Sandra whined.

"Accident or something...up ahead," her father said, trying to see around the cars in front of him by craning his neck out the side window.

"Oh, just dandy!" Sandra said.

"It'll be fine," her mother said, turning around in the front seat to pat her on the leg with an assuring smile.

"Mom, I have to get dressed. Do you know how long it's going to take me to put that gown on and get ready?"

"Well, we can't do anything about it, dear. There's an accident."

"No accident," her father announced. "Fire."

"A fire?" Sandra asked. "Where?"

"Looks like it's that little place on the corner of 25th and Garfield."

"What place?" her mother asked.

"That hot dog taco place," her father said.

"What!" Sandra asked, jumping forward in the back seat.

"Yeah…we're coming up to it now," her father said. "Don't worry, though, I think things are starting to loosen up."

"Pull over!" Sandra ordered.

"What—?"

"Pull over! Just do it, dad!"

Too confused to argue, Sandra's father guided the big Buick into a space just down the block from the smoldering building.

"Oh, my God," Sandra said, covering her face.

"What is it dear?" her mother asked.

"Stay here."

"But—"

"Just stay here!" And Sandra got out of the car and walked toward the fireman's blockade. Tears came to her eyes as she watched the remains of Fabulous Taco turn to charcoal.

Suddenly there was the sound of a collision in the street alongside the burning restaurant. A white stretch limousine had been just backended by the taxi behind it. The taxi driver was out of the car in a flash—face red with anger and fists forming.

"What the fuck was that!" he shouted. "What did you hit your fuckin' brakes for, you asshole."

Jack's driver just stood open-mouthed, left to deal with the irate cabbie, while Jack, who had ordered the sudden stop, ran toward the remains of his favorite restaurant. As he approached, he tried to shove his way past the blockade, as if he were a hero of some kind ready to rescue survivors.

"Where the hell do you think you're goin'?" a policeman said, pushing Jack back.

"Jack?" a woman's voice asked in surprise.
"Sandra!" Jack said recognizing the person standing next to him.
"Oh, Jack, it's gone!" Sandra said as the dam burst and she sobbed into Jack's chest as he held her.

On the other side, along Garfield, Colin was beside himself.
"How could this have happened?" he accused. "Who did this?"
"Calm down, young man, a fiftyish fire officer said to him. We think it was a grease fire."
"Anybody hurt?" someone from behind Colin asked.
"Just one," the fireman said. "The cook got out...but I guess the only customer didn't make it. According to the cook, there was plenty of time too. The cook—really just a young kid—said he pleaded with the guy to leave. Said the guy just sat there. Then the kid tried to move him, and the guy just said, 'I've finally got the courage.' Some nutcase, I figure. Anyway, the guy was too big for the kid to handle, so he just had to save himself."
"Oh shit!" Colin exclaimed. "Have you got some kind of identification from this guy?"
"There isn't anything left to identify—but the kid described him. Said he used to come there often with some young friends. Then he hadn't seen him for a long time. A guy about forty. Kid said he thought he might be an artist or somethin'. Said the guy had a strange smile on his face when he ordered his hot dogs. Like I said—some nutcase."
Colin went limp. His old friend...gone. And yet, if Doc had been such a good friend, why is it that Colin had not called him, if only to ask how he was doing? But Colin had been busy. Involved with his career. That was understandable; wasn't it?
Then Colin turned away from the ruins of Fabulous Taco and the remains of his friend; he just walked blindly in the direction of 25th. Here he left the sidewalk and began to walk down the center of the street—bumping into the front driver's side of the white limo where

the cop was trying to restrain a cab driver, past Sandra's bewildered parents, still sitting obediently in their big Buick.

Then he was awakened by his trance by someone calling his name.

"Colin! Colin!" the man's voice said. When it finally registered, he stopped and turned, vacant look on his face.

"Colin, it's us," Sandra said, running up to him. She put her arms around him as he stood there uncomprehending.

Then Jack walked up and also embraced his old friend.

"Jack?" Colin said weakly.

"Yeah, Colin. We're both back. We've all come home together."

And the three of them stood in the street, cars now backed up for blocks; and they wrapped their arms around each other as tightly as they could, holding on to each other as they desperately tried to hold on to something wonderful they had all had together.

But, there is never any going back. Things are never the same. The bad things that happen in our past have a way of stabbing us every so often, reminding us to be humble. But the good things in our past stab us also—because it can never be so good and innocent and real again—and that hurts more sometimes than reliving any pain.

CHAPTER 47

❦

Sandra did not arrive on time at the church that day. In fact, she never stepped foot in St. John's church again. There would be no wedding. Sean and his mother and the new lifestyle would never be. But it was not because Sandra would completely reject the world's facade. It was just that Doc's death showed her something about life—if only briefly and soon forgotten—and she could not go on with her plans. Something in her told her that she must stop and reevaluate. It was like a sign that she was looking for—hoping for—that would put an end to what she was doing and uncover herself.

When we get those revelations, those glimpses into the true meaning of our existence, they fortunately do not stay with us. If they did, we could not live comfortably—and, yes, happily, in the world that has been provided for us. We would constantly fight the hypocrisy, and be miserable in the process. We would end up like Doc.

No, Sandra went on to marry a quiet accountant, who provided her with a beautiful home in the suburbs and three loving children. Sandra opened a little studio in the garage and continued to put her artwork in the small shops in the area. Of course, the majority of her time was spent chauffeuring the children from activity to activity in her mini van, planning birthday parties, and helping the PTA at school with various fundraising projects.

Once in a while, when folding clothes in the laundry room or waiting for water to boil on the stove, Sandra would think about the times at Fabulous Taco; but she would always push the thoughts away after only a few moments. She had to—so she could be happy.

❦   ❦   ❦

Jack wrote an entire album of songs, which he dedicated to his old friend. All were done either acoustically or with minimal support from other musicians. The record company hated it, but Jack's previous success had given him the power to make some demands. The record sold big. In fact, the advance orders alone made Jack a fortune. But critically, it failed. And his fans turned against him. When he attempted to redeem himself on the next record, it was too late. Jack's career had reached an end.

But Jack had put his money away. He opened a string of record shops around his hometown and married a girl he had gone to high school with. His life was not simple, but it was happy.

❦   ❦   ❦

Colin's next book was the number one novel in sales in the country. It was a change from his normal material though. Gone was the frenetic anger of his previous writing. *Better Times* was about the simple things in life. In fact, the critics dismissed it as corny drivel. But Colin had to write what he felt—one had to be true to himself. So Colin wrote about a world that was not real—a world where there was integrity and true love and loyalty. Without this fantasy, he contended in his theme, we would not be able to tolerate the day to day. We somehow had to convince ourselves that this ideal life was a possibility. And even though it was unachievable, we had to convince ourselves that our current existence was similar.

Colin would never have a family. Though he now understood what it took to get through life, he just could not fool himself and go with the flow. No matter how much he wanted to join the mainstream, his demons would pull him back. It was as if a curse had been passed along to him by his old friend Doc. He would forevermore know the truth of things; and, therefore, he would never have peace of mind and contentment.

There was a big difference between Colin and Doc, though. Colin became enormously wealthy and was able to build himself a big home high in the mountains outside the city. Here he spent his days with his thoughts in his chosen solitude. Here he continued to write what he felt. He would be anxious, but physically comfortable the rest of his days.

About the Author

❀

The author was born in Gary, Indiana. He received his bachelor's degree from Indiana University and has been a teacher for 30 years.

Mr. Baran now teaches English at a small business school in Lancaster, PA where he lives with his wife of 30 years, his two daughters and his dog, Gelly.

0-595-23447-X